ALSO BY ROSS MACDONALD

*These are Borzoi Books, published in
New York by Alfred A. Knopf*

THE
UNDERGROUND
MAN

THE
UNDERGROUND
MAN

ROSS MACDONALD

Alfred A. Knopf · New York · 1971

THIS IS A BORZOI BOOK
PUBLISHED BY ALFRED A. KNOPF, INC.

Copyright © 1971 by Ross Macdonald
All rights reserved under International
and Pan-American Copyright Conventions.
Published in the United States by
Alfred A. Knopf, Inc., New York,
and simultaneously in Canada by
Random House of Canada Limited, Toronto.
Distributed by Random House, Inc., New York.
Library of Congress Catalog Card Number: 76-136337
Standard Book Number: 0-394-43467-6
Manufactured in the United States of America.

FIRST AND SECOND PRINTING BEFORE PUBLICATION

THIRD PRINTING, FEBRUARY 1971

To

Matthew J. Bruccoli

THE
UNDERGROUND
MAN

I

A rattle of leaves woke me some time before dawn. A hot wind was breathing in at the bedroom window. I got up and closed the window and lay in bed and listened to the wind.

After a while it died down, and I got up and opened the window again. Cool air, smelling of fresh ocean and slightly used West Los Angeles, poured into the apartment. I went back to bed and slept until I was wakened in the morning by my scrub jays.

I called them mine. There were five or six of them taking turns at dive-bombing the window sill, then retreating to the magnolia tree next door.

I went into the kitchen and opened a can of peanuts and threw a handful out the window. The jays swooped down into the yard of the apartment building. I put on some clothes and went down the outside stairs with the rest of the can of peanuts.

It was a bright September morning. The edges of the sky had a yellowish tinge like cheap paper darkening in the sunlight. There was no wind at all now, but I could smell the inland desert and feel its heat.

I threw my jays another handful of peanuts and watched the birds scatter on the grass. A little boy in a blue cotton suit opened the door of one of the downstairs apartments, the one that was normally occupied by a couple named Waller. The boy looked about five or six. He had dark close-cropped hair and anxious blue eyes.

"Is it all right if I come out?"

"It's all right with me."

Leaving the door wide open, he moved toward me with exaggerated caution, so as not to frighten the birds. The jays were swooping and screeching, intent on outwitting each other. They paid no attention to him.

"What are you feeding them? Peanuts?"

"That's right. Do you want some?"

"No thanks. My daddy's taking me to visit my grandma. She always gives me a lot of stuff to eat. She feeds birds, too." After a silence, he added: "I wouldn't mind feeding the jays some peanuts."

I offered him the open can. He took a fistful of peanuts and flung them on the grass. The jays came swooping. Two of them started to fight, raucously, bloodlessly.

The boy turned pale. "Are they killing each other?" he said in a tense small voice.

"No. They're just fighting."

"Do jays kill other birds?"

"Sometimes they do." I tried to change the subject: "What's your name?"

"Ronny Broadhurst. What kind of birds do they kill?"

"Young birds of other species."

The boy lifted his shoulders and held his folded arms close to his chest, like undeveloped wings. "Do they kill children?"

"No. They're not big enough."

This seemed to encourage him. "I'll try one of the peanuts now. Okay?"

"Okay."

He placed himself in front of me, face up and squinting against the morning light. "Throw it and I'll catch it in my mouth."

I threw a peanut, which he caught, and after that quite a few others. Some he caught and some fell in the grass. The jays were all around him like chunks of broken sky.

A young man in a peppermint-striped sport shirt came into the yard from the street. He looked like a grown-up version of the boy and gave the same impression of anxiety. He was puffing rapidly on a thin brown cigarillo.

As if she had been watching for the man, a woman with her dark hair in a pony-tail stepped out through the open door of the Wallers' apartment. She was pretty enough to make me conscious that I hadn't shaved.

The man pretended not to see her. He spoke to the boy formally: "Good morning, Ronald."

The boy glanced at him but didn't turn. As the man and the woman moved on him from different directions, the boy's face had lost its look of reckless pleasure. His small body seemed to grow smaller as if under the pressure of their meeting. He answered the man in a tiny voice:

"Good morning."

The man turned brusquely to the woman. "He's afraid of me. What have you been telling him, for God's sake?"

"We haven't been talking about you, Stan. For our own sake."

The man thrust his head forward. Without moving his feet, he gave the impression of attacking. "What does that mean, 'for our own sake'? Is that an accusation?"

"No, but I can think of a few if you like."

"So can I." His eyes moved in my direction. "Who's Ronny's playmate? Or is he *your* playmate?" He brandished the hot-tipped cigarillo in his hand.

5

"I don't even know this gentleman's name."

"Would that make a difference?" He didn't look at me.

The woman's face lost its color, as if she had become suddenly ill. "This is hard to take, Stan. I don't want trouble."

"If you didn't want trouble, why did you move out on me?"

"You know why." She said in a thin voice: "Is that girl still in the house?"

"We won't discuss her." Abruptly he turned to the boy. "Let's get out of here, Ron. We have a date with Grandma Nell in Santa Teresa."

The boy was standing between them with his fists clenched. He looked at his feet. "I don't want to go to Santa Teresa. Do I have to?"

"You have to," the woman said.

The boy edged in my direction. "But I want to stay here. I want to stay with the man." He took hold of my belt and stood with his head down, his face hidden from all adults.

His father moved on the boy. "Let go of him."

"I won't."

"Is he your mother's boyfriend? Is that what he is?"

"No."

"You're a little liar."

The man threw down his cigarillo and drew back his hand to slap the boy. I took hold of the boy under the arms, swung him out of reach, and held him. He was trembling.

The woman said: "Why don't you let him be, Stan? You can see what you're doing to him."

"What *you're* doing to him. I came here to take him on a nice trip. Mother's been looking forward to it. So what happens?" His voice rose in complaint. "I run into a nasty family scene, and Ron's all fixed up with a substitute father."

"You're not making too much sense," I said. "Ron and I are neighbors—very new neighbors. I only just met him."

"Then put him down. He's my son."

I put the boy down.

"And keep your dirty hands off him."

I was tempted to slug the man. But it wouldn't do the boy any good, and it wouldn't do the woman any good. I said in the quietest tone I knew:

"Go away now, mister."

"I've got a right to take my son with me."

The boy said to me: "Do I have to go with him?"

"He's your father, isn't he? You're lucky to have a father who wants to take you places."

"That's right," his mother put in. "Go along now, Ronny. You always get along better with your father when I'm not around. And Grandma Nell will be sad if you don't visit her."

The boy went to his father, head down, and put his hand in the man's hand. They headed for the street.

The woman said: "I apologize for my husband."

"You don't need to. He means nothing to me."

"He does to me, though, that's the trouble. He's so terribly aggressive. He wasn't always like this."

"He couldn't have been. He wouldn't have survived."

I meant this to be a light remark, but it fell heavily. The conversation died. I tried to revive it.

"Are the Wallers friends of yours, Mrs. Broadhurst?"

"Yes. Professor Waller was my adviser when I was in school." She sounded nostalgic. "As a matter of fact he still is my adviser. He and Laura both are. I called them at Lake Tahoe last night when I—" She failed to finish the sentence. "Are they friends of yours?"

"Good neighbors. My name is Archer, by the way. I live upstairs."

She nodded. "Laura Waller mentioned you last night, when

she offered me the use of their apartment. She said if I needed any kind of help, that I could call on you." She gave me a small cool smile. "In a way I have already, haven't I? Thank you for being so kind to my little boy."

"It was a pleasure."

But we were ill at ease. As angry people do, her husband had left his impression on the morning. The scene he had made still echoed dismally in the air. As if to dispel it, she said:

"I just perked some coffee. It's Laura Waller's special grind, and it looks as if it isn't going to get used. Would you like a cup?"

"Thanks, but it wouldn't be a good idea. Your husband might come back." In the street I had heard a car door open and then close, but no engine starting up. "He's pretty close to violence, Mrs. Broadhurst."

"Not really." But her tone was questioning.

"Yes, really. I've seen a lot of them, and I've learned not to stir them up when I can help it."

"Laura said that you're a detective. Is that right?" Something that looked like a challenge had come up into her face.

"Yes, but this is my day off. I hope."

I smiled, but I had said the wrong thing. A hurt look darkened her eyes and pinched her mouth. I blundered on:

"May I have a raincheck, Mrs. Broadhurst?"

She shook her head, not so much at me as at herself. "I don't know—I don't know if I'm going to stay here."

In the street the car door had opened. Stanley Broadhurst came back into the yard alone.

"Don't let me interrupt anything."

"There's nothing *to* interrupt," the woman said. "Where's Ronny?"

"In the car. He'll be all right after a little time with his father." He spoke as if the boy's father was someone else.

"You forgot to give me his toys and animals and stuff. He said you packed them."

"Yes, of course." Looking offended with herself, she hurried into the apartment and came out with a blue nylon airline bag. "Give my best regards to your mother."

There was no warmth in her voice and none in his answer: "Of course."

They sounded like a couple who never expected to see each other again. A pang of fear went through me—dull, because I was used to suppressing fear. I think it was mainly fear for the boy. At any rate, I wanted to stop Broadhurst and bring the boy back. But I didn't.

Broadhurst went out to the street. I climbed the outside stairs two at a time and walked quickly along the gallery to the front. A fairly new black Ford convertible was standing at the curb. A blond girl or woman in a sleeveless yellow dress was sitting in the front seat. Her left arm was around Ronny, who seemed to be holding himself in a strained position.

Stanley Broadhurst got into the front seat. He started the engine and drove away in a hurry. I didn't get a look at the girl's face. Foreshortened by the height, she was all bare shoulders and swelling breasts and flowing blond hair.

The pang of fear I felt for the boy had become a nagging ache. I went into my bathroom and looked at my face as if I could somehow read his future there. But all I could read was my own past, in the marks of erosion under my eyes, the mica glints of white and gray in my twenty-four-hour beard.

I shaved and put on a clean shirt and started downstairs again. Halfway down I paused and leaned on the handrail and told myself that I was descending into trouble: a pretty young woman with a likable boy and a wandering husband. A hot wind was blowing in my face.

ꝏꝏꝏꝏꝏꝏꝏꝏꝏꝏ

II

ꝏꝏꝏꝏꝏꝏꝏꝏꝏꝏ

I walked past the closed door of the Wallers' apartment and down the street to the nearest newsstand, where I bought the weekend edition of the Los Angeles *Times*. I lugged it home and spent most of the morning reading it. All of it, including the classified ads, which sometimes tell you more about Los Angeles than the news.

I had a cold shower. Then I sat down at the desk in my front room, looked at the balance in my checkbook, and paid the phone and light bills. Neither was overdue, and it made me feel dominant and controlled.

While I was putting my checks in envelopes, I heard a woman's steps approaching the door.

"Mr. Archer?"

I opened the door. Her hair was up, and she had on a short stylish multicolored dress and white textured stockings. There was blue shadow on her eyelids and carmine lipstick on her mouth. Behind all this she looked tense and vulnerable.

"I don't want to disturb you if you're busy."

"I'm not busy. Come in."

She stepped into the room and gave it a sweeping glance which lit up its contents like radar blips, one thing after another, and made me realize that the furniture was rather worn. I closed the door behind her and pulled the chair out from the desk.

"Won't you sit down?"

"Thank you." But she remained standing. "There's a fire in Santa Teresa. A forest fire. Did you know that?"

"No, but it's fire weather."

"According to the radio report it flared up quite near to Grandma Nell's—to my mother-in-law's estate. I've been trying to get her on the phone. Nobody answers. Ronny's supposed to be there, and I'm terribly worried."

"Why?"

She bit her lower lip and got a trace of lipstick on her teeth. "I don't trust Stanley to look after him properly. I should never have let him take Ronny away."

"Why did you?"

"I have no right to deprive Stanley of his son. And a boy needs his father's companionship."

"Not Stanley's, in his present mood."

She looked at me soberly and leaned toward me with one tentative hand extended. "Help me to get him back, Mr. Archer."

"Ronny," I said, "or Stanley?"

"Both of them. But it's Ronny I'm most concerned about. The man on the radio said they may have to evacuate some of the houses. I don't know what's going on in Santa Teresa."

She raised her hand to her forehead and covered her eyes. I led her to the chesterfield and persuaded her to sit down. Then I went out to the kitchen and rinsed a glass and filled it with water. Her throat vibrated as she drank. Her long white-stockinged dancer's legs protruded into the shabby room as if from some more theatrical dimension.

I sat at the desk, half-turned to face her. "What's your mother-in-law's number?"

She gave it to me, with the area code, and I dialed direct.

The phone at the other end buzzed urgently nine or ten times.

The gentle crash of the receiver being lifted took me by surprise. A woman's voice said: "Yes?"

"Is that Mrs. Broadhurst?"

"Yes, it is." Her voice was firm but polite.

"Stanley's wife wants to talk to you. Hold on."

I handed the receiver to the young woman, and she took my place at the desk. I went into the bedroom, closing the door behind me, and picked up the extension phone by my bed.

The older woman was saying: "I haven't seen Stanley. Saturday is my Pink Lady day, as he well knows, and I just got back from the hospital."

"Aren't you expecting him?"

"Perhaps later in the day, Jean."

"But he said he had a date with you this morning, that he had promised to take Ronny to see you."

"Then I presume he will." The older woman's voice had become guarded and more precise. "I fail to see why it's so important—"

"They left here hours ago," Jean said. "And I understand there's a fire in your neighborhood."

"There is. It's why I rushed home from the hospital. You'll forgive me now if I say goodbye, Jean."

She hung up, and so did I. When I went back into the living room, Jean was frowning at the receiver in her hand, as if it was a live thing which had died on her.

"Stan lied to me," she said. "His mother was at the hospital all morning. He took that girl to an empty house."

"Are you and Stanley breaking up?"

"I guess maybe we are. *I* don't want to."

"Who is the blond girl?"

She lifted the receiver in her hand and slammed it down rather violently. I felt as if she was hanging up on me.

"We won't discuss it," she said.

I changed the subject, slightly. "How long have you and Stanley been separated?"

"Just since yesterday. We're not really separated. I thought if Stanley talked to his mother—" She paused.

"That she'd take your side? I wouldn't count on it."

She looked at me in some surprise. "Do you know Mrs. Broadhurst?"

"No. But I still wouldn't count on it. Does Mrs. Broadhurst have money?"

"Am I—is it so obvious?"

"No. But there has to be a reason for everything. Your husband sort of used his mother's name to get Ronny away from you."

It sounded like an accusation, and she bowed her head under it. "Someone's been talking to you about us."

"You have."

"But I didn't say anything about Mrs. Broadhurst. Or the blond."

"I thought you did."

She went into deep thought. It sat prettily on her, softening the anxious angularity of her posture. "I know. Last night, after I called the Wallers in Tahoe, they called you and filled you in on me. What did Laura say, or was it Bob?"

"Nothing. They didn't call me."

"Then how do you know about the blond girl?"

"Isn't there always a blond girl?"

"You're putting me on," she said in a younger voice. "And under the circumstances it isn't very nice."

"Okay. I saw her." I realized as I spoke that I was volunteering as a witness—her witness—and my last hope or pretense of staying out of her life was being talked away. "She was in the car with them when they left here."

"Why didn't you tell me? I would have stopped them."

"How?"

"I don't know how." She looked at her hands. All of a sudden her face was disorganized by a rueful flash of humor. "I could carry a wife sign, I guess, or sit down in front of the car. Or write a letter to an astronaut."

I interrupted her before she got hysterical. "At least he's being open about it. And with the boy along, they're not likely to do anything—" I let the sentence trail off.

She shook her lovely head. "I don't know what they're likely to do. The fact that they're being so open, as you say, is one of the things that worries me. I think they're both crazy. I mean it. He brought her home from the office last night, and asked her to stay for dinner without consulting me. She was high on something when she arrived, and pretty vague in her answers."

"What kind of an office does Stanley have?"

"He works for an insurance firm in Northridge—that's where we live. She doesn't work in the office—I don't mean that. She wouldn't last a day. Possibly she's a student at the college or even a high school student. She's young enough."

"How young?"

"She can't be more than nineteen. That was one of the things that made me suspicious right off. According to Stanley, she was an old school friend who'd got in touch with him at the office. But he's at least seven or eight years older than she is."

"What was she high on?"

"I have no idea. But I didn't like the things she said to Ronny. I didn't like them at all. I asked Stanley to get rid of her. He refused. So I called Laura Waller—and came here."

"Maybe you shouldn't have."

"I know that now. I should have stayed in my own house and had it out with them. The trouble is, Stanley and I haven't been close for a long time. He's been wrapped up in his own concerns and completely uninterested in me. It sort of deprives a girl of any ground to stand on."

"Did you want out of the marriage?"

She considered the question soberly. "It never occurred to me. But maybe I do. I'll have to think about it." She stood up, leaning like a model on my desk, with one hip out. "But not now, Mr. Archer. I have to go to Santa Teresa. Will you drive me there, and help me get Ronny back?"

"I'm a private detective. I do these things for a living."

"Laura Waller told me. It's why I asked you. And of course I expect to pay you."

I opened the door and set the self-lock. "What else did Mrs. Waller tell you about me?"

She said with her bright disorganized smile: "That you were a lonely man."

III

I waited for her in the front room of the Wallers' apartment. The walls were lined with books, many of them in foreign languages, like insulation against the immediate present. She came out carrying a large handbag, and coats for herself and the absent boy.

I got my car out of the garage at the rear of the building, and we headed inland for the Ventura Freeway. The early afternoon sun glared on the traffic, flashing unpredictably on windshields and chromium. I turned up the air conditioning.

"That feels good," she said. Her presence beside me sustained an illusive feeling that there was an opening there into another time-track or dimension. It had more future than the world I knew, and not so bloody much traffic.

After I made the turn onto Sepulveda, I spent a little time preparing a remark.

"I seem to be getting less lonely, Mrs. Broadhurst."

"Call me Jean. Mrs. Broadhurst sounds like my mother-in-law."

"Is that bad?"

"Not necessarily. She's a pretty good woman—a lady, in fact, and a good sport. But underneath all that she's terribly sad. I suppose that's what manners are for, to cover up."

"What's she so sad about?"

"A lot of things." She looked at the side of my face, my one visible eye. "You're quite inquisitive, aren't you, Mr. Archer?"

"It's my working habit."

"And you're working?"

"You asked me to. Did the fact that I live where I do have anything to do with your moving in below?"

"The fact that you're a detective?"

"Roughly, yes."

"It may have. You may have been part of the whole Gestalt. Does it matter?"

"To me it does. I don't believe in coincidences. And I like to know exactly where I stand."

"You're lucky if you do."

"Is that a threat?" I said.

"It's more of a confession. I was thinking about myself—and where I stand."

"While you're confessing—did you send Ronny out this morning to help me feed the birds?"

"No." Her tone was definite. "That was his own idea." She added: "If you don't believe in coincidence, there's not much room for spontaneity, either. In your world."

"It isn't *my* world. I'm interested in the whole Gestalt you mentioned. Tell me about it."

She said haltingly: "I don't know what you want me to tell you."

"Everything that led up to this."

"You take it seriously, don't you?" I could hear the slight edge of surprise in her voice.

"Yes."

"I take it seriously, too. After all it's my life, and it's going to pieces. But as for explaining it, I wouldn't know where to begin."

"Just give me the pieces. You've already started, with Mrs. Broadhurst. What's she so sad about?"

"She's getting old."

"So am I, and I'm not sad."

"Aren't you? Anyway, it's different for a woman."

"Isn't Mr. Broadhurst getting old?"

"There is no Mr. Broadhurst. He ran away with another woman some years ago. Stanley seems to be repeating the pattern."

"How old was he when his father took off?"

"Eleven or twelve. Stanley never talks about it, but it was the main event of his childhood. I have to remember that when I'm judging him. When his father left, I think he felt even worse than his mother did."

"How do you know, if he never talks about it?"

"You ask good questions," she said.

"Give me a good answer, Jean."

She took her time. I couldn't see her face, but peripheral vision made me aware of her sitting beside me with her hands in her lap. Her head was bowed over her empty hands as if she was trying to untie a knot or unwind a ball of string.

"My husband has been looking for his father for some time," she said, "and gradually breaking up. Or maybe I've got it turned around. He's been looking for his father in the hope that it would put him back together."

"Did Stanley have a breakdown?"

"Nothing as definite as that. But his whole life has been a kind of breakdown. He's one of those overconfident people who turns out to have no confidence at all. And it makes him stupid. He barely got through the university. As a matter of fact, that was how I met him. I was in his French class, and he hired me to tutor him." She added with a kind of ironic precision: "The tutorial relationship persisted into our marriage."

"It can be tough on a man, to be married to a woman smarter than he is."

"It can be tough on the woman, too. But I didn't say I was smarter than Stanley, exactly. He's just a man who hasn't found himself."

"Is he looking?"

"He's been looking terribly hard, for a long time."

"For his father."

"That's the way he puts it to himself. He seems to feel that when his father ran out on him, it robbed his life of its meaning. That sounds like nonsense, but it isn't really. He's angry at his father for abandoning him; at the same time he misses him and loves him. The two together can be paralyzing."

The depth of feeling in her voice surprised me. She cared for her husband more than she admitted.

We crossed the low pass and began the descent into the valley. Above its floor, layers of brown dust were stacked in the air, obscuring the mountains on the far side. Like something in an old movie, a World War Two bomber labored up from Van Nuys Airport and turned north. It was probably headed for the fire in Santa Teresa.

I didn't mention this to the woman beside me. Another thought had begun to nag at my mind. If Stanley was following in his father's footsteps and running away with a girl, he wouldn't be likely to head straight for the town where his mother lived. Las Vegas, or possibly Mexico, was a more likely destination.

We passed a "Northridge" sign. I glanced at the woman. She was bent forward, unwinding her invisible ball of string.

"How far is your house from the freeway?"

"About five minutes. Why?"

"We ought to check there. We don't know that Stanley took the boy to Santa Teresa."

"You think they may be at the house?"

"It isn't likely, but it's possible. Let's have a look, anyway."

It was on a street named College Circle, one of a group of brand new houses with two-story porticoes supported by large wooden pillars. They were differentiated by their colors. The Broadhurst house was dark blue with light blue pillars.

Jean went in at the front door. I found when I followed the driveway around to the back that behind its imposing front it was just another tract house, as if the architect had tried to combine a southern plantation mansion with the slave quarters. A grape-stake fence separated the back yard from the neighbors'.

The garage door was locked. I went around to the window

at the side. The only car in the double garage, a green Mercedes sedan, bore no resemblance to the black convertible Stanley had been driving.

Jean opened the back door of the house from the inside. She gave me an appalled look, and came running across the grass to the garage window.

"They're not *in* there, are they?"

"No."

"Thank heaven. I thought for a minute they'd committed suicide or something." She stood beside me at the window. "That's not our car."

"Whose is it?"

"It must be hers. I remember now—she and Stanley came in separate cars last night. She has her nerve—leaving her car in my garage." Jean turned toward me, her face hardening. "Incidentally, she slept in Ronny's bed. I don't like that."

"Show me."

I followed her in through the back door. The house was already showing signs of abandonment. In the kitchen, unwashed dishes were piled in the sink and on the counters. On the top of the free-standing stove were a skillet half full of congealed grease and a saucepan containing something that smelled like pea soup but looked like cracked green mud. And there were flies.

The boy's room on the second floor was papered with pictures of friendly animals. The bedclothes were rumpled and twisted, as if the girl visitor had spent a troubled night. The red marks of her mouth were on the pillow, like a signature, and under the pillow was a copy of the novel *Green Mansions* bound in faded green cloth.

I examined the flyleaf of the book. It had a bookplate with an engraving of an angel or a muse writing in a scroll with a peacock-plume pen. The name on the bookplate was

Ellen Strome. Under it another name was inscribed in pencil: Jerry Kilpatrick.

I closed the book and slipped it into my jacket pocket.

ᴓᴓᴓᴓᴓᴓᴓᴓᴓᴓᴓᴓᴓ

IV

ᴓᴓᴓᴓᴓᴓᴓᴓᴓᴓᴓᴓᴓ

Jean Broadhurst came into the room behind me. "At least he didn't sleep with her."

"Where did your husband sleep?"

"In his study."

She showed me the little room on the ground floor. It contained a few shelves of books, a closed rolltop desk, an unmade daybed, and a gray steel filing cabinet standing like a cenotaph at the head of the bed. I turned to the woman:

"Does Stanley usually sleep in here?"

"You ask some pretty personal questions."

"You'll get used to it. I take it that he does usually sleep in here."

She colored. "He's been working at night on his files. He doesn't like to disturb me."

I gave the top drawer of the filing cabinet a tentative pull. It was locked.

"What kind of files does he keep in this?"

"It's his father's file," she said.

"His father's file?"

"Stanley keeps a file on his father—everything he's been

able to dig up about him, which isn't much. And all the false leads—the dozens of people he's talked to or written to, trying to find out where his father is. It's been his main occupation these last couple of years." She added wryly: "At least I've known where he was keeping himself nights."

"What sort of a man was his father?"

"I don't actually know. It's funny, with all this information"—she tapped the metal side of the filing cabinet—"Stanley doesn't really talk about him at all. He has long silences on the subject. His mother has even longer silences. I do know he was a captain of infantry in the Pacific. Stanley has a picture of him in uniform. He was a good-looking man with a nice smile."

I looked around at the paneled plywood walls. They were empty except for a business calendar which alleged that it was still the month of June.

"Where does he keep the picture of his father?"

"In plexiglass, so it doesn't get worn out."

"What would wear it out?"

"Showing it to people. He also has pictures of him playing tennis, and riding a polo pony, and one at the wheel of his yacht."

"I gather his father had a lot of money?"

"Quite a lot. At least Mrs. Broadhurst has."

"And her husband walked out on it and her for the sake of a woman?"

"So I've been told."

"Who was the woman?"

"I have no idea. Stanley and his mother don't discuss the subject. All I know is that Mr. Broadhurst and the woman eloped to San Francisco. Stanley and I spent two weeks in San Francisco last June. Stanley tramped around the city with his pictures. He covered most of the downtown district before he was through. I had quite a time getting him to come back with us. He wanted to quit his job and go on searching the Bay area."

"Assuming he finds his father, what then?"

"I don't know. I don't think Stanley knows, either."

"You said he was eleven or twelve when his father left. How long ago was that?"

"Stanley's twenty-seven now. Fifteen years."

"Can he afford to quit his job?"

"No, he can't. We owe a good deal of money, to his mother and other people. But he's getting so irresponsible, it's all I can do to keep him on the job." She was quiet for a moment, looking at the blank walls of the room, the calendar which hadn't been changed in several months.

I said: "Do you have a key to the filing cabinet?"

"No. There's only the one, and Stanley keeps it. He keeps the rolltop desk locked, too. He doesn't like me to look at his correspondence."

"Do you think he's been corresponding with the girl?"

"I have no idea. He gets letters from all over. I don't open them."

"What's her name, do you know?"

"She said her name was Sue, at least she told Ronny that."

"I'd like to take a look at the registration of that Mercedes. What about a key to the garage?"

"That I have. I keep it in the kitchen."

I followed her out to the kitchen, where she opened a cupboard and took the key off a nail. I used it to open up the garage. The key of the Mercedes was in the ignition. There was no registration, but crumpled in the back of the dash compartment I found an auto insurance invoice made out to a Mr. Roger Armistead of 10 Crescent Drive in Santa

Teresa. I copied the name and address in my black notebook and climbed out of the car.

"What did you find?" Jean said.

I showed her my open notebook. "Do you know Roger Armistead?"

"I'm afraid not. Crescent Drive is a good address, though."

"And that Mercedes is worth a lot of money. Stanley's old school friend seems to be loaded. Or else she stole it."

Jean made a quick quelling motion with her hand. "Please don't talk so loudly." She went on in a voice that was conscious of the neighbors beyond the grape-stake fence: "That story of his was ridiculous. She couldn't possibly be his old school friend. She's at least six or seven years younger, as I said. Besides, he attended a private boys' school in Santa Teresa."

I flipped open my notebook again. "Give me a description of her."

"She's a good-looking blond girl, about my height, five foot six. Nice figure. Perhaps she weighs 115 pounds or so. Her eyes are a shade of blue. They're her best feature, really—and also her strangest."

"Strange in what way?"

"I couldn't read them," she said. "I couldn't tell if she was absolutely innocent or absolutely cold and amoral. That isn't an afterthought, either. It was my first reaction when she came in with Stanley."

"Did he give any clue as to why he brought her home with him?"

"He said she needed food and rest, and he expected me to serve her dinner. Which I did. But she hardly ate a thing—a little pea soup."

"Did she talk much?"

"Not to me. She talked to Ronny."

"What about?"

"It was nonsense talk, really. She told him a wild story about a little girl who was left alone all night in a house in the mountains. Her parents were killed by monsters and the little girl was carried off by a big bird like a condor. She said that had happened to her when she was his age. She asked my son if he would like it to happen to him. It was fantasy, of course, but it had an ugly element, as if she was trying to unload her hysteria on Ronny."

"What was his reaction? Was he frightened?"

"Not exactly. He seemed to be kind of fascinated by her. I was not. I broke it up and sent him to his room."

"Did she say anything about taking him away?"

"She didn't say it directly. But that was the message, wasn't it? It scared me at the time. I should have acted on it and got rid of her."

"What scared you?"

She looked up at the sky, which was full of blowing dust. "She was afraid, I think, and I caught it from her. Of course, I was upset already. It was so unusual for Stanley to do what he did, bringing her home like some kind of child bride. I realized that here my life was changing, and there was nothing I could do about it."

"It's been changing for some time, hasn't it? Since June."

Her gaze came down, full of darkened sky. "June was the month we went to San Francisco. Why do *you* say June?"

"It was the last month your husband tore off the calendar in his study."

A car with a noisy engine pulled up in front, and a man appeared at the corner of the house. His body seemed ill at ease in his dark rumpled suit. His long pale face had cornices of scar tissue over the eyes.

He came toward us along the driveway. "Is Stanley Broadhurst here?"

"I'm afraid he isn't," Jean said uneasily.

"Would you be Mrs. Broadhurst, by any chance?" The man spoke with elaborate politeness, but an undertone of aggression buzzed in his voice.

"Yes, I'm Mrs. Broadhurst."

"When do you expect your husband back?"

"I really don't know."

"You must have a rough idea."

"I'm afraid I don't."

"If you don't, who does?"

He sounded like a man who was full of trouble. I stepped between him and Jean:

"Broadhurst's left town for the weekend. Who are you and what do you want?"

The man didn't answer me right away. He went into an intense quiet rage, swinging his hand up and slapping his own face. The blow left a four-fingered mark burning red on his cheek.

"Who I am is my concern," he said. "I want my money. You better get in touch and tell him that. I'm blowing this town tonight and taking the money with me."

"What money are you talking about?"

"That's between he and I. Just give him the message. I'm willing to take the even thousand if I get it by tonight. Otherwise the sky will be the limit. Tell him that."

His cold eyes didn't believe what his mouth was saying. I guessed he was an old con. He had the prison pallor, and he appeared ill at ease in the open daylight. He was sticking close to the wall as if he needed something to contain him.

"My husband doesn't have that kind of money."

"His mother has."

"What do you know about his mother?" Jean said in a thin voice.

26

"I happen to know she's loaded. He said he'd get it from her today and have it for me tonight."

I said: "You're a little early, aren't you?"

"It's a good thing I am, with him out of town and all."

"What's he buying from you?"

"If I told you, I couldn't sell it, could I?" He gave me the tricky look of a half-smart man who had never learned the limits of his own intelligence. "Tell him I'll be back here tonight. If he don't pay me then, the sky's the limit."

"There may not be anyone here then," I said. "Why don't you give me your name and address, and we'll get in touch with you?"

He considered my proposal, and finally said: "You can reach me at the Star Motel. That's below Topanga Canyon on the coast highway. Ask for Al."

I made a note of the address. "No phone?"

"You can't deliver money over the phone."

He gave us a dim eroded smile and went. I followed him to the corner of the house and watched him drive off in an old black Volkswagen. It had a missing front fender and a license plate so dirty I couldn't read it.

"Do you think he's telling the truth?" Jean said.

"I doubt if he knows, himself. He'd have to take a lie-detector test to find out. And he'd probably flunk it."

"What's Stanley doing with that kind of person?"

"You know Stanley better than I do."

"I'm beginning to wonder."

We went into the house, and I asked Jean's permission to use the phone in the study again. I wanted to get in touch with the owner of the Mercedes. Santa Teresa Information gave me Armistead's number, and I dialed it.

A woman's voice answered impatiently: "Yes?"

"May I talk to Mr. Armistead?"

"He isn't here."

"Where can I find him?"

"That depends on what you want him for," she said.

"Are you Mrs. Armistead?"

"Yes." She sounded ready to hang up on me.

"I'm trying to trace a young woman. An unnatural blond—"

She cut in in a much more interested voice: "Did she spend Thursday night on a yacht in the Santa Teresa marina?"

"I don't know."

"What *do* you know about her?"

"She was driving a green Mercedes. Apparently it's your husband's."

"It's *my* car. It's my yacht, too, for that matter. Did she wreck the Mercedes?"

"No."

"I want it back. Where is it?"

"I'll tell you if you let me come and talk to you."

"Is this some kind of a shakedown? Did Roger put you up to this?" There was a tremolo of anger and hurt in her voice.

"I've never seen him in my life."

"Count yourself fortunate. What's your name?"

"Archer."

"What do you do for a living, Mr. Archer?"

"I'm a private detective."

"I see. And what do you want to talk to me about?"

"The blond girl. I don't know her name. Do you?"

"No. Is she in trouble?"

"She seems to be."

"How old is she?"

"Eighteen or nineteen."

"I see," she said in a smaller, thinner voice. "Did Roger give her the car, or was it stolen?"

"You'll have to ask Roger. Shall I bring you the car?"

"Where are you calling from?"

"Northridge, but I'm on my way to Santa Teresa. We can have a talk, perhaps."

There was a short silence. I asked Mrs. Armistead if she was there.

"I'm here. But I'm not sure I want to talk to you. However," she added in a stronger voice, "the car belongs to me and I want it back. I'm willing to pay you, reasonably."

"We'll discuss that when I see you."

I backed the Mercedes out of the garage and put my car in its place. When I made my way back to the study, Jean was talking again on the phone to her mother-in-law.

She set the receiver down and told me that Stanley and Ronny and the girl had visited the ranch that morning in Mrs. Broadhurst's absence. "The gardener gave them the key to the Mountain House."

"What's that?"

"A guest cabin in the hills back of the ranch. Where the fire is."

∽₯₯∽₯₯∽₯₯∽₯₯∽₯₯∽₯₯∽

V

∽₯₯∽₯₯∽₯₯∽₯₯∽₯₯∽₯₯∽

Before we reached Santa Teresa I could smell smoke. Then I could see it dragging like a veil across the face of the mountain behind the city.

Under and through the smoke I caught glimpses of fire like the flashes of heavy guns too far away to be heard. The illusion of war was completed by an old two-engine bomber which flew in low over the mountain's shoulder. The plane was lost in the smoke for a long instant, then climbed out trailing a pastel red cloud of fire retardant.

On the freeway ahead the traffic thickened rapidly and stopped us. I reached over to turn on the car radio but then decided not to. The woman beside me had enough on her mind without having to listen to fire reports.

At the head of the line, a highway patrolman was directing the movement of traffic from a side road onto the freeway. There were quite a few cars coming down out of the hills, many of them with Santa Teresa College decals. I noticed several trucks piled with furniture and mattresses, children and dogs.

When the patrolman let us pass, we turned onto the road that led to the hills. It took us in a gradual climb between lemon groves and subdivisions toward what Jean described as Mrs. Broadhurst's canyon.

A man wearing a Forest Service jacket and a yellow hard hat stopped the Mercedes at the entrance to the canyon. Jean climbed out and introduced herself as Mrs. Broadhurst's daughter-in-law.

"I hope you're not planning to stay, ma'am. We may have to evacuate this area."

"Have you seen my husband and little boy?" She described Ronny—six years old, blue-eyed, black-haired, wearing a light-blue suit.

He shook his head. "I've seen a lot of people leaving with their kids. It isn't a bad idea. Once the fire starts spilling down one of these canyons she can outrace you."

"How bad is it?" I said.

"It depends on the wind. If the wind stays quiet we could get her fully contained before nightfall. We've got a lot of equipment up on the mountain. But if she starts to blow—" He lifted his hand in a kind of resigned goodbye to everything in sight.

We drove into the canyon between fieldstone gate posts emblazoned with the name Canyon Estates. New and expensive houses were scattered along the canyonside among the oaks and boulders. Men and women with hoses were watering their yards and buildings and the surrounding brush. Their children were watching them, or sitting quietly in cars, ready to go. The smoke towering up from the mountain stood over them like a threat and changed the color of the light.

The Broadhurst ranch lay between these houses and the fire. We went up the canyon toward it, and left the county road at Mrs. Broadhurst's mailbox. Her private asphalt lane wound through acres of mature avocado trees. Their broad leaves were shriveling at the tips as if the fire had already touched them. Darkening fruit hung down from their branches like green hand grenades.

The lane broadened into a circular drive in front of a large and simple white stucco ranchhouse. Under the deep porch, red fuchsias dripped from hanging redwood baskets. At a red glass hummingbird feeder suspended among the baskets, a hummingbird which also seemed suspended was sipping from a spout and treading air.

The bird didn't move perceptibly when a woman opened the screen door and came out. She had on a white shirt and dark slacks which showed off her narrow waist. She moved across the veranda with rapid disciplined energy, making the high heels of her riding boots click.

"Jean darling."

"Mother."

They shook hands briefly like competitors before a match of some kind. Mrs. Broadhurst's neat dark head was touched with gray, but she was younger than I'd imagined, no more than fifty or so.

Only her eyes looked older. Without moving them from Jean's face, she shook her head from side to side.

"No, they haven't come back. And they haven't been seen in the area for some time. Who's the blond girl?"

"I don't know."

"Is Stanley having an affair with her?"

"I don't know, Mother." She turned to me. "This is Mr. Archer."

Mrs. Broadhurst nodded curtly. "Jean mentioned on the telephone that you're some kind of detective. Is that correct?"

"The private kind."

She raked me with a look that moved from my eyes down to my shoes and back up to my face again. "I've never set much store by private detectives, frankly. But under the circumstances perhaps you can be useful. If the radio can be believed, the fire has passed the Mountain House and left it untouched. Would you like to come up there with me?"

"I would. After I talk to the gardener."

"That won't be necessary."

"But I understand he gave your son a key to the Mountain House. He may know why they wanted it."

"He doesn't. I've questioned Fritz. We're wasting time, and I've already wasted a good deal. I stayed by the telephone until you and Jean got here."

"Where is Fritz?"

"You're persistent, aren't you? He may be in the lath house."

We left Jean standing white-faced and apprehensive in the shadow of the veranda. The lath house was in a walled garden behind one wing of the ranchhouse. Mrs. Broadhurst followed me in under the striped shadows cast by the roof.

"Fritz? Mr. Archer wants to ask you a question."

A soft-looking man in dungarees straightened up from the plants he was tending. He had emotional green eyes and a skittish way of holding his body, as if he was ready to avoid a threatened blow. There was a livid scar connecting his mouth and his nose which looked as if he had been born with a harelip.

"What is it this time?" he said.

"I'm trying to find out what Stanley Broadhurst is up to. Why do you think he wanted the key to the guest house?"

Fritz shrugged his thick loose shoulders. "I don't know. I can't read people's minds, can I?"

"You must have some idea."

He glanced uncomfortably at Mrs. Broadhurst. "Am I supposed to spit it all out?"

"Please tell the truth," she said in a forced tone.

"Well, naturally I thought him and the chick had hanky-

33

panky in mind. Why else would they want to go up there?"

"With my grandson along?" Mrs. Broadhurst said.

"They wanted me to keep the boy with me. But I didn't want the responsibility. That's the way you get in trouble," he said with stupid wisdom.

"You didn't mention that before. You should have told me, Fritz."

"I can't remember everything at once, can I?"

"How was the boy behaving?" I asked him.

"Okay. He didn't say much."

"Neither do you."

"What do you want me to say? You think I did something to the boy?" His voice rose, and his eyes grew moist and suddenly overflowed.

"Nobody suggested anything like that."

"Then why do you keep at me and at me? The boy was here with his father. His father took him away. Does that make me responsible?"

"Take it easy."

Mrs. Broadhurst touched my arm. "We're getting nowhere."

We left the gardener complaining among his plants. The striped shadow fell from the roof, jailbirding him.

The carport was attached to an old red barn at the back of the house. Below the barn was a dry creekbed at the bottom of a shallow ravine which was thickly grown with oaks and eucalyptus. Band-tailed pigeons and sweet-voiced red-winged blackbirds were foraging under the trees and around a feeder. I stepped on fallen eucalyptus pods which looked like ornate bronze nailheads set in the dust.

An aging Cadillac and an old pickup truck stood under the carport. Mrs. Broadhurst drove the pickup, wrestling it angrily around the curves in the avocado grove and turning left on the road toward the mountains. Beyond the avocados were ancient olive trees, and beyond them was pasture gone to brush.

We were approaching the head of the canyon. The smell of burning grew stronger in my nostrils. I felt as though we were going against nature, but I didn't mention my qualms to Mrs. Broadhurst. She wasn't the sort of woman you confessed human weakness to.

The road degenerated as we climbed. It was narrow and inset with boulders. Mrs. Broadhurst jerked at the wheel of the truck as if it was a male animal resisting control. For some reason I was reminded of Mrs. Roger Armistead's voice on the phone, and I asked Mrs. Broadhurst if she knew the woman.

She answered shortly: "I've seen her at the beach club. Why do you ask?"

"The Armistead name came up in connection with your son's friend, the blond girl."

"How?"

"She was using their Mercedes."

"I'm not surprised at the connection. The Armisteads are *nouveaux riches* from down south—not my kind of people." Without really changing the subject, she went on: "We've lived here for quite a long time, you know. My grandfather Falconer's ranch took in a good part of the coastal plain and the whole mountainside, all the way to the top of the first range. All I have left is a few hundred acres."

While I was trying to think of an appropriate comment, she said in a more immediate voice: "Stanley phoned me last night and asked me for fifteen hundred dollars cash, today."

"What for?"

"He said something vague, about buying information. As you may or may not know, my son is somewhat hipped on the subject of his father's desertion." Her voice was dry and careful.

"His wife told me that."

"Did she? It occurred to me that the fifteen hundred dollars might have something to do with you."

"It doesn't." I thought of Al, the pale man in the dark suit, but decided not to bring him up right now.

"Who's paying you?" the woman said rather sharply.

"I haven't been paid."

"I see." She sounded as if she distrusted what she saw. "Are you and my daughter-in-law good friends?"

"I met her this morning. We have friends in common."

"Then you probably know that Stanley and she have been close to breaking up. I never did think that their marriage would last."

"Why?"

"Jean is an intelligent girl but she comes from an entirely different class. I don't believe she's ever understood my son, though I've tried to explain something about our family traditions." She turned her head from the road to glance at me. "Is Stanley really interested in this blond girl?"

"Obviously he is, but maybe not in the way you mean. He wouldn't have brought your grandson along—"

"Don't be too sure of that. He brought Ronny because he knows I love the boy, and because he wants money from me. Remember when he found I wasn't here, he tried to leave Ronny with Fritz. I'd give a lot to know what they're up to."

VI

At the base of a sandstone bluff where the road petered out entirely, she stopped the pickup and we got out.

"This is where we shift to shanks' mare," she said. "Ordinarily we could have driven around by way of Rattlesnake Road, but that's where they're fighting the fire."

In the lee of the bluff was a brown wooden sign, "Falconer Trail." The trail was a dusty track bulldozed out of the steep side of the canyon. As Mrs. Broadhurst went up ahead of me, she explained that her father had given the land for the trail to the Forest Service. She sounded as if she was trying to cheer herself in any way she could.

I ate her dust until I was looking down into the tops of the tallest sycamores in the canyon below. A daytime moon hung over the bluff, and we went on climbing toward it. When we reached the top I was wet under my clothes.

About a hundred yards back from the edge, a large weathered redwood cabin stood against a grove of trees. Some of the trees had been blackened and maimed where the fire had burned an erratic swath through the grove. The cabin itself was partly red and looked as if it had been splashed with blood.

Beyond the trees was a black hillside where the fire had

browsed. The hillside slanted up to a ridge road and continued rising beyond the ridge to where the fire was now. It seemed to be moving laterally across the face of the mountain. The flames that from a distance had looked like artillery flashes were crashing through the thick chaparral like cavalry.

The ridge road was about midway between us and the main body of the fire. Toward the east, where the foothills flattened out into a mesa, the road curved down toward a collection of buildings which looked like a small college. Between them and the fire, bulldozers were crawling back and forth on the face of the mountain, cutting a firebreak in the deep brush.

The road was clogged with tanker trucks and other heavy equipment. Men stood around them in waiting attitudes, as if by behaving modestly and discreetly they could make the fire stay up on the mountain and die there, like an unwanted god.

As Mrs. Broadhurst and I approached the cabin I could see that part of its walls and roof had been splashed from the air with red fire retardant. The rest of the walls and the shutters over the windows were weathered gray.

The door was hanging open, with the key in the Yale lock. Mrs. Broadhurst walked up to it slowly, as if she dreaded what she might find inside. But there was nothing unusual to be seen in the big rustic front room. The ashes in the stone fireplace were cold, and might have been cold for years. Pieces of old-fashioned furniture draped with canvas stood around like formless images of the past.

Mrs. Broadhurst sat down heavily on a canvas-covered armchair. Dust rose around her. She coughed and spoke in a different voice, low and ashamed:

"I came up the trail a little too fast, I'm afraid."

I went out to the kitchen to get her some water. There were cups in the cupboard, but when I turned on the tap in the tin sink no water came. The butane stove was disconnected, too.

I walked through the other rooms while I was at it: two downstairs bedrooms and a sleeping loft which was reached by steep wooden stairs. The loft was lit by a dormer window, and there were three beds in it, covered with canvas. One of them looked rumpled. I stripped the canvas off it. On the heavy gray blanket underneath there was a Rorschach blot of blood which looked recent but not fresh.

I went down to the big front room. Mrs. Broadhurst had rested her head against the back of the chair. Her closed face was smooth and peaceful, and she was snoring gently.

I heard the rising roar of a plane coming in low over the mountain. I went out the back door in time to see its red spoor falling on the fire. The plane grew smaller, its roar diminuendoed.

Two deer—a doe and a fawn—came down the slope in a dry creek channel, heading for the grove. They saw me and rockinghorsed over a fallen log into the trees.

From the rear of the cabin a washed-out gravel lane overgrown with weeds meandered toward the ridge road. Starting along the lane toward the trees, I noticed wheel tracks in the weeds leading off toward a small stable. The wheel tracks looked new, and I could see only one set of them.

I followed them to the stable and peered in. A black convertible that looked like Stanley's stood there with the top down. I found the registration in the dash compartment. It was Stanley's all right.

I slammed the door of the convertible. A noise that sounded like an echo or a response came from the direction of the trees. Perhaps it was the crack of a stick breaking. I went out and headed for the partly burned grove. All I could hear was the sound of my own footsteps and a faint sighing which came from the wind in the trees.

Then I made out a more distant noise which I didn't recognize. It sounded like the whirring of wings. I felt hot wind on my face, and glanced up the slope.

The wall of smoke that hung above the fire was leaning out from the mountain. At its base the fire was burning more brightly and had changed direction. Outriders of flame were leaping down the slope to the left, and firemen were moving along the ridge road to meet them.

The wind was changing. I could hear it rattling now among the leaves—the same sound that had wakened me in West Los Angeles early that morning. There were human noises, too—sounds of movement among the trees.

"Stanley?" I said.

A man in a blue suit and a red hard hat stepped out from behind the blotched trunk of a sycamore. He was a big man, and he moved with a kind of clumsy lightness.

"Looking for somebody?" He had a quiet cool voice, which gave the effect of holding itself in reserve.

"Several people."

"I'm the only one around," he said pleasantly.

His heavy arms and thighs bulged through his business clothes. His face was wet, and there was dirt on his shoes. He took off his hard hat, wiping his face and forehead with a bandana handkerchief. His hair was gray and clipped short, like fur on a cannonball.

I walked toward him, into the skeletal shadow of the sycamore. The smoky moon was lodged in its top, segmented by small black branches. With a quick conjurer's motion, the big man produced a pack of cigarettes from his breast pocket and thrust it toward me.

"Smoke?"

"No thanks. I don't smoke."

"Don't smoke cigarettes, you mean?"

"I gave them up."

"What about cigars?"

"I never liked them," I said. "Are you taking a poll?"

"You might call it that." He smiled broadly, revealing several gold teeth. "How about cigarillos? Some people smoke them instead of cigarettes."

"I've noticed that."

"These people you say you're looking for, do any of them smoke cigarillos?"

"I don't think so." Then I remembered that Stanley Broadhurst did. "Why?"

"No reason, I'm just curious." He glanced up the mountainside. "That fire is starting to move. I don't like the feel of the wind. It has the feel of a Santa Ana."

"It was blowing down south early this morning."

"So I've heard. Are you from Los Angeles?"

"That's right." He seemed to have all the time he needed, but I was tired of fooling around with him. "My name is Archer. I'm a licensed private detective, employed by the Broadhurst family."

"I was wondering. I saw you come out of the stable."

"Stanley Broadhurst's car is in there."

"I know," he said. "Is Stanley Broadhurst one of the people you're looking for?"

"Yes, he is."

"License?"

I showed him my photostat.

"Well, I may be able to help you."

He turned abruptly and moved in among the trees along a rutted trail. I followed him. The leaves were so dry under my feet that it was like walking on cornflakes.

We came to an opening in the trees. The big sycamore

which partly overarched it had been burned. Smoke was still rising from its charred branches and from the undergrowth behind it.

Near the middle of the open space there was a hole in the ground between three and four feet in diameter. A spade stood upright beside it in a pile of dirt and stones. Off to one side of the pile, a pickax lay on the ground. Its sharp tip seemed to have been dipped in dark red paint. Reluctantly I looked down into the hole.

In its shallow depth a man's body lay curled like a foetus, face upturned. I recognized his peppermint-striped shirt, glad rags to be buried in. And in spite of the dirt that stuffed his open mouth and clung to his eyes, I recognized Stanley Broadhurst, and I said so.

The big man absorbed the information quietly. "What was he doing here, do you know?"

"No. I don't. But I believe this is part of his family's ranch. You haven't explained what you're doing here."

"I'm with the Forest Service. My name's Joe Kelsey, I'm trying to find out what started this fire. And," he added deliberately, "I think I have found out. It seems to have flared up in this immediate area. I came across *this*, right there." He indicated a yellow plastic marker stuck in the burned-over ground a few feet from where we were standing. Then he produced a small aluminum evidence case and snapped it open. It contained a single half-burned cigarillo.

"Did Broadhurst smoke these?"

"I saw him smoke one this morning. You'll probably find the package in his clothes."

"Yeah, but I didn't want to move him until the coroner sees him. It looks as if I may have to, though."

He squinted uphill toward the fire. It blazed like a displaced sunset through the trees. The black silhouettes of men fighting it looked small and futile in spite of their tanker trucks and bulldozers. Off to the left the fire had spilled over the ridge and was pouring downhill like fuming acid eating the dry brush. Its smoke blew ahead of it and spread across the city toward the sea.

Kelsey took the spade and started to throw dirt into the hole, talking as he worked.

"I hate to bury a man twice, but it's better than letting him get roasted. The fire's coming back this way."

"Was he buried when you found him?"

"That's correct. But whoever buried him didn't do much of a job of covering up. I found the spade and the pick with the blood on it—and then the filled hole with loose dirt around. So I started digging. I didn't know what I was going to find. But I sort of had a feeling that it would be a dead man with a hole in his head."

Kelsey worked rapidly. The dirt covered Stanley's striped shirt and his upturned insulted face. Kelsey spoke to me over his shoulder:

"You mentioned that you were looking for several people. Who are the others?"

"The dead man's little boy is one. And there was a blond girl with him."

"So I've heard. Can you describe her?"

"Blue eyes, five foot six, 115 pounds, age about eighteen. Broadhurst's widow can tell you more about her. She's at the ranchhouse."

"Where's your car? I came out on a fire truck."

I told him that Stanley's mother had brought me in her pickup, and that she was in the cabin. Kelsey stopped spading dirt. His face was running with sweat, and mildly puzzled.

"What's she doing in there?"

"Resting."

"We're going to have to interrupt her rest."

Beyond the grove, in the unburned brush, the fire had grown almost as tall as the trees. The air moved in spurts and felt like hot animal breath.

We ran away from it, with Kelsey carrying the spade and me carrying the bloody pick. The pick felt heavy by the time we reached the door of the cabin. I set it down and knocked on the door before I went in.

Mrs. Broadhurst sat up with a start. Her face was rosy. Sleep clung to her eyes and furred her voice:

"I must have dozed off, forgive me, but I had the sweetest dream. I spent—we spent our honeymoon here, you know, right in this cabin. It was during the war, quite early in the war, and traveling wasn't possible. I dreamed that I was on my honeymoon, and none of the bad things had happened."

Her half-dreaming eyes focused on my face and recognized the signs, which I couldn't conceal, of another bad thing that had happened. Then she saw Kelsey with the spade in his hands. He looked like a giant gravedigger blocking the light in the doorway.

Mrs. Broadhurst's normal expression, competent and cool and rather strained, forced itself down over her open face. She got up very quickly, and almost lost her balance.

"Mr. Kelsey? It's Mr. Kelsey, isn't it? What's happened?"

"We found your son, ma'am."

"Where is he? I want to talk to him."

Kelsey said in deep embarrassment: "I'm afraid that won't be possible, ma'am."

"Why? Has he gone somewhere?"

Kelsey gave me an appealing look. Mrs. Broadhurst walked toward him.

"What are you doing with that spade? That's my spade, isn't it?"

"I wouldn't know, ma'am."

She took it out of his hands. "It most certainly is. I bought it for my own use last spring. Where did you get hold of it, from my gardener?"

"I found it in the clump of trees yonder." Kelsey gestured in that direction.

"What on earth was it doing there?"

Kelsey's mouth opened and shut. He was unwilling or afraid to tell her that Stanley was dead. I moved toward her and told her that her son had been killed, probably with a pickax.

I stepped outside and showed her the pickax. "Is this yours, too?"

She looked at it dully. "Yes, I believe it is."

Her voice was a low monotone, hardly more than a whisper. She turned and began to run toward the burning trees, stumbling in her high-heeled riding boots. Kelsey ran after her, heavily and rapidly like a bear. He took her around the waist and lifted her off her feet and turned her around away from the fire.

She kicked and shouted: "Let me go. I want my son."

"He's in a hole in the ground, ma'am. You can't go in there now, nobody can. But his body won't burn, it's safe underground."

She twisted in his arms and struck at his face. He dropped her. She fell in the brown weeds, beating at the ground and crying that she wanted her son.

I got down on my knees beside her and talked her into getting up and coming with us. We went down the trail in single file, with Kelsey leading the way and Mrs. Broadhurst between us. I stayed close behind her, in case she tried to do something wild like throwing herself down the side of the bluff. She moved passively with her head down, like a prisoner between guards.

VII

Kelsey carried the spade in one hand and the bloody pickax in the other. He tossed them into the back of the truck and helped Mrs. Broadhurst into the cab. I took the wheel.

She rode between us in silence, looking straight ahead along the stony road. She didn't utter a sound until we turned at her mailbox into the avocado grove. Then she let out a gasp which sounded as if she'd been holding her breath all the way down the canyon.

"Where is my grandson?"

"We don't know," Kelsey said.

"You mean that he's dead, too. Is that what you mean?"

Kelsey took refuge in a southwestern drawl which helped to soften his answer. "I mean that nobody's seen hide nor hair of him, ma'am."

"What about the blond girl? Where is she?"

"I only wish I knew."

"Did she kill my son?"

"It looks like it, ma'am. It looks like she hit him over the head with that pickax."

"And buried him?"

"He was buried when I found him."

"How could a girl do that?"

"It was a shallow grave, ma'am. Girls can do about anything boys can do when they set their minds to it."

A whine had entered Kelsey's drawl under the pressure of her questioning and the greater pressure of her fear. Impatiently she turned to me:

"Mr. Archer, is my grandson Ronny dead?"

"No." I said it with some force, to beat back the possibility that he was.

"Has that girl abducted him?"

"It's a good assumption to work on. But they may simply have run away from the fire."

"You know that isn't so." She sounded as if she had crossed a watershed in her life, beyond which nothing good could happen.

I stopped the pickup behind my car on the driveway. Kelsey got out and offered to help Mrs. Broadhurst. She pushed his hands away. But she climbed out like a woman overtaken by sudden age.

"You can park the truck in the carport," she said to me. "I don't like to leave it out in the sun."

"Excuse me," Kelsey said, "but you might as well leave it out here. The fire's coming down the canyon, and it may get to your house. I'll help you bring your things out if you like, and drive one of your cars."

Mrs. Broadhurst cast a slow look around at the house and its surroundings. "There's never been fire in this canyon in my lifetime."

"That means it's ripe," he said. "The brush up above is fifteen and twenty feet deep, and as dry as a chip. This is a fifty-year fire. It could take your house unless the wind changes again."

"Then let it."

Jean came to meet us at the door, a little tardily, as if she dreaded what we were going to say. I told her that her husband was dead and that her son was missing. The two women exchanged a questioning look, as if each of them was looking into the other for the source of all their troubles. Then they came together in the doorway and stood in each other's arms.

Kelsey came up behind me on the porch. He tipped his hard hat and spoke to the younger woman, who was facing him over Mrs. Broadhurst's shoulder.

"Mrs. Stanley Broadhurst?"

"Yes."

"I understand you can give me a description of the girl who was with your husband."

"I can try."

She separated herself from the older woman, who went into the house. Jean rested on the railing near the hummingbird feeder. A hummingbird buzzed her. She moved to the other side of the porch and sat on a canvas chair, leaning forward in a strained position and repeating for Kelsey her description of the blue-eyed blond girl with the strange eyes.

"And you say she's eighteen or so?"

Jean nodded. Her reactions were quick but mechanical, as if her mind was focused somewhere else.

"Is—was your husband interested in her, Mrs. Broadhurst?"

"Obviously he was," she said in a dry bitter voice. "But I gathered she was more interested in my son."

"Interested in what way?"

"I don't know what way."

Kelsey switched to a less sensitive line of questioning. "How was she dressed?"

"Last night she had on a sleeveless yellow dress. I didn't see her this morning."

"I did," I put in. "She was still wearing the yellow dress. I assume you'll be giving all this to the police."

"Yessir, I will. Right now I want to talk to the gardener. He may be able to tell us how that spade and pick got up on the mountain. What's his name?"

"Frederick Snow—we call him Fritz," Jean said. "He isn't here."

"Where is he?"

"He rode Stanley's old bicycle down the road about half an hour ago, when the wind changed. He wanted to take the Cadillac, but I told him not to."

"Doesn't he have a car of his own?"

"I believe he has some kind of jalopy."

"Where is it?"

She shrugged slightly. "I don't know."

"Where was Fritz this morning?"

"I can't tell you. He seems to have been the only one here for most of the morning."

Kelsey's face saddened. "How does he get along with your little boy?"

"Fine." Then his meaning entered her eyes and darkened them. She shook her head as if to deny the meaning, dislodge the darkness. "Fritz wouldn't hurt Ronny, he's always been kind to him."

"Then why did he take off?"

"He said that he was worried about his mother. But I think he was scared of the fire. He was almost crying."

"So am I scared of the fire," Kelsey said. "It's why I'm in this business."

"Are you a policeman?" Jean said. "Is that why you're asking me all these questions?"

"I'm with the Forest Service, assigned to investigate the causes of fires." He dug into an inside pocket, produced the aluminum evidence case, and showed her the half-burned cigarillo. "Does this look like one of your husband's?"

"Yes it does. But surely you're not trying to prove that he started it. What's the point if he's dead?" Her voice had risen a little out of control.

"The point is this. Whoever killed him probably made him drop this in the dry grass. That means they're legally and financially responsible for the fire. And it's my job to establish the facts. Where does this man Snow live?"

"With his mother. I think their house is quite near here. My mother-in-law can tell you. Mrs. Snow used to work for her."

We found Mrs. Broadhurst in the living room, standing at a corner window which framed the canyon. The room was so large that she looked small at the far end of it. She didn't turn when we moved up to her.

She was watching the progress of the fire. It was in the head of the canyon now, slipping downhill like a loose volcano, and spouting smoke and sparks above the treetops. The eucalyptus trees behind the house were momentarily blanched by the gusty wind. The blackbirds and pigeons had all gone.

Kelsey and I exchanged glances. It was time that we went, too. I let him do the talking, since it was his territory and his kind of emergency. He addressed the woman's unmoving back:

"Mrs. Broadhurst? Don't you think we better get out of here?"

"You go. Please do go. I'm staying, for the present."

"You can't do that. That fire is really on its way."

She turned on him. Her face had sunk on its bones; it made her look old and formidable.

"Don't tell me what I can or can't do. I was born in this house. I've never lived anywhere else. If the house goes, I might as well go with it. Everything else has gone."

"You're not serious, ma'am."

"Am I not?"

"You don't want to get yourself burned, do you?"

"I think I'd almost welcome the flames. I'm very cold, Mr. Kelsey."

Her tone was tragic, but there was a note of hysteria running through it, or something worse. A stubbornness which could mean that her mind had slipped a notch, and stuck at a crazy angle.

Kelsey cast a desperate look around the room. It was full of Victorian furniture, with dark Victorian portraits on the walls, and several cabinets full of stuffed native birds under glass.

"Don't you want to save your things, ma'am? Your silver and bird specimens and pictures and mementos?"

She spread her hands in a hopeless gesture as if everything had long since run through them. Kelsey was getting nowhere trying to sell her back the pieces of her life.

I said:

"We need your help, Mrs. Broadhurst."

She looked at me in mild surprise. "My help?"

"Your grandson is missing. This is a bad time and place for a little boy to be lost—"

"It's a judgment on me."

"That's nonsense."

"So I'm talking nonsense, am I?"

I disregarded her angry question. "Fritz the gardener may know where he is. I believe you know his mother. Is that correct?"

Her answer came slowly. "Edna Snow used to be my housekeeper. You can't seriously believe that Fritz—" she stopped, unwilling to put her question into words.

"It would be a great help if you'd come along and talk to Fritz and his mother."

"Very well, I will."

We drove out the lane like a funeral cortege. Mrs. Broadhurst was leading in her Cadillac. Jean and I came next in the green Mercedes. Kelsey brought up the rear, driving the pickup.

I looked back from the mailbox. Sparks and embers were blowing down the canyon, plunging into the trees behind the house like bright exotic birds taking the place of the birds that had flown.

VIII

The residential district called Canyon Estates had been almost depopulated. A few men were up on their roofs with running hoses and defiant expressions.

Two roads crossed at the mouth of the canyon, and Mrs. Broadhurst took the right-hand turn. The neighborhood changed abruptly. Black and Chicano children stood beside the road and watched us go by as if we were a procession of foreign dignitaries.

Mrs. Snow lived in an old stucco cottage on a street of old stucco cottages made almost beautiful by flowering jacaranda trees. Kelsey and I and Mrs. Broadhurst went to the door. Jean stayed in the Mercedes.

"I don't trust myself," she said.

Mrs. Snow was a quick-moving gray-haired woman wearing a fussy black outfit which looked as if she had dressed for the occasion. The eyes behind her rimless spectacles were dark, and hardened by anxiety.

"Mrs. Broadhurst! What brings you here?" Her voice hurried on as if she didn't really want to know: "It's very nice to see you. Won't you come in?"

The door opened directly into the meager front room, and we went in. Mrs. Broadhurst introduced Kelsey and me. But Mrs. Snow's scared eyes refused to look at us, resisting the notion that we were there at all. Which left her only Mrs. Broadhurst to deal with.

"Can I get you something, Mrs. Broadhurst? A nice cup of tea?"

"No thanks. Where's Fritz?"

"I believe he's in his room. The poor boy isn't feeling too well."

"He isn't a boy," Mrs. Broadhurst said.

His mother corrected her. "He is, emotionally. The doctor said he's emotionally immature."

She glanced quickly at Kelsey and me to see if we were picking this up. I sensed the beginning of a psychiatric copout.

"Get him out here," Mrs. Broadhurst said.

"But he isn't up to facing people now. He's terribly upset."

"What about?"

"The fire. He's always been afraid of fire." She gave Kelsey and me another seeking look. "Are you gentlemen from the police?"

"More or less," I said. "I'm a detective. Mr. Kelsey is investigating the fire for the Forest Service."

"I see." Her small body seemed to grow smaller and at the same time denser and heavier. "I don't know what kind of trouble Frederick is in, but I can assure you he isn't responsible."

53

"What kind of trouble is he in?" Kelsey said.

"I'm sure you know, or you wouldn't be here. I don't."

"Then how do you know that he's in trouble?"

"I've been looking after him for thirty-five years." Her look turned inward, as if she was registering each of the thirty-five years and each of her son's troubles.

Mrs. Broadhurst stood up. "We're wasting time. If you won't bring him out of his room, we'll go in and talk to him there. I want to know where my grandson is."

"Your grandson?" The little woman was appalled. "Has something happened to Ronald?"

"He's missing. And Stanley is dead. He was buried with my spade."

Mrs. Snow put her fingers to her mouth. A gold wedding band was sunk in the flesh of one finger like a scar.

"Buried in the garden?"

"No. At the top of the canyon."

"And you think Frederick did this?"

"I don't know."

I said: "We were hoping your son could help us."

"I see." Her face brightened surprisingly, like the lights just before a power failure. "Why don't I ask him? He isn't afraid of me—I can get more out of him."

Mrs. Broadhurst shook her head and started for the door that opened into the back of the house. Mrs. Snow danced out of her chair and intercepted her, backing into the doorway and talking quickly.

"Don't go into his room, please. It hasn't been cleaned, and Frederick isn't himself. He's in a bad state."

Mrs. Broadhurst spoke in a guttural voice: "So is Stanley. So are we all."

For the second or third time, she lost her balance and staggered a little. Her mouth was pulled to one side in a half-grin which seemed to call attention to some secret joke.

Mrs. Snow, who moved and changed like mercury, was at her side in a moment, taking her arm and helping her into an old platform rocker.

"You're feeling faint," she said. "And I don't wonder, if all these things are true. I'll get you a glass of water. Or would you like a cup of tea after all?"

She sounded genuinely concerned. But I suspected she was also a master of delaying tactics. She'd hold us off for a week if we played along with her.

I pushed through the door into the kitchen and called her son by name. A muffled answer came through a further door which opened off the kitchen. I knocked on it and looked in. The air in the room smelled sweet and rotten.

All I could see at first were the narrow shafts of sunlight that came through the holes in the blind drawn over the window. They were thrust across the room like the swords of a magician probing a basket to demonstrate that his partner had disappeared. As if he would like to disappear indeed, the gardener crouched in the corner of the iron bed with his feet pulled up under him.

"I'm sorry to bother you, Fritz."

"That's all right." His voice was hopeless.

I sat down on the foot of the bed facing him. "Did you take the spade and the pickax up the canyon?"

"Up the canyon?" he asked.

"To the Mountain House. Did you take them up there, Fritz?"

He considered his answer and finally said: "No."

"Do you know who did?"

"No." But his eyes shifted away from mine. He was a poor liar.

Moving as softly as a shadow, Kelsey appeared in the doorway. His large face was empty and waiting.

"The spade and pickax," I said to Fritz, "were used to bury

Stanley Broadhurst this morning. If you know who took the spade and pickax, you probably know who killed Stanley."

He shook his head so hard that his face blurred. "He took them himself, when he came to get the key. He put them in the back of his convertible."

"Is that true, Fritz?"

"Cross my heart and hope to die." He crossed his breast with his finger.

"Why didn't you tell us before about the spade and the pickax?"

"He told me not to."

"Stanley Broadhurst told you not to?"

"Yessir." He nodded profoundly. "He gave me a dollar and made me promise not to."

"Did he say why?"

"He didn't have to. He's afraid of his mother. She doesn't like people messing with her garden tools."

"Did he tell you what he wanted the tools for?"

"He said that he was going to dig for arrowheads."

"Did you believe him?"

"Yessir."

"And then he drove up the mountain in his car?"

"Yessir."

"With the blond girl and the little boy?"

"Yessir."

"Did the girl say anything to you?"

"No sir. Not then."

"What do you mean, 'not then'? Did she talk to you some other time?"

"No sir. She never did."

But his eyes shifted away again. He peered at the swords of light thrust through the chinks in the blind as if they were in fact the probes of a rational universe finding him out.

"When did you see her again, Fritz?"

He was perfectly silent for a while. His eyes were the only living things in the room. His mother appeared in the doorway behind Kelsey.

"You have no right in there," she said to me. "You're violating his legal rights and nothing that he says can be used against him. In addition to which he's non compos, and I can prove it over and over with medical facts."

"You're assuming he's done something wrong, Mrs. Snow," I said.

"You mean he hasn't?"

"Not that I know of. Please go away and let me talk to him. He's a very important witness."

IX

She gave her son a sad dubious look, which he returned. But she backed away into the kitchen. Then I heard water running in a pan, and a gas burner blooping on.

"Did the girl come back, Fritz?"

He nodded.

"When was this?"

"Around noon, or a little later. I was eating my lunch."

"What did she say?"

"She said Ronny was hungry. I gave him a half of a peanut butter sandwich. I gave her the other half."

"Did she mention Stanley Broadhurst?"

"No. I didn't ask her. But she was scared."

"Did she say so?"

"She didn't have to say so. I can tell. The boy was scared, too. I can tell."

"What happened after that?"

"Nothing. She went away down the canyon."

"On foot?"

"Yeah." But his eyes were avoiding mine again.

"Are you sure she didn't take your car?"

His head sank lower. He sat perfectly still like a yogi studying the center of his body.

"All right. She took my car. They drove away in my car."

"Why didn't you tell us that before?"

"I never thought of it. I was fertilizing—I had a lot on my mind."

"Come off it, Fritz. The boy is gone and his father is dead."

"I didn't kill him!"

"I think I believe you. Not everybody will."

He lifted his head and looked past Kelsey. His mother was moving around in the kitchen. He listened to the sounds she made, as if they might tell him what to say and think.

"Forget about your mother, Fritz. This is between you and me."

"Close the door then. I don't want her to hear me. Or him either."

Kelsey stepped back out of the doorway and closed the door. I said to Fritz: "Did you let her take your car?"

"Yeah. She said Mr. Broadhurst wanted her to have it."

"There's more to it than that, Fritz, isn't there?"

Shame suffused his face. "Don't tell *her*." He waved a loose hand toward the kitchen.

"Don't tell her what?" I said.

"She let me touch her." The memory, or the fantasy, shuddered through him. His scarred mouth smiled, leaving his eyes still sad. "I mean, she looked like a girl I used to know."

"And you let her take your car."

"She said she'd bring it back. But," he added in a grieved tone, "she never did yet."

"Did she say where she was going?"

"No." He sat for a moment in a listening attitude. "I heard her drive down the canyon."

"And the boy was with her?"

"Yessir. She made him go along with her."

"Didn't he want to go?"

"No." He shook his head furiously, as if he were the boy himself. "But she made him."

"How did she make him?"

"She said the bogy man would get him. She picked him up and put him on the seat and drove away with him."

I got out my notebook and pen. "What kind of a car is it?"

"1953 Chevrolet sedan. She still runs good."

"What color?"

"It's partly the same old blue and partly red primer. I started to paint her, but I got too busy."

"License?"

"You better ask my mother. She keeps track of everything around here. But don't *tell* her." He touched his mouth.

I went out into the kitchen. Mrs. Snow was at the gas stove, pouring boiling water into a brown teapot. The steam had clouded her glasses, and she turned to me in blank apprehension like a blind woman taken by surprise.

"The girl took your son's car."

She set down the teakettle with a crash. "I *knew* he did something wrong."

"That's not the point, Mrs. Snow. If you can give me the license number we'll put out an alarm."

59

"What will they do to Frederick?"

"Nothing. *Can* you give me the license number?"

She rummaged in a kitchen drawer, found an old leatherette memorandum book, and read aloud from it: "IKT 447."

I wrote down the number. Then I returned to the front room and reported to Kelsey. Mrs. Broadhurst was slumped in the platform rocker. Her color was high and her eyes were partly closed.

"Has she been drinking?" I asked Kelsey.

"Not that I know of."

Mrs. Broadhurst sighed, and made an effort to get up. She fell back onto the platform rocker, which creaked under her weight.

Mrs. Snow backed through the doorway from the kitchen. She was balancing a tray which held the brown teapot, containers of milk and sugar, and a bone-china cup and saucer which looked as if they had been worn thin. She set the tray on a table beside the platform rocker, and filled the teacup from the pot. I could see the dark tea rising through the cup.

She spoke to Mrs. Broadhurst with forced cheerfulness: "A spot of tea is good for whatever ails you. It will clear your brain and pep you up. I know just how you like it, with milk and sugar—isn't that right?"

Mrs. Broadhurst said in a thick voice: "You're very kind."

She reached for the teacup. Her arm swung wide and loose, sweeping the teacup and the milk and sugar off the tray. Mrs. Snow got down on her knees and gathered the pieces of the broken cup as if it was a religious object. She darted into the kitchen for a towel and blotted up some of the tea from the threadbare carpet.

Kelsey had lifted Mrs. Broadhurst by the shoulders and kept her from falling out of the chair.

"Who's her doctor?" I asked Mrs. Snow.

"Dr. Jerome. Do you want me to look up the number for you?"

"You could call him yourself."

"What shall I say is the matter?"

"I don't know. It could be a heart attack. Maybe you better call an ambulance, too."

Mrs. Snow stood motionless for a second, as if all her responses had been used up. Then she went back into the kitchen. I heard her dialing.

I was getting restless. The missing boy was the main thing, and he was long gone by now. I gave Kelsey the license number of the gardener's old car and suggested that he put out an all-points on it. He called the sheriff's office.

I went outside. Jean was pacing back and forth on the broken sidewalk. Her short skirt and her long white legs gave her a harlequin aspect, like a sad clown caught on a poor street under a smoky sky.

"What on earth is going on in there?"

I told her what the gardener had told me and added that her mother-in-law was ill.

"She's never been ill in her life."

"She is now. We're getting an ambulance for her." As I spoke, I could hear it coming in the distance like the memory of a scream.

"What am I going to do?" Jean said, as if the ambulance was coming for her.

"Go with Mrs. Broadhurst to the hospital."

"Where are you going?"

"I don't know yet."

"I'd rather go with you."

I didn't know exactly what she meant, and neither, I thought, did she. I gave her my business card and an all-purpose answer: "We'll keep in touch. Let my answering service know where you're staying."

She looked at the card as if it was in a foreign language. "You're quitting on me, aren't you?"

"No. I'm not."

"Do you want money, is that it?"

"It can wait."

"What do you want from me, then?"

"Nothing."

She looked at me as if she knew better. People always wanted something.

The ambulance turned the corner. Its animal scream sank to a growl before it stopped in the road.

"This the Snow residence?" the driver called.

I said it was. He and his partner took a stretcher into the house and came out with Mrs. Broadhurst on it. As they lifted her into the back of the ambulance, she tried to sit up.

"Who pushed me?"

"Nobody, dearie," the driver said. "We'll give you a sniff of oxygen and that'll perk you up."

Jean said without looking at me: "I'll follow along in her car. I can't let her go to the hospital by herself."

I decided it was time to deliver the green Mercedes to Mrs. Roger Armistead. Kelsey pointed out Crescent Drive, on the first ridge overlooking the city. There was smoke above it, pre-empting most of the sky.

Kelsey turned to me, the flesh around his eyes still crinkled by the long look he had taken. "Be careful if you're going up that way. The fire is still on the move."

I said I would be careful. "Can I drop you anywhere?"

"No thanks. I can use the pickup to get downtown. But first I want to do some further checking on Fritz."

"Don't you believe him?"

"Up to a point I do. But you never get all the facts on the first go-round."

62

He went back toward the house. Mrs. Snow was standing framed in the doorway like a faded vestal virgin guarding a shrine.

๛๛๛๛๛๛๛๛๛๛๛๛๛

X

๛๛๛๛๛๛๛๛๛๛๛๛๛

On my way up to Crescent Drive I punched on the car radio. It was tuned to a local station which was broadcasting continuous fire reports. The Rattlesnake Fire, as the announcer called it, was threatening the northeastern side of the city. Hundreds of residents were being evacuated. Smoke-jumpers were being flown in and additional firefighting equipment was on its way. But unless the Santa Ana stopped blowing, the announcer said, Rattlesnake might strike across the city all the way to the sea.

The Armistead house, like the Broadhurst house, was in debatable territory. I parked in the courtyard beside a black Continental. The fire was so close that I could sense its fibrillation when the engine died. Ashes like scant gray snow were sifting down onto the blacktop in the courtyard. I could hear water gushing somewhere at the rear.

The house was white and one-storied, set like a classical temple against a grove of cypress trees. It was so nicely proportioned that I didn't realize how big it was until I hiked around it to the back. I passed a fifty-foot swimming pool at the bottom of which lay a blue mink coat, like the headless pelt of a woman, anchored by what looked like jewel boxes.

A tanned woman with short gray hair was spraying the cypresses with a hose. Beyond the cypresses, in the dry brush, a dark-haired man in dungarees was digging a furrow and beating out falling embers with his spade.

The woman was talking to the fire as if it was a crazy man or a wild dog—"Get back, you crummy bastard!"— and she turned to me almost gaily when I called her name.

"Mrs. Armistead?"

I saw when she turned that her gray hair was premature. Her face was a hot brown, cooled by slanting green eyes. Her body was elegant in a white slack-suit.

"Who are you?"

"Archer. I brought your Mercedes."

"Good. I'll send you a check, provided the car's in good shape."

"It is, and I'll send you a bill."

"In that case you might as well help out here." Her downward smile made a white gash in her face. She gestured toward a spade which lay on brown cypress needles under the trees. "You could help Carlos dig that ditch."

It sounded like a poor idea. I was in city clothes. But I peeled off my jacket and picked up the spade and went through the trees to help Carlos.

He was a sawed-off middle-aged Chicano who took my arrival as a matter of course. I worked behind him, broadening and deepening his furrow. It was almost certainly hopeless, a token scratch in the dirt across the base of the chaparral-covered hill. I could hear the fire very plainly now, breathing on the far side of the hill. Behind me the wind was soughing in the cypresses.

"Where's Mr. Armistead?" I said to Carlos.

"I guess he moved onto the boat."

"Where would that be?"

"In the marina."

He gestured toward the sea. After a few more spadefuls, he added: "Her name is Ariadne." He pronounced the name slowly and carefully.

"The girl?"

"The boat," he said. "Mrs. Armistead told me it's a Greek name. She's crazy about Greece."

"She looks a little like a Greek."

"Yeah, I guess she does," he said with a ruminative smile. The sound of the fire became louder, and his face changed. We spaded some more. I was beginning to feel the work in my shoulders and in the palms of my hands. My shirt was pasted to my back.

"Is Mr. Armistead all by himself on the boat?"

"No. He's got a boy with him. He calls him a crew, but I never seen him do any work on the boat. He's one of these long-hairs, they call 'em." Carlos raised his grimy hand to his head and caressed imaginary locks.

"Doesn't Mr. Armistead like girls?"

"Yeah, he likes girls." He added thoughtfully: "There was a girl on the boat the other night."

"Blond girl?"

"Yeah."

"Did you see her?"

"My friend Pedro saw her when he was going out of the harbor yesterday morning. Pedro's a fisherman—he gets up before the daylight. The girl was 'way up the mast and yelling like she was going to jump. The boy was trying to talk her down."

"What did Pedro do?"

Carlos shrugged. "Pedro, he's got children to feed. He don't have time to stop and fool around with crazy girls."

Carlos went back to his work with renewed concentration, as if he was digging a foxhole that would shelter him against the contemporary world. I worked along behind him. But it was clear that we were wasting our time.

The fire appeared at the top of the hill like a brilliant omniform growth which continued to grow until it bloomed very large against the sky. A sentinel quail on the hillside below it was ticking an alarm.

Carlos looked up at the fire and crossed himself. Then he turned his back on it and beckoned to me and walked away from his furrow through the trees.

One of the cypresses was beginning to smoke, high beyond the reach of Mrs. Armistead's hose. She told Carlos to climb the tree.

He shook his head. "It wouldn't do no good. The trees are gonna go, and maybe the house, too."

The fire was coming down the hill, gathering speed and size. The trees had begun to sway. From the undergrowth beneath them, a bevy of stubby-winged quail flew up fighting for altitude over the house. Smoke like billowing darkness followed them.

Mrs. Armistead went on spraying the trees with her ineffectual hose. Carlos moved past her to the faucet and turned it off. She stood with the dripping nozzle in her hand, facing the fire.

It made a noise like a storm. Enormous and hot and wild, it leapt clumsily into the trees. The cypress that had been smoking burst into flames. Then the other trees blazed up like giant torches in a row.

I took Mrs. Armistead by the hand and pulled her away. She resisted jerkily, instinctively, like a woman who had trouble taking direction. She held onto the hose as long as she could, and finally dropped it in the grass.

Carlos was waiting impatiently by the pool. Fire was falling around him, sputtering and turning black in the blue water.

"We better get out of here," he said. "We might could be cut off if she jumps the driveway. What do you want me to do about the fur coat?"

"Leave it in the pool," she said. "It's too hot for mink."

I didn't exactly like the woman, but I was beginning to take her personally. I gave Carlos the key to the Mercedes and went with her to the Lincoln Continental.

"You can drive if you like," she said. "I'm a little done in."

She grimaced. The admission cost her pain. As we followed the Mercedes down the driveway, she added a kind of explanation: "I love those quail. I've been feeding them and watching them ever since we built the house. They were finally beginning to feel safe. They brought their chicks right into the yard this spring."

"The quail will come back."

"Maybe so. I wonder if I will."

We came to a turnaround which overlooked the city. Carlos pulled the Mercedes off the road, and I followed him. Smoke hung over the city, giving it a sepia tint like an old photograph. We climbed out of the cars and looked back at the house.

The fire bent around it like the fingers of a hand, squeezing smoke out of the windows and then flame. We got back into our cars and turned downhill. It was my second evacuation of the day, and it made me feel slightly paranoid until I thought of the reason. The people I was getting involved with could afford to live in the open outside the city, right up against nature.

There was only one good thing about the fire. It made people talk about the things that really concerned them. I asked Mrs. Armistead how long she had lived in the house.

"Just four years. Roger and I came up here from Newport and built it. It was part of an attempt to hold our marriage together, on the analogy of having a child."

"Do you have any children?"

"Only each other," she answered in a wry voice. Then she added: "I wish I had a daughter. I wish even more that my husband had a daughter."

"On account of the blond girl?"

She turned toward me suddenly, with a kind of suppressed violence. "Just what do you know about the girl?"

"Very little. I've only seen her once, at a distance."

"I've never seen her at all," the woman said. "She sounds like a kook. But it's hard to tell about young people nowadays."

"It always was."

She was still watching my face. "You said that you're a detective. Just what has the girl done?"

"I'm trying to find out."

"But you didn't just pick her at random. She must have done something wrong, besides taking the Mercedes. What did she do?"

"Ask Roger."

"I intend to. But you haven't explained why *you're* so interested in her."

"She ran away with a six-year-old boy. It amounts to child stealing." I held back the rest of the story.

"Why would she do a thing like that?" When I failed to answer that question, she asked another: "Is she on acid or some other drug?"

"She may be."

"I thought so." She spoke with a kind of bitter satisfaction. "She went off the deep end the night before last, literally. She ended up jumping into the harbor. Jerry had to go in after her."

"Who's Jerry?"

"The boy who lives on the boat. Roger calls him his crew, for want of a better word."

"What do you call him?"

"His last name is Kilpatrick."

I remembered the book in my pocket, with "Jerry Kilpatrick" inscribed on the flyleaf in pencil. "Do you know who he is?"

"He's the son of Brian Kilpatrick, a real estate man in town. As a matter of fact Mr. Kilpatrick sold us that piece of property on the ridge."

"Is that how your husband met Jerry?"

"I think so. You could ask Roger."

"When will we be seeing Roger?"

"Quite soon, if he's at the beach house."

We were passing through the center of the city. The main street was clogged with traffic, and the sidewalks were crowded. It was strange to see the people going about their business without apparent concern for the fire at the edges of the town. The people were moving more quickly than usual, perhaps, as if their lives had speeded up and might come to an end suddenly.

Following Carlos in the Mercedes, I turned onto Maritime Drive, which took us along the ocean to a row of beach houses curving around a bay. Carlos led me into a parking lot behind the houses, and I drew up beside the Mercedes. "While I'm thinking about it," Mrs. Armistead said, "I'll pay you now. How much?"

"A hundred will do it."

She produced a money clip made of gold in the shape of a dollar-sign and laid a hundred-dollar bill across my upper leg. Then she put a fifty on top of it.

"That's a tip," she said.

I took the money, since I needed it for expenses, but I felt vaguely declassed by the transaction, like a repossession man. It gave me a certain sympathy for Roger, even before I met him.

The Armisteads' beach house was a driftwood-gray building which we entered at the rear on the second-floor level. We moved past an open stairwell into the main room. It was furnished nautically, with brass, a wall barometer, captain's chairs.

Through the sliding glass windows at the front I could see a youngish man sitting on the balcony. He was sportily clad in a blue T-shirt and a boating cap, but he was watching the people on the beach from a distance, like a spectator sitting in a theatre box.

"Hello, Roger." The woman's voice had changed. It was soft and musical, as if she was listening to it, tuning it carefully.

The young man got up and took off his cap, showing neither surprise nor pleasure. "I didn't expect a visit from you, Fran."

"The house on Crescent Drive just burned to the ground."

His face lengthened. "With all my clothes?"

"You can always buy more clothes." Her voice was partly serious and partly mocking, waiting for him to decide which way he wanted the meeting to go.

He said a little belatedly: "Too bad about the house. You liked it, didn't you?"

"I liked it as long as you liked it."

"Are you planning to build again?"

"I don't know, Roger. What do you think?"

He moved his heavy shoulders, shrugging off the threat of responsibility. "It's really up to you, isn't it?"

"Well, I feel like traveling." She spoke with a kind of fake decisiveness, like a woman improvising. "I may go to Yugoslavia."

He turned and stared at me, as if he'd just discovered my presence. He was a good-looking man, perhaps ten years younger than his wife, with a strong impatient body. I noticed that his dark hair was thinning. He noticed that I noticed and ruffled it up with his hand.

"This is Mr. Archer," his wife said. "He's a detective. He's looking for the girl you had aboard the sloop."

"What girl?" But he looked at me with instant dislike and flushed.

"The one who tried to fly too near the sun. Or was it the moon?"

"I wouldn't know. I had nothing to do with her."

"Do you know her full name?" I said.

"Susan, I think. Sue Crandall."

His wife brightened up alarmingly. "I thought you said you had nothing to do with her."

"I didn't. I chewed Jerry out for having her aboard, and he told me what her name was. I had to force it out of him."

"The story came to me differently," she said. "I heard she spent Thursday night on *Ariadne* with you. The marina's rather a public place for that sort of thing, isn't it?"

He answered somberly: "I don't mess with young chicks. I spent Thursday night here by myself, drinking. The girl was taken aboard without my knowledge and without my permission."

"Where's she from?" I said.

"I don't really know. Somewhere down south, according to Jerry—"

His wife cut in: "How long have you known her?"

He gave her a hard dull look. "Don't be a broken record, Fran. I never met the Crandall girl. Ask Jerry Kilpatrick if you don't believe me. The girl is his little friend."

"Who gave her the use of the Mercedes, if you didn't?"

"That was Jerry's doing, too. I hate to blame it all on him, but that's the truth. I chewed him out for it."

"I don't believe you. You're not going to have the Mercedes from now on."

"To hell with you then."

He moved past her to the open stairs and stamped down to the ground floor. There were sounds like drawers being opened and shut, and closet doors being slammed.

The house was frame, with open rafters and without insulation, so that the angry sounds reverberated through it. Fran Armistead winced at them, as if the violence was being inflicted on her body. She was afraid of her husband, I thought, and probably in love with him.

She went down after him, looking strained and intent, like a woman descending voluntarily into hell. Their voices floated up the stairs, clearly audible in the intervals between the sounds of the surf.

"Don't be angry," she said.

"I'm not angry."

"You can have the Mercedes."

"I need some transportation," he said reasonably. "Not that I'm going anywhere."

"No. You stay with me. I felt absolutely ghastly when the house burned. I felt as if my life was burning down. But it wasn't, was it?"

"I don't know. What's this about going to Yugoslavia?"

"Don't you want to go?"

"What's in Yugoslavia?"

"We'll stay here then. Does that suit you?"

"For the present," he said. "I may have had it with this town."

"On account of the girl? What's her name—Susan?"

"Listen. Do we have to go on about her? I never even saw her."

A door closed, and their voices became muffled. I began to hear more private sounds, and decided to go outside.

It was late on a Saturday afternoon, and the beach was littered with bodies. It was like a warning vision of the future, when every square foot of the world would be populated. I found a place to sit in the sand beside a youth with a guitar who lay propped against a girl's stomach. I could smell her sun-tan oil, and I felt as if everybody but me was paired off like the animals in the ark.

I got up and looked around me. Under the stratum of smoke which lay over the city, the air was harshly clear. The low sun was like a spinning yellow frisbee which I could almost reach out and catch.

The thrusting masts of the marina looked dark and calcined against the light in the west. I took off my shoes and socks and carried them along the beach in that direction.

XI

A concrete breakwater extended by a sandbar curved like a sheltering arm around the harbor and marina. A few boats, under motor or sail, were coming in from the sea through the marked channel. A multitude of other boats lay in the slips, from racing yachts to superannuated landing craft.

I walked along beside the high woven-wire fence which divided the marina from the public parking lot. There were several gates in it but they all had automatic locks. I found a boat rental dock near the foot of the breakwater and asked the man in charge how to get to *Ariadne*.

He gave me a suspicious look which took in my bare feet and the shoes I had tied together and slung over my shoulder.

"Mr. Armistead's not aboard, if he's the one you're looking for."

"What about Jerry Kilpatrick?"

"I wouldn't know about him. Go down to the third gate and try giving him a yell. You can see the boat from there, about halfway along the float on the left."

I put on my shoes and found the gate and the boat. She was a white sloop, poised on the quiet water in a way that made my breath come a little faster. A thin young man with straggling hair and a furred lower face was working over the auxiliary motor near her stern. I called to him through the locked gate.

"Jerry?"

His head came up. I waved him toward me. He jumped down onto the slip and moved along it in a swift barefoot shamble. He was naked to the waist, and he walked with his bearded head thrust forward as though to cancel out his boy's shoulders and his narrow hairless chest. His hands were so fouled with engine oil that he seemed to be wearing black gloves.

He regarded me somberly through the wire gate. "What can I do for you?"

"You lost your book." I got out the copy of *Green Mansions* with his name on the flyleaf. "This is yours, isn't it?"

"Let me see." He started to open the gate, then clicked it emphatically shut again. "If my father sent you, he can drop dead. And you can go back and tell him that I said that."

"I don't know your father."

"Neither do I know him. I never knew him. And I don't want to know him."

"That takes care of your father. What about me?"

"That's your problem."

"Don't you want your book?"

"Keep it, if you can read. It'll improve your mind, if you have a mind."

He was a very hostile young man. I reminded myself that he was a witness, and there was no point in getting angry with him through a fence.

"I can always get somebody to read it to me," I said.

He smiled quickly. The smile in the midst of his reddish beard seemed extraordinarily bright.

I said:

"There's a small boy missing. His father was killed this morning—"

"You think I killed him?"

"Did you?"

"I don't believe in violence." His look implied that I did.

"Then you'll want to help me find whoever killed him. Why don't you let me in? Or come out and we can talk."

"I like it this way." He fingered the wire gate. "You look like the violent type to me."

"The situation isn't funny," I said. "The missing boy is six years old. His name is Ronald Broadhurst. Do you know anything about him?"

75

He shook his tangled head. The beard that covered his lower face seemed to have overgrown his mouth and left him only his eyes to speak with. They were brown, and slightly starred, like damaged glass.

"A girl was with him," I went on. "She was reading this book of yours last night in bed. Her name is Sue Crandall."

"I don't know her."

"I've been told you do. She was here night before last."

"I wouldn't know about that."

"I think you would. You lent her this book, and you lent her Armistead's Mercedes. What else did you lend her?"

"I don't understand what you mean."

"She got stoned on something and climbed the mast. What did you give her, Jerry?"

A shadow of fear crossed his face. He converted it into anger. His brown eyes became reddish and hot, as if there was fire behind them. "I thought you were fuzz," he said in a stylized way. "Why don't you go away?"

"I want to talk to you seriously. You're in trouble."

"Go to hell."

He trotted away along the slip. His hairy head seemed enormous and grotesque on his boy's body, like a papier-mâché saint's head on a stick. I stood and watched him vault into the cockpit of the boat and go back to work on the motor.

The sun was almost down now. When it reached the water, the entire sea and sky seemed to ignite, burning red in a larger fire than Rattlesnake.

Before it got dark I went through the parking lot looking for Fritz Snow's old Chevrolet sedan. I couldn't find it, but I had a persistent feeling that it had to be in the neighborhood. I began to search along the boulevard which paralleled the shore.

The western sky lost its color like a face going suddenly pale. The light faded gradually from the air. It clung for a long time to the surface of the water, which stretched out like a faint and fallen sky.

I walked for several blocks without finding the old Chevrolet. Street lights came on, and the waterfront was bleakly lit by the neon signs of motels and hamburger joints. I crossed to one of the latter and had a double hamburger with a paper sack of French fried potatoes, and coffee. I ate and drank like a starved man, and remembered that I hadn't eaten since morning.

When I turned away from the bright counter, it was almost fully dark. I glanced up at the mountains, and was shocked by what I saw. The fire had grown and spread as if it fed on darkness. It hung around the city like the bivouacs of a besieging army.

I took up my search for the Chevrolet again, working through the motel parking lots and up the side streets toward the railroad tracks. As soon as I left the boulevard, I was in a ghetto. Black and brown children were playing quiet games in the near-darkness. From the broken-down porches of the little houses, their mothers and grandmothers watched them and me.

I found Fritz Snow's half-painted Chevrolet in a rutted lane behind a dusty oleander hedge. There was music leaking out of it. A small man in a baseball cap was sitting behind the wheel.

"What are you doing, friend?"

"Playing my organ." He put a mouth organ to his lips again and played a few bars of wheezy blue music. I'm guilty, it seemed to say, but I've suffered enough—so have you.

"You play very well."

"It's a gift."

He pointed skyward through the roof of the car. Then he blew a few more bars, and shook the spit out of his mouth organ. He smelled of wine.

"Is this your car?" I asked him.

"I'm watching it for a friend."

I got in beside him. The key was in the ignition, and I took it. He gave me a glinting apprehensive look.

"My name is Archer. What's your name?"

"Amos Johnstone. You got no right or reason to bust me. I'm really and truly watching it for a friend."

"I'm not a cop. Is your friend a young woman with a little boy?"

"That's her. She gave me a dollar—told me to sit in the car till she came back."

"How long ago was that?"

"I dunno, I don't carry a watch. Only thing I can swear to, it was today."

"Before dark?"

He peered at the sky as if nightfall had taken him by surprise. "Must have been. I bought some wine with the dollar, and it's gone." He glanced around at me. "I could use another dollar."

"Maybe we'll get to that. Where did the young lady go?"

"Down the street." He gestured in the direction of the marina.

"And she took the boy with her?"

"Yessir."

"Was he all right?"

"He was scared."

"Did he say anything?"

"He didn't say a word to me. But he was shivering like a puppy."

I gave the man a dollar and started back to the marina.

He played me some farewell music which merged with the voices of the children playing in the dark.

There were a few scattered lights on the boats along the slips. A steadier, more brilliant light shone over the wire gate from the top of a metal pole. I took a quick look around and went over the gate, snagging one leg on the barbed wire across the top of it and coming down hard on my back on the slanting gangway. It shook me, and I stayed down for a minute.

My blood was beating in my ears and eyes as I approached the sloop. There was a light in the cabin, but no one on deck that I could see. In spite of the circumstances, there was something secret and sweet about the dark water, and something beautiful about the boat, like a corralled horse at night. I climbed over the railing into the cockpit. The mast towered up against the obscure sky.

There was a scuffling noise in the cabin. "Who's that?" It was Jerry's voice. He opened the hatchway and stuck out his head. His eyes were wide and glaring, and his open mouth was like a dark hole in his beard. He looked like Lazarus coming out of the tomb.

I reached for him, got hold of his body under the arms, lifted him up, and set him down hard in the cockpit on his back. He stayed down, as if he had hit his head. I felt a twinge of shame at hurting a boy.

I went down the ladder into the cabin, past a ship-to-shore radio and a chart table. On one of the two lower bunks a girl-shaped body was lying under a red blanket with only its blond hair showing, spilling like twisted gold across the pillow.

I pulled the blanket off her face. Her expression was queerly impassive. Her eyes looked at me from some other place, almost as if she was ready to die or perhaps already had.

79

Something besides her body was moving under the blanket. I stripped it off. She was holding the small boy against her, with one arm curled around his head and her hand over his mouth. He lay still beside her. Even his round blue eyes were perfectly still.

They flickered past me. I turned in the cramped space. Jerry was crouched on the ladder with a revolver held in both his hands.

"Get off this boat, you grungy pig."

"Put the gun away. You'll hurt somebody."

"You," he said. "Unless you get off here now. I'm in charge of this boat, and you're trespassing."

It was hard to take him seriously, but the gun helped. He waved it at me, and moved to one side. I climbed out past him, undecided whether I should try to take him or pass.

My indecision made me slow. Out of the corner of my eye I saw him shift the gun in his hands and swing it up by the barrel. I failed to avoid its fall. The scene spun away.

XII

I was watching the cogwheels of the universe turning. It resembled, on a large scale, one of those boxes of gears that engineers fool around with in their spare time. I seemed to be able to see the whole apparatus at once, and to understand that the ratio of output to input was one to one.

Quiet water lapped at the edge of my attention. The side of my face was against a flat rough surface which seemed to rise and fall. The air seemed cooler, and I thought for a while that I was on the boat. Then I got up onto my hands and knees and saw that I was on the slip and that the space where *Ariadne* had lain was an oblong of dark water.

I dipped up some of the water in my hand and splashed it on my face. I was dizzy and depressed. I hadn't taken the bearded boy seriously enough, and mishandled both him and the situation. I checked my wallet: the money was still in it.

I made my way up the gangway to a public rest station in the parking lot. I washed my face again, without looking too closely at it, and decided not to mess with the swelling on my head, which had stopped bleeding.

I found a pay phone, with a directory chained to it, on the outside wall of the building and called the sheriff's office. The deputy on duty told me that the sheriff and most of his officers were in the fire zone. He was swamped with calls and had no one to send out.

I dialed the local Forest Service number. The female voice of an answering service informed me that no calls were taken after business hours, but she agreed to accept a message for Kelsey. I dictated a telegraphic version of recent events and listened to the operator read it back to me in a bored voice.

Next I looked up Brian Kilpatrick in the Real Estate section of the yellow pages. Both home and business numbers were listed for him. I called Kilpatrick's home, got him immediately, and asked him if I could come and see him. He sighed.

"I just sat down with a drink. What's on your mind?"

"Your son Jerry."

"I see. Are you an officer?" His carefully modulated voice had flattened out.

"A private detective."

"Does this have to do with the trouble at the harbor yesterday morning?"

"I'm afraid it does, and it's getting worse. May I come and talk to you?"

"You still haven't said what about. Is a girl involved in this?"

"Yes. She's a young blond named Susan Crandall. Susan and your son and a little boy named Ron Broadhurst have taken off—"

"Is that Mrs. Broadhurst's grandson?"

"Yes, it is."

"Where in the name of heaven have they gone?"

"To sea. They took the Armistead yacht."

"Does Roger Armistead know about this?"

"Not yet. I called you first."

"Thank you," he said. "You'd better come over as you suggest. Do you know where I live?" He gave me the address, twice.

I called a cab and repeated the address to the driver. He was one of the loquacious ones. He talked about fires and floods, earthquakes and oil spills. Why, he wanted to know, would anyone want to live in California? If things got any worse, he was going to move his family back to Motown. That was a city.

He took me to an upper-middle residential area on the side of the city which was not yet threatened by the fire. Kilpatrick's modern ranch house lay on a floodlit pad on the side of a brush-covered slope. I had left the cool air lower in the city, and hot wind blew in my face when I got out of the cab. I told the driver to wait.

Kilpatrick came out to meet me. He was a big man wearing an open-necked sport shirt over slacks. There was graying red hair on both his head and his chest. In spite of the drink in his hand, and the dead-fish gleam of previous drinks in his eyes, his large handsome face was sober, almost lugubrious.

He offered me his hand, and peered at my injured head. "What happened to you?"

"Your son Jerry happened to me. He hit me with a gunbutt."

Kilpatrick made a commiserating face. "I want to say right now I'm heartily sorry. But," he added, "I'm not responsible for what Jerry does. He's gotten beyond my control."

"So I gather. Can we go inside?"

"By all means. You'll be wanting a drink."

He ushered me into a bar and game room which overlooked a brilliantly lighted pool. Beside the pool a woman with black hair and gleaming copper-colored legs was sitting in a long chair which concealed the rest of her. A portable radio on a table beside her was talking to her like a familiar spirit. A silver cocktail shaker stood by the radio.

Kilpatrick closed the venetian blinds before he turned up the light. He said that he was drinking martinis, and I asked for scotch and water, which he poured. We sat facing each other across a round table which had a chessboard made of light and dark squares of wood inlaid in its center.

He said in a cautious measured voice: "I suppose I better tell you that I heard from the girl's father earlier today. He found my son's name in his daughter's address book."

"How long has the girl been missing from home? Did Crandall say?"

Kilpatrick nodded. "A couple of days. She walked out on her parents Thursday."

"Did Crandall say why?"

"He doesn't know why, any more than I do." He added

83

in a discouraged voice which made him sound like an old man: "We're losing a whole generation. They're punishing us for bringing them into the world."

"Do the Crandalls live in town here?"

"No."

"How do your son and their daughter happen to know each other?"

"I have no idea. All I know is what Crandall told me."

"What's Crandall's full name and where does he live?"

Kilpatrick lifted his palm in a traffic-halting gesture. "Before I tell you anything more, you'd better fill me in on the ramifications. How does the Broadhurst boy come into this? What are they planning to do with him?"

"There may not be any plan at all. It looks as if they're playing it by ear. But on the other hand it may be a kidnaping. It is now, in the legal sense."

"For money? Jerry claims that he despises money."

"Money isn't the only motive for kidnaping."

"What else is there?" Kilpatrick said.

"Revenge. Power. Kicks."

"That doesn't sound like Jerry."

"What about the girl?"

"I gather she's a fairly nice girl from a fairly nice family. Maybe not a happy girl, her father said, but a girl you can depend on."

"That's what Lizzie Borden's father used to say about her."

Kilpatrick gave me a shocked look. "It's a pretty far-fetched comparison, isn't it?"

"I hope so. The man she was traveling with today—the little boy's father—was killed with a pickax."

Kilpatrick's face grew pale, setting its broken veins in relief. He finished his martini, and sucked audibly at the dry glass.

"Are you telling me Stanley Broadhurst has been killed?"

"Yes."

"You think she murdered him?"

"I don't know. But if she did, the Broadhurst boy is probably a witness."

"Was Jerry there?"

"I don't know."

"Where did this murder take place?"

"At the head of Mrs. Broadhurst's canyon, near a cabin called Mountain House. Apparently the fire was started at the same time."

Kilpatrick began to drum on the table with his glass. He got up and went to the bar, searching along the shelves of bottles behind it for something guaranteed to relieve anxiety. He came back to the table empty-handed, and soberer than ever.

"You should have told me about this when you called me in the first place. I never would have—" His voice broke off, and he glared at me distrustfully.

"You never would have let me in or talked to me," I said. "Where does Crandall live?"

"I'm not saying."

"You might as well. None of this will be a secret for long. The only positive thing we can do is try and head off Jerry and the girl before they make more trouble."

"What more could they do?"

"Lose the boy," I said. "Or kill him."

He looked at me narrow-eyed. "Just what's your interest in the boy?"

"Mrs. Stanley Broadhurst hired me to get him back."

"So you're on the other side."

"The boy's side."

"Do you know him?"

"Slightly."

"And you care about him personally?"

85

"Yes, I do."

"Then you have some faint idea of how I feel about my son."

"I'd have a better idea if you'd cooperate fully. I'm trying to head off trouble for you and your son."

"You smell like trouble to me," he said.

That stopped me for a minute. He had a salesman's insight into human weakness, and he'd touched on a fact which I didn't always admit to myself—that I sometimes served as a catalyst for trouble, not unwillingly.

With some idea of changing the subject a little, I brought out the green-covered book with his son's name penciled on the flyleaf.

"How did Sue Crandall get hold of this?"

After some thought, he said: "I suppose Jerry took it when he left. I don't pay too much attention to the books. My wife was the intellectual in the family. She graduated from Stanford."

"Is Mrs. Kilpatrick at home?"

He shook his head. "Ellen left me years ago. The girl out by the pool is my fiancée."

"How long ago did Jerry leave?"

"A couple of months. He moved onto the yacht in June. But actually he left me a year ago, as far as any real relationship is concerned. That was when he went away to college."

"He's in college?"

"Not any more," Kilpatrick said in a disappointed voice. "He could have handled it easily. I was all set to send him right through to a master's in business administration. But he refused to make the effort. Don't ask me why, because I don't know the answer." He reached across the table for the book and closed it on his son's name.

"Is Jerry on drugs?"

"I wouldn't know about that."

But his eyes were dubious and avoided mine. The conversation was running down, and it wasn't hard to guess why. He was afraid of involving his son in murder.

"You knew about the incident on the yacht," I said. "When the girl jumped overboard."

"That's right. I got the word from the harbor people. But I didn't know that drugs were involved."

Kilpatrick leaned toward me abruptly and took hold of my untouched scotch and water. "If you're not going to use that, I am," he said, and drank it down.

We sat in opposing silences. He was studying the inlaid board as if there were chessmen on it, most of them mine. Finally he looked up and met my eyes.

"You think she got drugs from Jerry, don't you?" he said.

"You're the authority on Jerry."

"No more," he said. "But I suspected he was using drugs. It was one of the bones of contention between us."

"What kind of drugs?"

"I don't really know. But he talked and acted as if he had blown his mind." The phrase was strange on his lips, and somehow touching, like a statement of fellow-feeling with his lost son. He added nervously: "I've told you more than I should have."

"You might as well tell me the rest of it."

"There is no rest of it. That's all there is. I had a bright promising boy and one day he decided to change all that and go and live like a waterfront bum."

"What's his in with Roger Armistead?"

"I sold some property to Armistead, and Armistead's always liked him. He taught him to sail. Last year Jerry crewed for him in the Ensenada race."

87

"Jerry must be a pretty good sailor."

"He is. He could sail that sloop to Hawaii if he had to." His mood swung down: "Unless he's forgotten his navigation along with everything else."

He rose and went to the blinded window, separating the slats with his fingers and peering out, like a man in a building under attack.

"Dammit," he said. "I was supposed to take my fiancée to dinner." He turned on me in quick anger. "I suppose you realize you're wrecking my evening?"

The question didn't deserve an answer, and he knew it. He drifted to the bar as if he might find a ghostly bartender to complain to. There was a telephone on the bar, with a little blue book beside it. He opened the book as if to look up a number, then dropped it again. Instead he got out a fresh glass and poured a scotch and water and rapped it down in front of me.

I thanked him for the gesture, though I didn't need the drink. I could feel a long night coming on. So could Kilpatrick. He stood above me leaning on the table, his hands splayed out, his face expanding with emotion.

"Look," he said. "I'm not the swinging bastard I—you think I am. When Jerry was just a tot my wife ran out on me. I never gave her any good reason to leave me, except that I couldn't provide the life romantic. But Jerry blamed me for the breakup. He's always blamed me for everything." He drew in a deep mournful breath. "I really do care about him. I wanted the best for him, and knocked myself out to provide it. But things don't work out like that any more, do they? No more happy endings."

He leaned above me, listening to the silence as if he was hearing it for the first time. I said:

"What can we do to get him and Susan back?"

"I don't know."

"I thought of calling the FBI."

"Don't do that. It would be the end of Jerry."

I felt his heavy hand on my shoulder. He removed it and went to the bar again, moving like a caged animal that had paced out the short distance many times. He poured himself a scotch and resumed his place at the round table.

"Give him a chance to bring the sloop back on his own. We don't have to make a federal case out of it."

"We're going to have to tell the local police."

"Let me do that," he said. "I'll talk to Sheriff Tremaine—he's a friend of mine."

"Tonight?"

"Of course tonight. I'm more concerned than you are. Jerry's my son. What happens to him happens to me." He sounded as if he wanted to mean it, but couldn't quite feel the full sense of the words.

"Then tell me where I can reach Sue Crandall's parents. I particularly want to talk to her father."

"I'm sorry. I wouldn't feel right about it."

I hit him with the hardest words I could think of: "You may never feel right about anything again. The situation is going to hell in a handcar, and you won't lift a finger to stop it. Still you expect some kind of happy ending."

"I don't expect one. I said that." He wiped his eyes and cheeks with a downward motion of his palms, which stayed pressed together at his chin in a prayerful attitude. "You've got to give me time to think this through."

"Sure. Take several hours. I'll sit here and wonder what's happening to the Broadhurst boy."

Kilpatrick gave me a grave look across his peaked fingers. I caught a glimpse of the broken seriousness which lived in him like a spoiled priest in hiding.

The doorbell chimed, and he left the room, closing the door behind him. I picked up the small blue book beside the phone. It contained a handwritten list of numbers. A Lester Crandall was listed among the C's, with a Pacific Palisades number. The listing probably wasn't new—there were other names below it on the page.

As I was making a note of it, the door was flung open behind me. It was the dark-haired woman from the poolside. She was a handsome woman, but a little old for the bikini she was wearing. And she was smashed.

"Where's the action?" she said boisterously.

"There is none."

The corners of her mouth drooped like a disappointed child's. "Brian promised to take me dancing."

She did a few experimental steps, and almost fell down. I led her to one of the chairs, but she didn't want to sit still. She wanted to dance.

Kilpatrick came into the room. He gave no sign of noticing the woman. Moving like something mechanical and pre-aimed, he went behind the bar and opened a drawer and took out a heavy revolver.

"What goes on?" I asked him.

He gave no answer, but I didn't like the look of inert cold anger on his face. I followed him out to the front of the house, letting him know I was there. A rather wild-eyed young man with soot on his forehead was waiting at the front door.

Kilpatrick showed him the gun. "Get out of here. I don't have to put up with this kind of nonsense."

"You call it nonsense, do you?" the young man said. "I lost my house and my furniture. My family's clothes. Everything. And I'm holding you responsible, Mr. Kilpatrick."

"How am I responsible?"

"I talked to a fireman after my house burned down—too bad he wasn't there when it burned, but he wasn't—and he said that canyon should never have been built in, with the high fire hazard. You never even mentioned that when you sold it to me."

"It's a risk we all run," Kilpatrick said. "I could be burned out tonight or tomorrow myself."

"I hope you are. I hope your house burns down."

"Is that what you came here to tell me?"

"Not exactly." The young man sounded a little ashamed. "But I've got no place to spend the night."

"You're not going to spend it here."

"No. I realize that."

He ran out of words. With a parting look at the gun in Kilpatrick's hand, he walked quickly to a station wagon which was parked beside my taxicab. A number of children peered out through the back windows of the wagon, like prisoners wondering where they might be taken next. A woman sat in the front seat, looking straight ahead.

I said to Kilpatrick: "I'm glad you didn't shoot him."

"I had no intention of shooting him. But you should have heard the names he was calling me. I don't have to take—"

I cut in: "What area did he live in?"

"Canyon Estates. I'm the developer."

"Did the canyon go?"

"Not all of it. But several houses burned, including his." Kilpatrick jerked his angry head toward the departing station wagon. "He isn't the only one who took a beating. I'm still paying interest on some of those houses, and I'll never be able to move them now."

"Do you know what happened to Elizabeth Broadhurst's house?"

"The last I heard it was still standing. Those old Spanish-type structures were built to resist fire."

The dark-haired woman came up behind Kilpatrick. She had put on a light coat over her bikini and she looked quite sober, but sick.

"For heaven's sake," she said to him, "put that gun away. It scares the living hell out of me when you wave that gun around."

"I'm not waving it around." But he shoved it down out of sight in his pocket.

The three of us stepped out onto the asphalt pad. The cabdriver was watching us like an observer from Mars.

Kilpatrick wet his finger in his mouth and held it up. A cool wind was blowing up the canyon.

"That's sea air," he said. "If it keeps blowing from that direction we're going to be A-O.K."

I hoped he was right. But the eastern edges of the sky were still burning like curtains.

XIII

It cost me fifty dollars, paid in advance, to be driven to Northridge, where I'd left my car in Stanley Broadhurst's garage. The driver wanted to talk, but I shut him off and caught an hour's sleep.

I woke up with a pounding head when we left the Ventura Freeway. I told the driver to stop at a public pay phone. He found one and gave me change for a dollar. I dialed Lester Crandall's number.

A woman's voice which sounded as if it was being kept under strict control said: "This is the Crandall residence."

"Is Mr. Crandall home?"

"I'm afraid he isn't. I don't know when he'll be back."

"Where is he?"

"On the Strip."

"Looking for Susan?"

Her voice became more personal. "Yes, he is. Are you a friend of Lester's?"

"No. But I've seen your daughter. She isn't in Los Angeles. May I come and talk to you, Mrs. Crandall?"

"I don't know. Are you a policeman?"

I told her what I was, and gave her my name, and she responded with her address. It was on a street I knew off Sunset Boulevard.

The cab took me under the freeway to Northridge. I'd kept the key to the Broadhurst garage. I asked the driver to wait while I used the key and made sure my car was still there. It was, and it started. I went out to the street and dismissed the driver.

When I went to the back of the house a second time, I looked around more carefully. Some light came from the neighbor's on the other side of the grape-stake fence. I noticed that the back door of Stanley Broadhurst's house was slightly ajar. I opened it all the way and turned on the kitchen lights.

There were marks in the wood around the lock which showed that it had been jimmied. It occurred to me that the man who had done the job might still be inside. I didn't want to run into him accidentally. Burglars seldom intended to kill anyone, but they sometimes killed when they were caught by surprise in their dark fantasy.

I turned off the kitchen lights and waited. The house was silent. From outside I could hear the pulsing hum of the arterial boulevard I had just left.

The neighbors were listening to the late news on television. In spite of these normal sounds, I felt a physical anxiety close to nausea. It got worse when I went into the hallway.

Perhaps I smelled or otherwise sensed the man in the study. In any case, when I switched on the light he was lying there in front of the broken desk, grinning up at me like a magician who had pulled off the ultimate trick.

I didn't recognize him right away. He had a black beard and mustache and long black hair which seemed to grow peculiarly low on his forehead. I found on closer inspection that the hair was a wig which didn't fit him too well. The beard and mustache were false.

Under the hair was the dead face of the man who called himself Al and had come to the house to ask for a thousand dollars. Come once too often. The front of his shirt was wet and heavy with blood, and there were stab wounds under it. He smelled of whisky.

The inside breast pocket of his cheap dark suit bore the label of a San Francisco department store. The pocket itself was empty, and so were his other pockets. I lifted him to feel for a wallet in his hip pockets. There was none.

I checked my notebook for the address he had given me: the Star Motel, on Pacific Coast Highway below Topanga Canyon. Then I looked at the rolltop desk which he had evidently broken open. The wood around the locking mechanism was splintered, and the rolltop section was stuck in a half-open position.

I couldn't force it far enough back to release the drawers, which stayed locked. But in one of the pigeonholes I found a pair of photographs of a young man and a young woman who at first glance looked alike. Clipped to the photographs was a piece of paper with the printed heading: "Memo from the desk of Stanley Broadhurst."

Someone, presumably Stanley, had written laboriously on it: "Have you seen this man and woman? According to witnesses they left Santa Teresa early in July, 1955, and traveled to San Francisco by car (red Porsche, Calif. license number XUJ251). They stayed in San Francisco one or two nights, and sailed July 6 en route to Honolulu via Vancouver on the English freighter *Swansea Castle*. A thousand-dollar reward will be paid for information about their present whereabouts."

I took another look at the pictures attached to it. The girl had dark hair and very large dark eyes which looked up rather dimly out of the old photograph. Her features seemed to be aquiline and sensitive, except for her heavy passionate mouth.

The man's face, which I took to be Captain Broadhurst's, was less open. There were well-shaped bones in his face and hard, staring eyes set obliquely in them. The resemblance between him and the girl turned out to be superficial when I compared them. His bold stare kept him hidden in a way, but I guessed that he was a taker. She looked like a giver.

I turned to the filing cabinet. Its top drawer had been forced, so violently that it couldn't be properly closed. It was full of letters carefully arranged among manila dividers. The postmarks ranged over the past six years.

I picked out a fairly recent one whose return address was the Santa Teresa Travel Agency, 920 Main Street.

Dear Mr. Broadhurst [the typed letter said]:

Have checked our files as per your request and confirm that your father, Mr. Leo Broadhurst, booked double passage on the *Swansea Castle*, due to sail from San Francisco for Honolulu (via Vancouver) on or about July 6, 1955. Passage paid for, but we cannot confirm that it was used. *Swansea Castle*

has changed to Liberian registry, and 1955 owners and master
are hard to trace. Please advise if you wish us to check
further.

> Faithfully yours,
> Harvey Noble, Proprietor

I looked at an older letter which was handwritten on the
stationery of a Santa Teresa church and signed by the
pastor, a Reverend Lowell Riceyman.

Dear Stanley [it said],

*Your father Leo Broadhurst was one of my parishioners, in
the sense that he sometimes attended Sunday services, as you
may recall, but I have to confess that I never knew him at all
well. I'm sure the fault must have been mine as much as his.
He gave the impression of being a sportsman, an active and
spirited man who enjoyed life. No doubt that is your recollection of him, too.*

*May I suggest in all good feeling and sympathy that you
be content with that recollection, and not pursue any further
the course you have embarked on, against my advice. Your
father chose to leave your mother and you, for reasons which
neither you nor I can fathom. The heart has its reasons that
the reason does not know. I think it is unwise for a son to
attempt to delve too deeply into his father's life. What man
is without blame?*

*Think of your own life, Stanley. You have recently taken on
the responsibilities of marriage—as I, having had the pleasure
of performing the ceremony, have good cause to remember.
Your wife is a fine and lovely girl, clearly more worthy of
your living interest than those old passions of which you have
written to me. The past can do very little for us—no more than
it has already done, for good or ill—except in the end to release us. We must seek and accept release, and give release.*

*Concerning the marital problems of which you write me,
believe me, they are not unusual. But I would prefer to discuss*

them with you personally, rather than commit my poor thoughts
to paper. Until I see you, then.

I looked down at the dead man, and thought of the
other dead man on the mountain. The Reverend Riceyman
had given Stanley good advice, which he had failed to
take. A feeling of embarrassment and regret went through
me. It wasn't exactly grief for Stanley, though it included
that.

It also included the realization that I had to call the police.
I left the phone in the study untouched and went back to the
kitchen. As soon as I switched on the lights, I noticed the
empty brown whisky bottle standing among the dishes in
the sink.

I called the Valley headquarters of the LAPD and
reported a homicide. During the nine or ten minutes that
the police took to answer the call, I walked halfway along
the block and found Al's Volkswagen, locked. At the very
last minute, when I could already hear the siren, I remembered that the engine of my car was running. I went out to
the garage and turned it off.

I had a light hat in the trunk. I used it to cover my damaged head, and met the patrol car out in front of the house.
The man next door came out and looked at us and went
back into his house without saying anything.

I took the officers in through the back door, pointing out
the jimmy marks. I showed them the dead man and told
them briefly how I had happened to find him. They made a
few notes and put in a call for a homicide team, suggesting
politely that I stick around.

I told my story in greater detail to a captain of detectives
named Arnie Shipstad, whom I had known since he was a
detective-sergeant with the Hollywood division. Arnie was

a fresh-faced Swede with shrewd sensitive eyes which registered the details of the study as precisely as the cameras of his photographer did.

The dead man had his picture taken with and without his wig and beard and mustache. Then he was carefully rolled onto a stretcher and carried out.

Arnie lingered. "So you think he came here for money?"

"I'm sure he did."

"But he got something different. And the man who promised him money is dead, too." He picked up Stanley's memo, which I had shown him, and read aloud: " 'Have you seen this man and woman?' Is this what it's all about?"

"It could be."

"Why do you think he came here in disguise?"

"I can think of a couple of possible reasons. He may be wanted. I'd lay even money that he is wanted."

Arnie nodded in agreement. "I'll check him out. But there's another possibility, too."

"What's that?"

"He may have been wearing the outfit for fun and games. Quite a few swingers use longhair wigs when they go quail-hunting. This one may have been planning to pick up his money and have a night on the town."

I had to admit there was something in the idea.

XIV

I left Sepulveda at Sunset and drove into Pacific Palisades. The Crandalls lived on a palm-lined street in a kind of Tudor manor with a peaked roof and brown protruding half-timbers.

The mullioned windows were all lighted as though a Saturday night party was going on. But the only sound I heard before I knocked was the sighing and scratching of the wind through the dry palm fronds.

A blond woman in black opened the ornately carved door. Her body was so trim against the light that I thought for a moment she was the girl. Then she inclined her head to look at me, and I saw that time had faintly touched her face and begun to tug at her throat.

She narrowed her eyes and peered past me into the darkness. "Are you Mr. Archer?"

"Yes. May I come in?"

"Please do. My husband is home now, but he's resting." Her speech was carefully correct, as if she had taken lessons in talking. I suspected that her natural speech was a good deal rougher and freer.

She led me into a formal sitting room with a blazing crystal chandelier which hurt my eyes and an unlit marble fireplace. We sat down in facing conversation chairs. Her body fell into a beautiful still pose, but her faintly pinched blond face seemed bored with it, or resentful, like an angel living with an animal.

"Was Susan all right when you saw her?"

"She wasn't hurt, if that's what you mean."

"Where is she now?"

"I don't know."

"You mentioned serious trouble." Her voice was soft and small, as if she was trying to minimize the trouble. "Please tell me what you mean, and please be frank. This is the third night now that I've been sitting by the telephone."

"I know how it is."

She inclined toward me. Her breasts leaned out from her body. "Do you have children?"

"No, but my clients do. Susan has one of those children with her now—a small boy named Ronald Broadhurst. Have you ever heard of him?"

She hesitated for a moment, in deep thought, then shook her head. "I'm afraid I haven't."

"Ronald's father was murdered this morning. Stanley Broadhurst."

She failed to react to the name. While she listened raptly like a child at a fairy tale, I gave her an account of the day. Her hands climbed from her lap like small independent creatures with red feet, and fastened on her breasts. She said:

"Susan couldn't have done what was done to Mr. Broadhurst. She's a gentle girl. And she loves children. She certainly wouldn't hurt the little boy."

"Why would she grab him?"

The word jolted the woman. She looked at me with some dislike, as if I'd threatened the dream she was living in. Her hands fell away from her breasts.

"There must be some explanation."

"Do you know why she left home?"

"I—Lester and I haven't been able to understand it. Everything was going along smoothly. She'd been accepted at UCLA and she was on a good summer program—tennis and diving lessons and conversational French. Then on Thursday morning, when we were out shopping, she left without any warning. She didn't even say goodbye to us."

"Did you report it to the police?"

"Lester did. They told him they couldn't promise much— there are dozens of missing young people every week. But I never thought my daughter would be one of them. Susan has had a really good life. We've given her every advantage."

I nudged her back toward the hard truth: "Have there been any radical changes in Susan lately?"

"What do you mean?"

"Any big change in her habits. Like sleeping a lot more— or a lot less. Getting excited and staying that way, or turning apathetic and letting her appearance go to pot."

"None of those things. She isn't on drugs, if that's what you have in mind."

"Think about it, though. Thursday night in Santa Teresa she had what sounds like a bad trip and jumped into the ocean."

"Was Jerry Kilpatrick with her?"

"Yes. Do you know him, Mrs. Crandall?"

"He's been here at the house. We met him at Newport. He seemed like a nice enough boy to me."

"When was he here?"

"A couple of months ago. He and my husband got into an argument, and he never came back after that." She sounded disappointed.

"What was the argument about?"

"You'll have to ask Lester. They just didn't take to each other."

"May I speak to your husband?"

"He's lying down. He's had a rough couple of days."

"I'm sorry, but maybe you'd better get him up."

"I don't believe I should. Lester is no longer young, you know."

She didn't move. She was one of those dreaming blonds who couldn't bear to face a change in her life. One of those waiting mothers who would sit forever beside the phone but didn't know what to say when it finally rang.

"Your daughter's at sea with a teen-age dropout, under suspicion of child-stealing and murder. And you don't want to disturb her father." I got up and opened the door of the sitting room: "If you won't call your husband, I think I'd better."

"*I* will, if you insist."

As she passed me in the doorway I could feel the small chill presence that lived like a stunted child in her fine body. The same cold presence reflected itself in the room. The chandelier for all its blaze was like a cluster of frozen tears. The white marble mantel was tomblike. The flowers in the vases were plastic, unsmellable, giving off a dull sense of artificial life.

Lester Crandall came into the room as if he was the visitor, not I. He was a short heavy-bodied man with iron gray hair and sideburns which seemed to pincer his slightly crumpled face and hold it out for inspection. His smile was that of a man who wanted to be liked.

His handshake was firm, and I noticed that his hands were large and rather misshapen. They bore the old marks of heavy work: swollen knuckles, roughened skin. He had spent his life, I thought, working his way to the top of a small hill which his daughter had abandoned in one jump.

He was wearing a figured red-silk bathrobe over undershirt and trousers, and his face was rosy-purplish, his hair damp from the shower. I told him I was sorry to disturb him.

He waved the thought away. "I'd be glad to get up at any hour of the night, believe me. I understand you have word of my little girl?"

I told him briefly what I knew. Under the pressure of my words his face seemed to be forced back on its bones. But he refused to admit the fear that was making his eyes water.

"There must be a reason for what she's doing. Susan's a sensible girl. I don't believe she's been taking drugs."

"What you believe won't change the facts," I said.

"But you don't know her. I spent most of the evening traipsing up and down the Sunset Strip. It gave me a real insight into what's happening to the youth of today. But Susan isn't like that at all. She's very organized at all times."

He sat down heavily in one of the conversation chairs, as if the little speech on top of the long evening had exhausted him. I sat in the other.

"We won't argue," I said. "One good lead is worth all the theories in the world."

"You're very right."

"May I see Susan's address book? I understand you have it."

He looked up at his wife, who was hovering near him. "Would you get it for me, Mother? It's on the desk in the library."

After she left the room, I said to Crandall: "When something like this happens in a family, there's nearly always some advance warning. Has Susan been in any kind of trouble lately?"

"None at all. Never in her life, if you want the truth."

"Any drinking?"

"She doesn't even like it. I give her a taste of my drink now and then, but she always makes a face."

He made one himself. It stayed imprinted in his flesh as an expression of dismay. I wondered what he was remembering or trying to forget.

"What does she do for fun?"

"We're a very close family," he said. "The three of us spend a lot of time together. I own some motels up and down the coast, and the three of us go on a lot of little trips combining business and pleasure. And of course Susan has her activity program—tennis and diving lessons and French conversation."

He was like a man with his eyes closed trying to put his hands on a girl that wasn't there. I began to think I had a glimmering of the problem. It was often the same problem—an unreality so bland and smothering that the children tore loose and impaled themselves on the spikes of any reality that offered. Or made their own unreality with drugs.

"Does she spend much time on the Strip?"

"No sir, she never goes there—not to my knowledge."

"Why did you?"

"A policeman suggested it to me. He said it's a port of missing girls and he thought I might see her there."

"What kind of boys does she run with?"

"She doesn't have too much to do with boys. She's gone to some supervised parties, of course, and we've sent her to dancing school for years—ballroom as well as ballet. But as for boys, frankly I've discouraged it, the state of the modern world being what it is. Most of her friends and acquaintances are girls."

"What about Jerry Kilpatrick? I understand he visited your daughter."

Crandall flushed. "Yes. He came here back in June. He and Sue seemed to have a lot to talk about, but they shut up when I came into the room. I didn't like that."

"Didn't you have an argument with him?"

He gave me a quick narrow look. "Who told you that?"

"Your wife did."

"Women always talk too much," he said. "Yes, we had an argument. I tried to straighten the boy out on his philosophy of life. I asked him in a friendly way what he planned to do with himself, and he said all he wanted was just to get by. I didn't think that was a satisfactory answer, and I asked him what would happen to the country if everybody took that attitude. He said it had already happened to the country. I don't know what he meant by that, but I didn't like his tone. I told him if that was his philosophy of life he could leave my home and not bother coming back. The little twerp said he'd be glad to. And he left and never did come back. Which was good riddance of bad rubbish."

Crandall's face was dusky red. A pulse at the side of his forehead throbbed. My sore head throbbed in sympathy.

"Mrs. Crandall thought at the time I'd made a mistake," he said. "You know how women are. If a girl isn't married or at least engaged by age eighteen, they think she's bound to be an old maid." Crandall lifted his head as if he'd picked up a signal that was inaudible to me. "I wonder what Mother's doing in the library."

He got up and opened the door of the room, and I followed him down the hall. His body moved heavily and dolefully, as if it was weighted down by a kind of despair which hadn't yet reached his consciousness.

The sound of a woman crying came through the library door. Mrs. Crandall was standing up and sobbing against a wall of empty shelves. Crandall went to her and tried to quiet her shaking back with his hands.

"Don't cry, Mother. We'll get her back."

"No." She shook her head. "Susan will never come back here. We had no right to bring her here in the first place."

"What do you mean?"

"We don't belong in this place. Everybody knows it except you."

"That's not true, Mother. I've got a higher net worth than anybody on this block. I could buy and sell most of them."

"What good is net worth? We're like fish out of water. I've got no friends on this street—and neither has Susan."

His large hands grasped her shoulders and forced her to turn and face him. "That's just your imagination, Mother. I always get a friendly smile and nod when I drive past. They know who I am. They know I've got what it takes."

"Maybe you have. It doesn't help Susan—or me."

"Help you do what?"

"Just live," she said. "I've been trying to pretend that everything is okay. But now we know it isn't."

"It will be. I guarantee it. Everything will be hunky-dory again."

"It never was."

"That's nonsense, and you know it."

She shook her head. He reached up and stopped her movement of denial with his hands, as if it was merely a physical accident. He pushed the hair back from her forehead, which looked clear and untroubled in contrast with her tear-streaked face.

She leaned on him, letting him hold her up. Her face on his shoulder was inert, and unaware of me, like that of a woman who had drowned in her own life.

Walking in a kind of lockstep, they went out into the hallway and left me alone in the room. I noticed a small red-leather book lying open on a corner table, and I sat down to look at it. The word "Addresses" was stamped in gold on the cover, and inside on the flyleaf the girl had written her name in an unformed hand: "Susan Crandall."

There were three other girls' names in the book, and one boy's name, Jerry Kilpatrick. I realized what Susan's mother had been crying about. The family had been a lonely trio, living like actors on a Hollywood set, and now there were only two of them to sustain the dream.

Mrs. Crandall came into the room and startled me out of my thoughts. She had combed her hair and washed her face and made it up quickly and expertly.

"I'm sorry, Mr. Archer, I didn't mean to break down."

"Nobody ever does. But sometimes it's a good idea."

"Not for me. And not for Lester. You wouldn't think it to look at him, but he's an emotional man, and he loves Susan."

She came over to the table. Her grief still clung to her body like a perfume. She was one of those women whose feminine quality persisted through any kind of emotional weather.

"You hurt your head," she said.

"Jerry Kilpatrick did."

"I admit I made a mistake about him."

"So did I, Mrs. Crandall. What are we going to do about Susan?"

"I don't know what to do." She stood above me sighing, leafing over the empty pages of the address book. "I've talked to the girls she knows, including the ones in here. None of them were really friends. All they ever did together was go to school or play tennis."

"That wasn't much of a life for an eighteen-year-old girl."

"I know that. I've tried to promote things for her, but nothing worked. She was afraid."

"Afraid of what?"

"I don't know, but it's real. I've been fearful all along that she'd go on the run. And now she has."

I asked Mrs. Crandall to show me the girl's room, if she didn't mind.

"I don't mind. But don't mention it to Lester. He wouldn't like it."

She took me to a large room with a sliding glass door which opened onto a patio. In spite of its size, the room seemed crowded. The bedroom furniture, ivory with gold trim, was matched by stereo and television sets and a girl's work desk with a white telephone. The place suggested a pampered prisoner expected to live out her life in a single room.

The walls were hung with mass-produced psychedelic posters and pictures of young male singing groups which only seemed to emphasize the silence. There were no pictures or other traces of any actual people the girl might have known.

"As you can see," her mother said, "we gave her everything. But it wasn't what she wanted."

She opened the wardrobe closet for my inspection. It was stuffed with coats and dresses like a small army of girls crushed flat for storage and smelling of sachet. The chest of drawers was full of sweaters and other garments, like shed or unused skins. The single drawer of the dressing table was jammed with cosmetics.

There was a telephone directory lying open on the white desk. I sat on the cushioned chair in front of it and switched on the fluorescent desk lamp. The directory was open to the motel section of the yellow pages, and at the bottom of the righthand page was a small advertisement for the Star Motel.

I didn't think that this could be a coincidence, and I

pointed it out to Mrs. Crandall. It suggested nothing to her. Neither did my description of Al.

I asked her to give me a recent photograph of Susan. She took me into another room, which she called her sewing room, and produced a pocket-sized high school graduation picture. The clear-eyed blond girl in it looked as if she would never lose her purity or youth or grow old or die.

"That's the way I used to look," her mother said.

"There's still a strong resemblance."

"You should have seen me when I was in high school."

She wasn't boasting, exactly. But a little earthiness was asserting itself behind her careful manner. I said:

"I wish I had. Where did you go to high school?"

"Santa Teresa."

"Is that why Susan went up there?"

"I doubt it."

"Do you have relatives in Santa Teresa?"

"Not any more." She changed the subject. "If you get any word of Susan, will you let us know right away?"

I promised, and she handed me the picture as if to seal the bargain. I put it in my pocket along with the green-covered book, and left the house. The shadows of the palms lay like splash-marks of dark liquid on the pavement and across the roof of my car.

XV

The Star Motel stood with its rear end on pilings in a narrow crowded place between the highway and the sea. The lights of the all-night service station beside it shone on its yellow stucco walls and on the weathered "Vacancy" sign which hung on the office door.

I went in and tapped the hand bell on the counter. A man came plodding out of the back room and peered at me through his creased and sleepy face.

"Single or double?"

I told him I was looking for a man, and I started to give him a description of Al. He cut me short with a shake of his frowzy head. An anger that floated like a pollution near the surface of his life came up in his throat and almost choked him.

"You got no right to wake me up for that. This is a business establishment."

I laid two dollar bills on the counter. He sucked his anger back into his body and picked up the money.

"Many thanks. Your friend and his wife are in room seven."

I showed him Susan's picture. "Has she been here?"

"Maybe she has."

"You've seen her or you haven't."

"What's the rap?"

"No rap. She's just a floating girl."

"Are you her father?"

"Just a friend," I said. "Has she been here?"

"I think she was, a couple of days ago. I haven't seen her since. Anyway," he said with a slanted grin, "you got your two dollars' worth."

I left him and moved along the railed gallery. A high tide was slapping disconsolately at the pilings. The reflection of the neon from the service station floated on the water like iridescent waste.

I knocked on the door and made its tin 7 rattle. The narrow band of light which rimmed the door widened as it opened. The woman behind it tried to close it again when she saw my face, but I put my arm and shoulder in the opening and slid inside.

"Go away," she said.

"I only want to ask you a couple of questions."

"Sorry. I lost my memory." She seemed to mean it literally. "Some days I can't remember my own name."

Her voice was flat. Her face was without expression, though it was marked by the traces of past expressions around the eyes and at the corners of the mouth. She looked both young and old. Her body was muffled in a quilted pink robe, and I couldn't tell if she was a well-preserved middle-aged woman or a dilapidated girl. Her eyes were the color of the darkness in the corners of the room.

"What is your name?"

"Elegant."

"That's a striking name."

"Thank you. I picked it one day when I was feeling that way. I haven't felt that way for quite some time now."

She looked around the room as if to blame her environment for this. The bedclothes were tangled and dragging on the floor. Empty bottles stood on the dresser among tooth-marked pieces of old hamburgers. The chairs were hung with her discarded clothing.

"Where's Al?" I said.

"He should be back by now, but he isn't."

"What's his last name?"

"Al Nesters, he calls himself."

"And where's he from?"

"I'm not supposed to tell anybody that."

"Why not?"

She made a vague impatient gesture. "You ask too bloody many questions. Who do you think you are?"

I didn't try to answer that. "How long ago did Al leave here?"

"Hours. I don't know exactly. I don't keep track of the time."

"Was he wearing his longhair wig and mustache and beard?"

She gave me a blank look. "He doesn't wear any of those things."

"That you know of."

She showed a flicker of interest, even a little anger. "What is this? Are you trying to tell me he's doubletiming me?"

"He may be. When I saw him tonight, he was wearing a black wig and a beard to match."

"Where did you see him?"

"Northridge."

"Are you the man who promised him the money?"

"I represent that man." It was true in a way— I was working for Stanley Broadhurst's wife. But the statement made me feel as if I was mediating between two ghosts.

Another flicker of interest appeared in her eyes. "Do you have the thousand for him?"

"Not that much."

"You could leave me what you have."

"I don't think so."

"Enough for a bindle anyway."

"How much is that?"

"Twenty dollars would fix me up for tonight and all day tomorrow."

"I'll think about it. I'm not sure Al delivered on his side of the bargain."

"You know he did, if you're with it. He's been hanging around for days waiting to be paid off. How much longer do you expect him to wait?"

The answer was forever, but I didn't say it. "I'm not sure what he did was worth a grand."

"Don't tell me that. It was the figure mentioned." Her vague eyes narrowed. "Are you sure you're fronting for the money man? What's his name—Broadman?"

"Broadhurst. Stanley Broadhurst."

She relaxed on the edge of the bed. Before she got suspicious again, I showed her the photograph of Susan which Mrs. Crandall had given me. She looked at it with a kind of respectful envy and passed it back to me.

"I was almost as pretty as that at one time," she said.

"I bet you were, Elegant."

The sound of her name pleased her, and she smiled. "Not so long ago as you might think."

"I can believe it. Do you know this girl?"

"I've seen her once or twice."

"Recently?"

"I think so. I don't keep good track of time, I've got too much on my mind. But she was here in the last two or three days."

"What was she doing here?"

"You'll have to ask Al. He made me go out and sit in the bug. Fortunately, I'm not the jealous type, that's one good quality I have."

"Did Al make love to her?"

"Maybe he did. I wouldn't put it past him. But mainly he was trying to get her to talk. He made me mix up some acid in a Coke. That was supposed to loosen her up."

"What did she talk about?"

"I wouldn't know. He took her away someplace, and that was the last I saw of her. But I guess it had to do with the Broadman business. Broadhurst? That was what Al had on his mind all week."

"What day was she here? Thursday?"

"I don't remember offhand. I'll try to figure it out." Her lips moved in calculation, as if between that day and this she had crossed some sort of international dateline. "It was Sunday when we left Sac, I know that for certain. He took me to San Francisco to answer the ad, and we spent Sunday night there and came down here on Monday. Or was it Tuesday? What day is this again?"

"Saturday night. Early Sunday morning."

She counted on her fingers, the days and nights crossing her eyes like shadows. "I guess he made his contact Wednesday," she said. "He came back here and said we could cross the border by Saturday at the latest." She looked at me in sudden alienation. "Where is the money? What happened to it?"

"It hasn't been paid yet."

"When do we get it?"

"I don't know. I don't even know what Al was supposed to do for it."

"It's simple enough," she said. "There were this guy and this girl, and Al was supposed to locate them. You know that if you work for Broadhurst."

"Broadhurst doesn't confide in me."

"But you've seen the ad from the *Chronicle*, haven't you?"

"Not yet. Do you have a copy?"

I was moving too fast for her, and her face closed up. "Maybe I have and maybe I haven't. What do I get out of it?"

"I promise you'll get something. But if the ad came out in the San Francisco *Chronicle*, a million people must have seen it. You might as well show it to me."

She considered this proposition. Then she got a worn suitcase out from under the bed, opened it, and handed me a folded and refolded clipping. It was a two-column ad about six inches high, reproducing the pictures I had found in Stanley Broadhurst's rolltop desk. The accompanying text had been changed in part:

Can you identify this couple? Under the name of Mr. and Mrs. Ralph Smith, they arrived in San Francisco by car on or about July 5, 1955. It is believed they took passage for Vancouver and Honolulu aboard the *Swansea Castle*, which sailed from San Francisco July 6, 1955. But they may still be in the Bay area. A thousand-dollar reward will be paid for information leading to their present whereabouts.

I turned to the woman who called herself Elegant. "Where are they?"

"Don't ask me." She shrugged, and the movement disarranged her robe. She pulled it close about her. "I think maybe I saw the woman."

"When?"

"I'm trying to remember."

"What's her name?"

"Al didn't tell me that. He didn't tell me anything, really. But we stopped at her house on the way down here, and I got a look at her face when she came to the door. She's older now, but I'm pretty sure it's the same woman." She considered the question further. "Maybe not, though. It seems to me Al got that clipping from her."

"You mean the ad?"

"That's right. It doesn't make sense, does it? Maybe he was putting me on, or I'm remembering wrong."

"Can you tell me where her house is?"

"That," she said, "is worth money."

"How much do you want?"

"It says in the ad a thousand. If I took less, Al would kill me."

"Al won't be coming back here."

She met my eyes and held them. "You're telling me he's dead?"

"Yes."

She huddled on the edge of the bed, as if the knowledge of Al's death had chilled her. "I never thought we'd make it to Mexico." She gave me a cold darting look, like a harmless snake. "Did you kill him?"

"No."

"The cops?"

"What makes you say that?"

"He was on the run." She looked around the room. "I've got to get out of here." But she didn't move.

"Where was he on the run from?"

"He broke out of prison. He talked about it once when he was high. I should have left him when I had the chance." She stood up and made a frantic gesture. "What happened to my Volkswagen?"

"The cops probably have it by now."

"I've got to get out of here. You take me out of here."

"No. You can take a bus."

She called me a few names, which didn't bother me. But when I moved toward the door, she followed.

"How much money will you give me?"

"Nothing like a thousand."

"A hundred? That would take me back to Sac."

"Are you from Sacramento?"

"My parents live there. But they don't want to see me."

"What about Al?"

"He has no parents. He came out of an orphanage."

"Where?"

"Some city north of here. We stopped there on the way down. He pointed out the orphanage to me."

"You stopped at the orphanage?"

"You're all mixed up," she said with condescension. "He showed me the orphanage when we passed it on the highway—we didn't stop there. We stopped in town to get some money for gas and food."

"What town?"

"One of those Santa places. Santa Teresa, I think it was."

"And how did you get the money for gas?"

"Al got it from a little old lady. She gave him twenty dollars. Al's very big with little old ladies."

"Can you describe her?"

"I dunno. She was just a little old lady in a little old house on a little old street. It was kind of a pretty street, with purple flowers in the trees."

"Jacarandas?"

She nodded. "Flowering jacarandas, yeah."

"Was her name Mrs. Snow?"

"I think that was the name."

"What about the woman in the ad? Where does she live?"

A look of stupid cunning took hold of her face. "That's worth money. That's what it's all about."

"I'll give you fifty."

"Let me see it."

I got out my wallet and gave her the fifty-dollar bill that Fran Armistead had tipped me with. I was sort of glad to get rid of it, though here again I was conscious of buying and being sold at the same time, as if I'd made a down payment on the room and its occupant.

She kissed the money. "I can really use it, it's my ticket out of here." But she looked around the room as if it was a recurrent nightmare she had.

"You were going to tell me where the woman lives."

"Was I?" She was stalling, and uncomfortable about it. She forced herself to say: "She lives in this big old house in the woods."

"You're making this up."

"I am not."

"What woods are you talking about?"

"It's on the Peninsula someplace. I didn't pay good attention on the way. I was strung out on an Einstein trip."

"Einstein trip?"

"When you go all the way out, past the last star, and space loops back on you."

"Where on the Peninsula?"

She shook her head, the way you shake a watch that has stopped ticking. "I can't remember. There's all these little cities strung together. I can't remember which one."

"What did the house look like?"

"It was very old, two-storied—*three*-storied. And it had two little round towers, one on each side." She erected her thumbs.

"What color?"

"Kind of gray, I think it was. It looked kind of grayish green through the trees."

"What kind of trees?"

"Oak trees," she said, "and some pines. But mostly oak trees."

I waited for a while.

"What else do you remember about the place?"

"That's about all. I wasn't really *there*, you know. I was out around Arcturus, looking down. Oh yeah, there was a dog running around under the trees. A Great Dane. He had a beautiful voice." She woofed in imitation.

"Did he belong to the house?"

"I don't know. I don't think so. He acted lost, I remember thinking that. Will that help?"

"I don't know. What day was it?"

"Sunday, I think. I said it was Sunday, didn't I, that we left Sac?"

"You haven't given me much for my fifty."

She was dismayed, and afraid I'd take it back. "You could make love to me if you want."

Not waiting for my answer, she stood up and dropped the pink robe to the floor. Her body was young, high-breasted, narrow-waisted, almost too slender. But there were bruises on her arms and thighs like the hash-marks of hard service. She was a dilapidated girl.

She looked up into my face. I don't know what she saw there, but she said: "Al roughed me up quite a bit. He was pretty wild after all that time in prison. I guess you don't want me, do you?"

"Thanks, I've had a hard day."

"And you won't take me with you?"

"No." I gave her my business card and asked her to call me collect if she remembered anything more.

"I doubt I will. I've got a mind like a sieve."

"Or if you need help."

"I always need help. But you won't want to hear from me."

"I think I can stand it."

Leaning her hands on my shoulders, she raised herself on her toes and brushed my mouth with her sad mouth.

I went outside and folded Stanley Broadhurst's ad into the green-covered book and locked up both of them in the trunk of my car. Then I drove home to West Los Angeles.

Before I went to bed I called my answering service. Arnie Shipstad had left a message for me. The man whose body I'd found in Stanley Broadhurst's house was a recent escapee from Folsom named Albert Sweetner, with a record of a dozen or so arrests. His first arrest occurred in Santa Teresa, California.

XVI

It was late at night, almost halfway to morning. I knocked myself out with a heavy slug of whisky and went to bed.

In the dream that took over my sleeping mind I was due to arrive someplace in a very short time. But when I went out to my car it had no wheels, not even a steering wheel. I sat in it like a snail in a shell and watched the night world go by.

The light coming through the bedroom blind changed from gray to off-white and woke me. I lay and listened to the early traffic. A few birds peeped. At full dawn the jays began to squawk and divebomb my window.

I'd forgotten the jays. Their sudden raucous reminder turned me cold under the sheet. I threw it off and got up and put on my clothes.

There was a last can of peanuts in the kitchen cupboard. I scattered the peanuts out the window and watched the jays come swooping into the yard. It was like watching a flashing blue explosion-in-reverse that put the morning world together again.

But the central piece was missing. I shaved and went out for breakfast and kept going.

Miles below Santa Teresa, sooner than I expected, the fire came into view above the freeway. It had burned southward and eastward along the mountains, which were black and rimmed with flames. But the mass of air which had moved in from the sea the night before seemed to be holding it back from the coastal plain and the city.

The wind was still coming from the sea. Where the freeway looped close to the water I could see the white spume drifting up from the shore and hear the surf crashing.

I stopped at the Armistead beach house. The tide was high, and the broken water slid up the beach and wet the pilings that the house stood on. I knocked at the second-floor entrance at the rear.

Fran Armistead came to the door wearing men's pajamas. Her face was swollen with sleep. Her hair was sticking up like ruffled feathers.

"Do I know you?" she said not unpleasantly.

"Archer," I prompted her. "I brought your car back. We were fellow-refugees from the fire."

"Of course. It's rather fun being a refugee, isn't it?"

"Maybe the first time. Is your husband here?"

"I'm afraid he isn't. He went out very early."

"Do you know where?"

"He's probably at the marina. Roger's dreadfully upset about his boat. When Mr. Kilpatrick phoned him this morning, he didn't even know that it was gone."

"I take it it hasn't been heard from."

"It hadn't been when he left here. Roger's terribly angry with the Kilpatrick boy. I don't know what he'll do to him when he catches him."

"Were Roger and Jerry Kilpatrick pretty close?"

She gave me a hard look. "Not in the way you mean. Roger is terribly masculine."

She shivered, and hugged herself. I drove to the marina and parked in the almost deserted public lot. It was still very early in the morning.

I could see through the wire fence that *Ariadne's* slip was still empty. Roger Armistead was standing on the float, looking out to sea in an attitude that seemed consciously statuesque. Brian Kilpatrick was near him, facing me. The two men seemed remote, yet tensely conscious of each other, as if they had quarreled.

Kilpatrick saw me at the gate. He came up the gangplank and let me through. He was wearing the same clothes, and he looked as if he had slept in them, or tried to.

"Armistead's in a filthy mood, I warn you," Kilpatrick said. "He blames *me* for this mess. Hell, I've barely seen Jerry in the last couple of months. He's been running out of my control. Armistead practically adopted him. *I* can't assume responsibility." But he moved his heavy shoulders as if the weight of his son was strapped to his back.

"Where would Jerry take the boat? Do you have any idea?"

"I'm afraid I don't. I'm not a yachtsman. Which is one of the reasons Jerry took up sailing. If I'd been interested in the sea, he'd have gone in for golf."

Kilpatrick had slipped in the course of the night. His voice was querulous.

"North or south?" I said.

"Probably south. Those are the waters he knew. Maybe out to the islands."

He pointed to the offshore islands which lay on the horizon like blue whales. In the twenty-mile span between them and the shore, there was nothing visible on the surface of the water.

"Have you informed the sheriff?"

He looked at me in some embarrassment. "Not yet."

"You said you were going to talk to him last night."

"I tried to, honestly. He was out on the fire line. As a matter of fact he still is."

"There must be other officers on duty."

"There are some. But all they can think about is the fire. They're involved in a major catastrophe, you know."

"So is Jerry."

"You don't have to tell me that. He's my son." He gave me an anxious sidelong look. "I heard from Crandall again, early this morning. I gather you went to see him after all."

"What did he have to say?"

"He blames the whole thing on Jerry, naturally. Boys always get the blame where a girl's concerned. According to Crandall's version, his daughter never caused them any trouble at all, until now. That's hard to believe."

"He may believe it. He and his wife seem to be slightly out of touch." My mind came up with a stereoscopic view of the girl alone in her white room at home, and the girl at the Star Motel with Al Sweetner.

"I wish you hadn't gone to Crandall," Kilpatrick said in an aggrieved voice. "It complicates things. He could make things rough for me if he wanted to."

"I'm sorry. I have to follow my case where it leads."

"It's your case, is it?"

"I'm willing to share it. If you'll wait a few minutes, we'll go and find your friend the sheriff. How about it?"

"If you say so."

I left Kilpatrick at the gate and spoke to Armistead's back. He turned deliberately. He looked both sad and angry in a strangled inexpressive way. He was wearing a yachting cap and blazer, and an ascot at his throat.

"Why didn't you tell me about this, last night? Now we may never get her back." Armistead sounded as if he was talking about a woman he had lost, or the dream of a woman. "She could be a hundred miles from here by now, or at the bottom of the sea."

"Have you told the Coast Guard?"

"Yes I have. They'll keep an eye out for her. But they're not exactly in the business of tracking down stolen boats."

"This isn't a simple case of theft," I said. "I guess you know the girl's aboard, and a little boy."

"Kilpatrick told me that."

Armistead's eyes narrowed and seemed to fasten on an ugly vision. He rubbed his knuckles in the sockets of his eyes, and turned his back on me again.

The waves were coming over the breakwater, shattering in green streaming water. Even the water in the marina was unquiet, lifting the float under our feet and letting it fall. The world was changing, as if with one piece missing the whole thing had come loose and was running wild.

Armistead walked out to the seaward end of the float. I followed him. He was a closed man, but I thought he might be getting more ready to open.

"I understand Jerry's a pretty good friend of yours."

"He was. I don't want to talk about it."

I went on anyway. "I don't blame you for being browned off. I feel the same way. He hit me over the head with a revolver last night. It looked and felt like a .38."

He said, after some hesitation: "I kept a .38 on the boat."

"And I suppose he took it with him?"

"I suppose he did. I'm not responsible."

"That's what Kilpatrick says, too. Nobody's responsible. The thing I'm trying to get at is Jerry's motivation. What do you think he's trying to accomplish?"

"Pure destruction, for all I know."

"I hope not."

"He broke faith with me." Armistead sounded resentful and betrayed, like a sailor who had come to the edge of a flat world. "I trusted him with my boat. I let him live aboard her all summer."

"Why?"

"He needed a place. I don't mean just a place to live. A place in the scheme of things. And I thought the sea would do it for him." He paused. "I was a yacht bum when I was Jerry's age. That was my main thing, if you want the truth. I couldn't stand life ashore any more than Jerry could. All I ever wanted was to get outside"—his arm swept seaward— "and be with the wind and the water. You know, the sea and the sky."

Like many divided and inarticulate men, Armistead had an old-fashioned poetic streak. I tried to keep him talking.

"Where did you live when you were a boy?"

"Near Newport. That's where I met my wife. I used to crew for her first husband."

"Jerry is supposed to have met Susan Crandall in Newport."

"He may have. We sailed down there in June."

I showed him the girl's picture, but he shook his head. "So far as I know, he never brought a girl aboard—her or any other girl."

"Until Thursday?"

"That's correct."

"What happened Thursday night? I'd like to get it straight."

"So would I. I gather from the scuttlebutt that the girl got high on something. She climbed the mast and dove into the water. She barely missed one of the pilings. This was about dawn on Friday morning."

"I understand Jerry's on drugs."

His face closed up. "I wouldn't know."

"His father admits he's been using them."

Armistead glanced toward the gate. Kilpatrick was still there.

"A lot of people use them," he said.

"The question may be important."

"All right. I tried to discourage it, but he was using pep pills and other dangerous drugs. It's one of the reasons I let him live aboard."

"I don't understand."

"He was less likely to get into trouble on the boat. At least, that was my theory." His face turned sullen again.

"You're fond of the boy."

"I tried to be a father to him, or a big brother. I know that sounds like corn. But I thought he was a good one, in spite of the drugs. What makes them so important?"

"I think the girl Susan had some kind of a breakdown. And she may have killed a man yesterday. Have you heard about the murder?"

"No, I haven't."

"The victim was a man named Stanley Broadhurst."

"I know a Mrs. Broadhurst who lives here."

"She's his mother. Do you know her well?"

"We don't know anyone here really well. The ones I know best are the harbor people. Fran has her own friends."

He glanced around the harbor restlessly like a sailor who had gone to sea in his youth and never moved back ashore. He looked at the town with uncomprehending eyes. It hung like a city made of fog or smoke between the restless sea and the black mountains.

"I'm not connected with any of this," Armistead said.

"Except through Jerry."

He frowned. "Jerry is finished and done with as far as I'm concerned."

I could have told him that it wasn't that easy. Jerry's real father seemed to know it already.

✺✺✺✺✺✺✺✺✺✺✺✺

XVII

✺✺✺✺✺✺✺✺✺✺✺✺

Kilpatrick was standing inside the wire gate. He looked at me like a suspect waiting to be released.

"Armistead's bitter, isn't he? He'll throw the book at Jerry."

"That I doubt. He's more let down than angry."

"I'm the one that's really let down," Kilpatrick said competitively.

I changed the subject. "Do you know where Sheriff Tremaine is this morning?"

"I know where he was an hour ago—at the main fire camp on the college grounds."

Kilpatrick volunteered to take me up there. Driving a new

black Cadillac, he led me in my not-so-recent Ford to the eastern edge of the city and onto a county road which climbed into the foothills through areas where the fire had been and gone. Just before we reached the campus, we passed a walled Forest Service compound where tanker trucks and tractors were being repaired.

We were stopped at double iron gates which stood open between iron gateposts. A brass sign was bolted to one post: Santa Teresa College. The ranger who stopped us knew Kilpatrick and told us to drive on through—the sheriff was on the athletic field with the fire boss. Joe Kelsey, whom I also asked him about, had passed that way not long before in a deputy coroner's truck.

Kilpatrick and I parked behind the bleachers that overlooked the athletic field. Before I left my car I got the green-covered book out of the trunk and put it in my jacket pocket. We made our way among official cars and trucks that had assembled from all over Southern California, from the Tehachapis in the north to the Mexican border.

The athletic field resembled a staging area just back of the lines in a major battle. On the grass oval inside the cinder track, bubble copters were landing and taking off with reinforcements.

Undisturbed by their din, smoke-jumpers lay on the grass with their closed and soot-blurred faces to the sky. There were men of every color there—Indians and blacks and weathered whites—hard-nosed, stoic, working stiffs with nothing to lose but their bedrolls and their lives.

We found Sheriff Tremaine in the main command post, which was a plain gray Forest Service trailer. The sheriff-coroner was a big-bellied man wearing a tan uniform and a Stetson. The flesh of his face hung in folds like a bloodhound's dewlaps and made his smile a strange and complex thing. He gave Kilpatrick an old-fashioned politician's hand-shake, with his left hand on the elbow as he pumped.

"What can I do for you, Brian?"

Kilpatrick cleared his throat. His voice came out tinny and uncertain. "My son Jerry's in a spot of trouble. He's taken Roger Armistead's sloop and gone to sea with a girl."

The Sheriff smiled his complicated smile. "It doesn't sound so serious. He'll come back."

"I was hoping you could alert the people up and down the coast."

"Maybe if there were two of me. Take it up with the men at the courthouse, Brian. We're planning to move base within twenty-four hours. And on top of everything else, I hear we've got a dead man on our hands."

"Stanley Broadhurst?" I said.

"Yessir. Do you know him?"

"I was with Joe Kelsey when his body was found. The girl that Mr. Kilpatrick is talking about is a material witness in that killing. And she and Jerry have Stanley Broadhurst's son with them."

Tremaine became more attentive, but he seemed too tired to react fully. "What do the two of you want me to do?"

"Put out an all-points alarm, as Kilpatrick suggested, with emphasis on the coastal cities and seaports. The missing boat is a sloop named 'Ariadne'." I spelled it out. "Do you have an aero-squadron?"

"I have, but the volunteer pilots are up to their necks."

"You could detach one plane and send it out to the islands. They may have anchored out there." From where I stood I could see the islands, embossed on the slanting sea.

"I'll consider it," the sheriff said. "If there's anything else, you can take it up with Joe Kelsey. He has the full coopera-tion of my office."

"There's one other thing, sheriff."

He bowed his head in weary patience. I produced the green-covered book and got out Stanley Broadhurst's ad from the San Francisco *Chronicle*.

The sheriff took the clipping in his hands and studied it. Kilpatrick moved to his shoulder and looked at it, too. The two men lifted their eyes at the same time and exchanged a glance of dubious recognition.

"The man is Leo Broadhurst, of course," the sheriff said. "Who's the woman, Brian? Your eyes are better than mine."

Kilpatrick swallowed. "My wife," he said. "My ex-wife, that is."

"I thought it was Ellen. Where is she now?"

"I have no idea."

The sheriff handed the clipping back to me. "Is this connected with Stanley Broadhurst's death?"

"I think so."

I started to tell Tremaine something about the background of the case, and the dead man Al. He waved me into silence. "Take it up with somebody else. Take it up with Kelsey. Will you do me that favor, both of you? The fire boss expects to be out of here before noon tomorrow, and I'm helping him plan the move."

"Where are you moving to?" Kilpatrick said.

"Buckhorn Meadow, about sixteen miles east of here."

"Does that mean that the city is out of danger?"

"I think it should be by tomorrow, anyway. But the worst is yet to come." He looked up at the bare black slope of the mountain above us. "The first real rain, and we'll all be drowning in mud."

The sheriff opened the door of the trailer. As he levered his bulk through the narrow opening, I caught a glimpse of a tall man in a Forest Service jacket bowed over a map. He had a graying Scandinavian head, and he looked like a Viking trying to navigate a sea of land.

I turned to Kilpatrick. "You didn't tell me Leo Broadhurst ran away with your wife."

"I told you last night she left me. I don't usually bare my bosom to strangers."

"Is she still with Broadhurst?"

"I wouldn't know about that. They don't report to me."

"Did you divorce her?"

"She divorced me soon after she left here."

"And married him?"

"I assume so. They didn't send me a wedding invitation."

"Where did she divorce you?"

"In Nevada."

"Where is she now—in the Bay area?"

"I haven't the slightest notion where she is. Now if you don't mind we'll change the subject."

But he couldn't leave it alone. Anger or some other emotion was running through him in a gross vibration which made his voice tremble.

"That was a dirty trick you pulled on me just now, showing that picture to Sheriff Tremaine."

"What was dirty about it?"

"It put me on the spot in front of him. You could at least have brought it up in private. You didn't have to shoot me down in public."

"I'm sorry. I didn't know it was your wife."

He gave me a look of disbelief so naked that it made me question myself. Perhaps I had had a hunch just below the level of consciousness.

"Let me have another look at that picture," he said.

I handed him the clipping. He stood and examined it,

oblivious of the action around him and the clatter of helicopters overhead, like a man on the rim of the present peering down into the deep past. When he looked up, his face had been changed by it. It seemed older and more defensive.

He gave me back the clipping. "Where did you get this? From Jerry?"

"No."

"Did Stanley Broadhurst put that ad in the *Chronicle?*"

"Apparently," I said. "Have you seen it before?"

"I may have. I don't remember if I did."

"Then how would you know it was printed in the *Chronicle?*"

He answered smoothly: "I simply took it for granted. The styling looks like the *Chronicle.*" After a moment's intense thought, he added: "San Francisco is mentioned in the text."

It was too good an answer, but I let it pass. "What made you ask if I got the ad from your son Jerry?"

"It was just a thought," he said with a one-sided grimace. "Jerry's been very much on my mind, and I happen to know he reads the *Chronicle.* He thinks San Francisco is the center of the known world."

"Did Jerry see a copy of this ad?"

"He may have. How would I know?"

"I think you do know, Kilpatrick."

"I don't give a damn what you think."

He brought up his clenched fist, ready to swing at me. I got ready to block it. He pulled his fist in to his chest and looked down at it as if it was a small animal which had momentarily got out of control. Then he turned abruptly and went behind the bleachers, moving in hurried uncertainty as if he was going to be sick.

I went after him at a little distance. He was leaning against a supporting post with his head hanging. The look I surprised on his face was one of terrible disappointment.

He straightened up and put on an expression of weary patience which fitted the lines of his face. "You're giving me a hard time," he said to me. "Why?"

"You're a hard man to get information from."

"Really? I've practically told you my life story. It isn't all that interesting."

"I think it is. You've as good as admitted that Jerry saw a copy of this ad. It could explain a number of things."

"I'm not admitting anything, but give me a for-instance."

"He may have got in touch with Stanley Broadhurst and helped to stir him up."

"Stanley didn't need any stirring up. He's been hipped on this subject for years. He never forgave his father for leaving him and his mother."

"Did you ever discuss it with Stanley?"

"Yes, I did."

"Did you tell him that your wife ran off with his father?"

"I didn't have to. He knew it very well. Everyone knew it."

"Who do you mean by 'everyone'?"

"All the people concerned. The affair was no great secret in town, but at least most people have forgotten it by now." Kilpatrick was beginning to look sick again. "Couldn't we forget it, too? It isn't my favorite subject."

"How does Jerry feel about it?"

"He blames me—I told you that. It suits him to believe that his mother left me because I deserved it."

"Has he ever visited her?"

"Not to my knowledge. You don't quite understand the situation. Ellen left me fifteen years ago and cut off all contact. The last word I had from her was her divorce notice, and that came from her lawyer in Reno."

"What was the lawyer's name?"

"I couldn't tell you at this late date."

I got out the green-covered book again, opened it to the flyleaf, and showed Kilpatrick the bookplate with the peacock-plume engraving.

"Ellen Strome was your ex-wife's maiden name, I gather."

"Yes."

"If Jerry hasn't seen her, where did he get this book?"

"She left it in the house. She left a lot of her things behind."

"Why did she go so abruptly?"

"It wasn't so abrupt. I saw it coming. She didn't really like me, and she didn't like my business. I was just another real estate salesman in those days. She didn't approve of my seven-day week, with the phone ringing all the time and having to be nice to little old ladies from Dubuque. Ellen wanted something more refined. More romantic." His voice was laced with sarcasm and regret.

"Is that what Leo Broadhurst was—romantic?"

"I wouldn't know, I'm not a woman. Broadhurst didn't come in on my wave-length that way."

"How did he come in?"

"He went for women the way some men go deer-hunting —pitting his skills, you know? Ellen shouldn't have taken him so seriously. Neither should his son Stanley. But I think maybe Stanley was trying to convince himself that there was some deep significance to his father's affair. He wanted to find his father and get an explanation out of him."

"Who killed Stanley?"

Kilpatrick lifted his heavy shoulders and let them drop. "Who knows? I doubt that the murder's connected with that old business."

"It almost has to be," I said.

Kilpatrick looked at me levelly. A kind of angry brotherhood had been growing between us. It was partly based on the fact, which he didn't know, that my wife had walked out on me and sent me divorce papers through a lawyer. And partly that we were two middle-aging men, and three young people had slipped away over the curve of the world.

"Okay," he said. "Jerry saw the ad in the *Chronicle.* That was around the end of June. He recognized his mother from her pictures, and he seemed to think I should do something about it. I told him he was simply making trouble for himself. It was his mother's choice to walk out on us. We couldn't do anything now but try to forget it."

"What was his reaction?"

"He walked out on me, too. But you know all this." Kilpatrick seemed to be losing interest in his own life.

∿∿∿∿∿∿∿∿∿∿∿∿

XVIII

∿∿∿∿∿∿∿∿∿∿∿∿

He got into his car and headed back toward the gate. I walked in the opposite direction, to the western side of the college grounds.

From the edge of the mesa a path meandered downhill toward the decimated grove where the fire had started. I could see a panel truck there, and two men moving around it, small in the distance. One of them moved with clumsy speed, like Kelsey.

I went down the path, which passed through burned-out areas in the brush. A firebreak had been bulldozed along a line that ran roughly parallel with the path, and below it. There were places where the fire had jumped the firebreak, but it had been put out on the other side, the side where the city lay. The live body of the fire, when I looked back, seemed to be far up the mountainside and moving away eastward.

The hillside path was littered with black sticks and gray ashes. Stepping carefully among the leavings of the fire, I worked my way down to the broad shelf where the Broadhurst family's mountain cabin had stood. It had been built of wood, and there was virtually nothing left but several sets of bedsprings, a stove, a blackened tin sink.

I passed the place where the stable had been. The burned-out body of Stanley's convertible was sitting in the open, its tireless rims sunk in the ashes of the building. It looked like a relic of an ancient civilization, ruined and diminished by the passage of centuries, already half buried among their droppings.

The panel truck had a sheriff-coroner's decal on the side. It was parked in the lane that led up to the ridge road. There was someone in the cab, but the morning glare on the windshield kept me from seeing who it was.

Beyond the truck, through the denuded trees, I could see a uniformed man digging and Kelsey watching him. There was a pile of dirt between them. A *déjà vu* feeling gave me a twinge of basic doubt, as if the burial and the digging-up might be repeated daily from now on.

Jean Broadhurst got down out of the truck and lifted her hand to me. She had on the same mod clothes as the day before, and against the surreal background of burned trees she looked more than ever like a lost and widowed Columbine. She was wearing no makeup. Even her mouth was pale.

"I didn't expect to see you here," I said.

"They asked me to come with them and identify Stanley's body."

"They're a little late about getting to it, aren't they?"

"Mr. Kelsey couldn't get a deputy coroner here until now. But it doesn't matter to Stanley. And it doesn't matter to me."

She was in a chancy mood, rational and composed and on the edge. I wanted to tell her I had seen her son, but I couldn't think of a way that wouldn't scare her. I asked her how her mother-in-law was doing.

"She's suffering from exhaustion. But Dr. Jerome says she has great recuperative powers."

"Does she remember about this?" I motioned toward the digging.

"I don't really know. The doctor told me not to bring up anything painful, which rather tends to limit the conversation."

Jean was trying hard to sustain a style. But the effort she was making had the effect of silencing me. We stood and looked at each other in embarrassment, as if we shared some guilty knowledge.

"I caught a glimpse of Ronny last night," I said.

"What are you trying to tell me? That he's dead?" Her somber eyes were ready for any horror.

"He was very much alive." I told her where, and when.

"Why didn't you let me know last night?"

"I was hoping to bring you better news."

"That means there isn't any."

"At least he isn't dead, and there was no sign that he was being mistreated."

"But why did they *take* him? What are they trying to do?"

"That isn't clear. It's a complex case involving a number of people, and at least one known criminal. Do you remember the man who came to your house in Northridge yesterday?"

"The one who wanted money? How could I forget him?"

"He came back later and broke into your house. I found him dead in your husband's study last night."

"Dead?"

"Somebody knifed him. Does anyone besides your family have access to your house?"

"No, not anyone." She was trying to comprehend this second death. "Is his body still in the house?"

"No, it was taken out. I called the police. But the study is pretty much of a shambles."

"It hardly matters," she said. "I've decided not to go back to that house, ever."

"This is a poor time to make a decision."

"It's the only time I have."

The rhythmic sound of spading had ceased in the grove, and Jean turned toward the sudden emptiness. The digging man was almost out of sight in the hole. Like a man growing laboriously out of the earth, he stood up with Stanley's body clasped in his arms. He and Kelsey laid the body on a stretcher and brought it toward us through the naked tree trunks.

Jean watched it come as if she dreaded its arrival. But when they laid it on the tail-gate of the truck she walked steadily toward it and looked down without flinching into the dirt-filled eyes. She pushed the dead man's hair back and bent over to kiss his forehead. The action had a heightened reality, as if she was an actress playing a tragic role.

She stayed beside her husband for some time. Kelsey didn't question her or disturb her. He introduced me to the deputy coroner, a serious-faced young man named Vaughan Purvis.

"What killed him, Mr. Purvis? The pickax wounds?"

"I'd say the pickax wounds were secondary. He was stabbed in the side with a sharp instrument, probably a knife."

"Has the knife been found?"

"No, but I plan to make a further search."

"I don't think you'll find it here."

I told Purvis and Kelsey about the dead man I'd found in Stanley's house in Northridge. Kelsey said he'd be getting in touch with Arnie Shipstad. Deputy Purvis, who had been listening quietly, broke into unexpectedly emotional speech:

"It looks like a conspiracy, probably the Mafia at work."

I said that I doubted the Mafia was involved. Kelsey pretended delicately not to have heard him.

"Then what do you make of it all?" Purvis asked me. "Who stabbed him and drove that pickax into the back of his head? Who dug that grave for him?"

"The blond girl is a prime suspect," I said experimentally.

"I don't believe it," Purvis said. "This ground is heavy adobe, and it's dry—almost like brick. That hole went down at least four feet. I don't believe any girl could have chopped it out."

"She may have had an accomplice. Or Stanley Broadhurst may have dug it himself. He was the one who borrowed the tools from the gardener."

Purvis looked puzzled. "Why would a man dig his own grave?"

"He may not have known it was going to be his," I said.

"You don't think he was planning to kill his son," Purvis said, "like Abraham with Isaac in the Bible?"

Kelsey let out a sardonic laugh, and Purvis went red with embarrassment. He trudged back toward the grave to pick up his spade.

When he was out of hearing, Kelsey said:

"The gardener may be lying about the tools. He may have come up here and used them himself. Don't forget he lent the girl his car, and lied about it."

"Fritz is still on your list of suspects, then."

Kelsey scratched at his short gray hair. "He has to be. I've been doing a little digging into his record."

"He has a record?"

"Not much of a one, but in my book it's significant. When Fritz was in his late teens he was convicted of a sex crime. It was a first offense—at least that was known of—and the judge allowed him juvenile status and sent him to the county forestry camp."

"What crime did he commit?"

"Statutory rape. I'm particularly interested, because these sex incidents sometimes crop up in the histories of firebugs. I'm not saying Fritz is a firebug—I have no evidence for that. But in camp he got interested in firefighting, and he even helped put out a couple of fires in the back country."

"Is that bad?"

"It's indicative," Kelsey said gravely. "Don't quote me to any firemen—as a matter of fact, I used to be one myself—but firemen and firebugs are sometimes brothers under the skin. They're both fascinated by fires. Apparently Fritz Snow was so fascinated that when he got out of camp he went to work for the Forest Service."

"I'm surprised they took him."

"He had some pretty good backing. Captain Broadhurst and his wife went to bat for him. The Forest Service didn't make a fireman out of him, but they gave him some training and a job running a bulldozer. As a matter of fact, he helped to build that trail." Kelsey pointed toward the trail which went down the side of the bluff into the canyon. "Fritz and his crewmates did a fair job—it's still in pretty good shape after fifteen years. But he didn't last long in the Forest Service. Too many personal problems, to put it mildly."

"Did they fire him on account of his personal problems?"

"I don't know why they fired him. There's no notation in the file, and it was before my time."

"Fritz could tell you."

"Yeah. But it isn't going to be easy. Yesterday afternoon, when I tried to talk to him again, his mother wouldn't let me back into the house. She defends that hopeless son of hers like a wildcat."

"Maybe she'll let me in. I want to talk to her anyway. The dead man in Northridge, Al Sweetner, picked up some money from Mrs. Snow last week."

"How much money?"

"We'll have to ask her." I looked at my watch. "It's ten-fifteen now. Can you meet me out in front of her house at eleven?"

"I'm afraid I can't," Kelsey said. "I want to get in on the preliminary examination of this body. You go and talk to Fritz. There has to be a reason for all the fear he has in him."

Kelsey's voice was cool and rather uncomprehending. He talked about fear as if he had never experienced that emotion. Perhaps the reason for his being a fire investigator, I thought, was a puzzled need to understand what made emotional types like Fritz commit their hot foolish crimes.

"Who was the girl he raped?"

"I don't know who she was. The case was handled in Juvenile Court, and the record of it is sealed. I picked up my information from the old-timers at the courthouse."

XIX

Jean was looking down into her husband's face as if she wondered how it felt to be dead. When Purvis came marching back, with his spade over his shoulder, she gave a start and turned away. Purvis set the spade down quietly and carefully.

He unbuttoned the breast pocket of his uniform and took out a black leather folder with Stanley's name printed in gold inside. It contained his driver's license and other identification, a number of credit cards and membership cards, and three dollar bills.

"He didn't have much left," the young man said.

I was struck by the feeling in his voice. "Did you know Stanley Broadhurst?"

"I knew him just about all my life, starting back in grade school."

"I thought he went to private school."

"He did, after he left grade school. He had some kind of trouble that summer, and his mother put him in a special school."

"The summer his father went away?"

"That's right. Stanley had a lot of bad luck in his life." He spoke with a certain awe. "I used to envy him back there in grade school. His people were rich, and we were as poor as Job's turkey. But I'll never envy him again."

I looked around for Jean. She had wandered off in the direction of the stable, and seemed to be searching for a means of escape. She reminded me of the frightened doe I had seen the day before, but there was no fawn with her.

When I reached her, she was standing beside the incinerated car. "Was this ours?"

"I'm afraid so."

"Do you have transportation, Mr. Archer? I've got to get out of here."

"Where do you want to go?"

"Elizabeth's house. I spent the night at the hospital."

I told Kelsey where we were going and said I might see him later, in the pathology department of the hospital. Jean and I started up the hillside path. She took the lead, moving quickly, like a woman trying to climb out of the present.

Near the bleachers where my car was parked, a number of plywood tables had been set up on trestles. A hundred or more men were seated at them, eating mulligan stew dispensed by a motorized chuckwagon.

Most of the men looked up as we passed. Some whistled; a few cheered. Jean kept going, her head down. She climbed into my car as if she was being pursued.

"It's my fault," she said in self-loathing. "I shouldn't be wearing these clothes."

We drove a long way around through the outskirts of the city. I tried to question her about her husband, but she was unresponsive. She sat with her head down, deep in her own thoughts.

When we entered Mrs. Broadhurst's canyon, she straightened up and began to look around her. The fire had come down nearly as far as the entrance to the canyon and left its scorch-marks on the trees and on the hillside brush.

Most of the houses in Canyon Estates were untouched. A few had been burned, as if picked out at random. There was nothing left of one house but a stone fireplace and a statue of Venus standing up out of rubble and wilted pipes. A man and a woman were poking among the ruins.

The random pattern of the fire persisted as we went further into the canyon. Mrs. Broadhurst's avocado trees seemed unharmed, but the olive trees beyond them had burned black. The eucalyptus trees that towered over the tile roof of the house had lost most of their branches and all their leaves. The barn had burned. The house itself was scorched but intact.

Jean had a key, and we went in together. The closed house was full of the bitter smell of fire, and seemed abandoned. The worn Victorian furniture looked ready for the junk heap.

Even the mounted birds in their glass cases looked as if they had seen better days. An acorn woodpecker had only one glass eye. The breasts of the robins had faded. They looked like imitation birds made to lend life to a dead and scruffy world.

"Excuse me," Jean said. "I've got to find something black."

She disappeared into the other wing of the house. I had decided to call Willie Mackey, a San Francisco detective who had worked with me on other cases. Looking for a telephone, I went into a kind of den adjoining the living room. There were ancestral tintypes on the walls. A man with mutton chop whiskers and a high winged collar glared at me from a black frame, as if daring me to make something of his whiskers.

His look reminded me of Mrs. Broadhurst, but it didn't help me to understand her. I had seen her young and forceful, then sick and doddering. I needed something to fill up the gap between those versions of her, something that would explain why her husband had left her or why her son hadn't been able to.

The room contained among other things a black leather couch which made me want to lie down, and a kneehole desk made of burnished cherrywood. There was a telephone on the desk, sitting on top of a worn leather folder.

I sat down at the desk, with my knees snug in the kneeholes, and dialed Willie Mackey's office on Geary Street in San Francisco. The girl on duty switched me to his apartment on the top floor of his building.

Another girl answered in a less businesslike voice, and then Willie came to the phone.

"Call me back, Lew. You caught me in the midst of the act of love."

"You call me." I read off Mrs. Broadhurst's phone number to him.

Then I lifted the phone and opened the leather folder under it. There were several sheets of foolscap in the folder, and a faded map drawn in ink on creased and yellowing paper. The map showed about half of the Santa Teresa coastal plain; roughly penned in at the back of it were foothills and mountains resembling thumb-prints and paw-prints.

In the upper righthand corner of the map, someone had written:

U.S. Land Commission
Robert Driscoll Falconer
Ex Mission Santa Teresa
Filed in office June 14, 1866
John Berry

The top sheet of foolscap was covered with Spencerian handwriting. Under the heading " 'Memories,' by Elizabeth Falconer Broadhurst," I read:

The Santa Teresa County Historical Society has asked me to set down some notes concerning my family. My paternal grandfather, Robert Driscoll Falconer, was the son of a Massa-

chusetts scholar and businessman and a student and disciple of Louis Agassiz. Robert Driscoll Falconer fought in the Union Army and on May 3, 1863, was wounded, almost mortally, at the Battle of Chancellorsville. But he lived to tell me about it in his old age.

He came to the Pacific Coast to recuperate from his injuries and acquired, in part through purchase but chiefly through marriage, a holding of several thousand acres which became known as Falconer Ranch. Much of this ranch was originally part of the Mission Lands, secularized in 1834 and becoming part of a Mexican Land Grant which passed by way of my grandmother to my grandfather, and thence to my father, Robert Falconer, Jr.

It is difficult for me to write objectively about my late father. He was the third in the male line of Falconers to attend Harvard College. He was more of a naturalist and scholar than a rancher or businessman. My father has been criticized for dissipating some of the family holdings. His reply would be that he had more important things to do with his life. He became a noted amateur ornithologist, author of the first checklist of native species to be found in the Santa Teresa region. His rich collection of skins both local and exotic became the nucleus of the bird collection of the Santa Teresa Museum.

At this point the Spencerian writing began to deteriorate:

I have heard false rumors that my father was a wanton killer of songbirds and that he killed them because he loved to kill. Nothing could be further from the truth! He killed birds only for scientific reasons, in order to preserve the evanescent beauty of their markings. He loved the colorful little fliers which science compelled him to shoot.

I can attest to this from personal observation. I accompanied my father on many of his expeditions here and abroad, and many were the times I came upon him weeping openly over the perforated body of the warbler, or the thrush, which he held in his kind masculine hand. Sometimes we wept together, he and I, hid in some wooded recess of our home canyon. He was a good man and a crack shot, and when he bestowed the gift of death he did so instantly, painlessly, with no mistake about it. Robert Driscoll Falconer, Jr., was a god come down to earth in human guise.

Toward the end, the handwriting went to pieces. It straggled across the lined yellow page like a defeated army.

I started to go through the drawers of the desk. The top one on the righthand side was stuffed with bills. Some of them had been unpaid for months and had special little messages written across them:—"Immediate payment will be appreciated," "In case of further delay, the matter will be placed in the hands of legal counsel."

In the second drawer I found an old wooden gun case and opened it. Fitted into its shaped felt lining were a pair of German target pistols. They were old, but oiled and gleaming like strange blue jewels.

I lifted one of the pistols out of the case and hefted it in my hand. It was so light and so well balanced that it seemed to come up of its own accord to eye level and let me sight along it. I aimed it at the picture of the man with the whiskers, but that only made me feel foolish. I carried it to the window to find something better to aim at.

No birds. But there was a circular bird feeder on a metal pole set in cement. A rat was eating the few kernels of grain left in the feeder. I pointed the empty gun at him. He ran down the pole and disappeared in the black ravine.

ᘓᘓᘓᘓᘓᘓᘓᘓᘓᘓᘓᘓᘓᘓ

XX

ᘓᘓᘓᘓᘓᘓᘓᘓᘓᘓᘓᘓᘓᘓ

"What in the world are you doing?" Jean said behind me.

"Playing games."

"Put it away, please. Elizabeth wouldn't like you to be handling her pistols."

I returned the gun to its case. "They're a pretty pair."

"I don't think so. I hate all guns."

She fell silent, but her eyes were full of further things to say. The girl had changed her short bright dress for a black one that covered her knees but didn't fit her. She reminded me of an actress again, this time a young woman playing the part of an older one.

"Do I look all right?" She sounded anxious, as if in the absence of her son, the death of her husband, she doubted who she was.

"You couldn't look any other way."

She pushed the compliment away as if it might contaminate her and backed onto the couch, pulling her legs up under her black skirt so that they were completely hidden.

I closed the gun case and put it away. "Were those her father's guns?"

"Yes. They belonged to Elizabeth's father."

"Does she use them?"

"If you mean does she shoot birds now, the answer is

no. The guns are precious relics of the great man. Everything in this house is some kind of a relic. I feel like one myself."

"Is that Elizabeth's dress?"

"Yes it is."

"Are you thinking of living in this house?"

"I may. It suits my mood."

She bowed her head and sat in a listening attitude as if the black dress was wired for sound like a space suit. "Elizabeth used to shoot a lot of birds. She taught Stanley to do it. It must have worried him, or he wouldn't have told me about it. Apparently it worried his mother, too. She gave up shooting entirely long before I knew her.

"But my father never did," she said surprisingly, "at least not as long as my mother stayed with him. My father loved to shoot at anything that moved. And mother and I had to pluck the quail he shot, and the pigeons. After my mother left my father, I never went back to see him."

She had jumped from Stanley's family to her own without any transition. Wondering why, I said:

"Are you thinking of going back to your family now?"

"I have no family. Mother's remarried and living in New Jersey. The last I heard of my father he was running a sport-fishing boat in the Bahamas. Anyway, I couldn't face either of them. They'd blame me for everything that's happened."

"Why?"

"They just would, that's all. Because I went away and put myself through school. Neither of them approved of my doing that. A girl is supposed to do what she's told." Her voice was stony with resentment.

"Who do you blame for everything that's happened?"

"Myself, of course. But I blame Stanley, too." She lowered her eyes again. "I know that's a dreadful thing to say. I can forgive him for the girl. And all that foolish business about his father. But why did he have to take—bring Ronny with him?"

"He wanted money from his mother, and Ronny's visit was part of the transaction."

"How do you know that?"

"Elizabeth said so."

"She would. She's a cold woman." She added as if in apology to the house: "I shouldn't say that. She's suffered a lot. And Stanley and I haven't been much comfort to her. We've taken a great deal, and haven't given much."

"What have you taken?"

"Money." She sounded angry at herself.

"Does Elizabeth have much money?"

"Of course—she's wealthy. She must have made a fortune out of the Canyon Estates development, and she still has hundreds of acres left."

"They're not producing much, except for a few acres of avocados. And she seems to have a lot of unpaid bills."

"That's just because she's rich. Rich people never pay their bills. My father used to run a small sports shop in Reno, and the ones who could best afford to pay were the very ones he had to threaten to take to court. Elizabeth has thousands a year from her grandfather's estate."

"How many thousands a year?"

"I don't really know. She's close-mouthed about her money. But she has it."

"Who gets it if she dies?"

"Don't say that!" Jean sounded scared and superstitious. She added in a more controlled voice: "Dr. Jerome says she's going to be okay. Her attack was just the result of overexertion and strain."

"Can she talk all right?"

"Of course. But I wouldn't bother her today if I were you."

"I'll take it up with Dr. Jerome," I said. "But you haven't answered my other question. Who gets her money when she dies?"

"Ronny does." Her voice was low, but her body was tense with feeling she couldn't hold. "Are you worried about who will pay you? Is that why you're hanging around here when you should be out looking for him?"

I didn't try to answer her, but sat and maintained a low profile for a while. Anger and grief were alternating in her like an electric current. She turned the anger against herself, taking the hem of her skirt between her hands and pulling at it as if she was trying to tear it.

"Don't do that, Jean."

"Why shouldn't I? I hate this dress."

"Then take it off and put on another one. You mustn't go to pieces."

"I can't stand waiting."

"It may stretch out for a while, and you've got to stand it."

"Isn't there anything more we can do? Can't you go out and find him?"

"Not directly. There's too much ground to cover. And too much water." She looked so cast down that I added: "But I do have one or two leads." I got out the advertisement again, with its picture of Stanley's father and Kilpatrick's wife. "Have you seen this?"

She bent her head over the clipping. "I didn't see it until some time after it came out. Stanley placed it in the *Chronicle* without telling me, when we were in San Francisco last June. He didn't tell his mother, either, and when she saw it she was furious."

"Why?"

"She said he was bringing the whole scandal back to life. But I don't suppose anyone cared, really, except for her and Stanley."

And Jerry Kilpatrick, I thought, and Jerry's father, and possibly the woman herself. "Do you know who this woman is?"

"Her name was Kilpatrick, according to Elizabeth. She was married to a local real estate man, Brian Kilpatrick."

"What kind of terms are he and Elizabeth on?"

"Very good terms, I think. They're partners, or co-investors, in Canyon Estates."

"What about Kilpatrick's son Jerry?"

"I don't think I know him. What does he look like?"

"He's a lanky boy about nineteen, with long reddish brown hair and a beard. Very emotional. He hit me over the head with a gun last night."

"Is he the one who took Ronny away on the yacht?"

"He's the one."

"I may know him after all." Her sight turned inward and stayed that way for a while, as if she was doing a sum in mental arithmetic. "He didn't have a beard then, but I think he came to our house one night last June. I only saw him for a moment. Stanley took him into the study and shut the door. But I believe he had that clipping with him." Her head came up. "Do you think he's trying to strike back at us? Because his mother eloped with Stanley's father?"

"It's possible. I think the boy really cares about his mother. In fact, he may be on his way to her now."

"Then we've got to find her," Jean said.

"I agree with you. If I can believe my informant, the ex-Mrs. Kilpatrick is living somewhere south of San Francisco, on the Peninsula."

She seized on the lead because it was the only one. "Will you go there for me? Today?"

The life was coming back into her face. I hated to disappoint her. "I'd better stay here until we get something definite. Jerry sailed in the Ensenada race last summer, and he may have gone that way."

"To Mexico?"

"A lot of young people are ending up there. But our lead on the Peninsula ought to be checked out."

She stood up. "I'll go myself."

"No. You stay here."

"Here in this house?"

"Here in town, anyway. I doubt that this is a kidnaping for ransom. But if it is, you're the one they'll be getting in touch with."

She looked at the phone as if it had just spoken. "I have no money."

"You've just been telling me about Mrs. Broadhurst's money. You can raise some if you have to. As a matter of fact, I'm glad you brought the subject up."

"Because I haven't paid you?"

"I'm not anxious. But we're going to need some actual cash pretty soon."

Jean was getting disturbed again. She moved around the little room, awkward and angry in her ill-fitting black dress.

"I'm not going to ask Elizabeth for money. Of course, I could go and look for a job."

"At the moment, that isn't very realistic."

She paused in front of me. We exchanged a quick stabbing glance. It carried the possibility that we could be passionate enemies or friends. There was angry heat stored up in her like deep hot springs beyond the reach of her marriage or her widowhood.

She said in a more confident voice, as if she had somehow taken my measure: "Speaking of realism, what are you going to do to get my son back?"

"I have a call in to a man named Willie Mackey who runs a detective agency in San Francisco. He knows the Bay area thoroughly and I'd like to co-opt him."

"Do that. I can raise the money." She seemed to have made a decision involving more than money. "What are *you* going to do?"

"Wait—and ask questions."

She made an impatient movement and sat on the couch again. "All you do is ask questions."

"I get tired of it, too. Sometimes people tell me things without being asked, but you're not one of them."

She looked at me distrustfully. "That's just another question, isn't it?"

"Not exactly. I was thinking you've had a strange marriage."

"And you want me to tell you about it," she stated.

"If you want to, I'm willing to listen."

"Why should I?"

"You got me into this."

The reminder touched off her anger again—it was very near the surface. "I've always known about voyeurs. But you're an auditeur, aren't you?"

"What are you so ashamed of?"

"I'm not ashamed," she said hotly. "Leave me alone. I don't want to talk about it."

I sat without speaking for a couple of minutes. I suspected I was half in love with her, partly because she was Ronny's mother but also because she was beautiful and young. The body sheathed in her tight black dress seemed infinitely poignant.

But her widowhood seemed to project around her a circle of shadow which I couldn't enter. Besides, as I reminded myself, I was nearly twice her age.

She was looking at me with candid eyes, as if she had heard my thoughts. "I hate to admit it," she said, "I never have admitted it until now. My marriage was a failure. Stanley lived in a world of his own, and I couldn't reach him. Maybe if he was alive, he would say the same thing about me. But we never actually discussed it. We just went our separate ways in the same house. I looked after Ronny, and Stanley got more and more wrapped up in searching for his father. I used to look in on him late at night sometimes, when he was working in his study. Sometimes he'd be just sitting there shuffling through his pictures and his letters. He looked like a man counting his money," she said with her quick disorganized smile.

"But I shouldn't be making light of him," she added. "I should have taken the whole thing much more seriously. The Reverend Riceyman advised me to. He said that Stanley was looking for his own lost self, and I'm beginning to realize he was right."

"I'd like to talk to Riceyman."

"So would I. Unfortunately he's dead."

"What did he die of?"

"Old age. I really miss him. He was a nice man, with a lot of understanding. But I didn't listen to him. I was angry, and jealous."

"Jealous?"

"Of Stanley and his parents, and their wrecked marriage. I felt as if it was competing with my own marriage, gradually edging it out of the picture. Stanley was living more and more in the past, and getting more and more impatient with me. Maybe if I had tried harder, I could have stopped him. Then all at once it was too late. That ad he placed in the *Chronicle* touched off this whole disaster, didn't it?"

155

I didn't have to answer her. The phone rang.

It was Willie Mackey. "Hello, Lew. Mission accomplished. Now what can I do for you?"

"I'm looking for a woman, aged forty or so. When she left Santa Teresa fifteen years ago her name was Ellen Strome Kilpatrick. She was traveling with a man named Leo Broadhurst. He may or may not be living with her now. According to my slightly freaked-out informant, she's staying on the Peninsula now, in an old house two or three stories high, with a pair of towers. And trees around it, oaks and some pines."

"Can't you pinpoint it any better? There are still a lot of trees on the Peninsula."

"There was a Great Dane in the neighborhood a week ago today. He acted lost."

"What's Ellen's background?"

"She's the divorced wife of a real estate man here in Santa Teresa. Brian Kilpatrick. He told me that she graduated from Stanford."

Willie uttered a clicking sound of satisfaction. "That means we start in Palo Alto. The Stanford grads go back there like homing pigeons. Do you have a picture of Ellen Strome Kilpatrick?"

"I have one from an ad in the *Chronicle* that came out late in June. It shows her and Leo Broadhurst as of fifteen years ago when they arrived in San Francisco, using the name Mr. and Mrs. Ralph Smith."

"I have the ad in my clipping file," Willie said. "As I recall, it offers a thousand-dollar reward."

"You have a good memory for money."

"Yes, I do. I just got married again. Am I in line for the reward?"

"Unfortunately the man who offered it is dead." I told him how Stanley had died, and the rest of it.

"What makes Ellen so important?"

"I intend to ask her. Don't you ask her, though. When you find her let me know and I'll take it from there."

I said goodbye to him and then to Jean. Her mood had changed, and she didn't want me to go and leave her alone. Before I closed the front door of the house I could hear her angry crying.

XXI

Along Mrs. Snow's street the jacaranda blossoms hung like purple clouds caught and condensing on the branches of the trees. I sat in my car for a minute and rested my eyes on them. Brown-skinned children were playing in the yard next door.

The curtain over Mrs. Snow's front window twitched like an eyelid with a tic. Then she came out and approached my car. She was wearing rusty silk that resembled armor and her face was blanched with powder, as if she was expecting an important visitor.

Not me. She said in controlled fury: "You have no right to do this. You're persecuting us."

I climbed out and stood with my hat in my hand. "That's not my intention, Mrs. Snow. Your son's an important witness."

"But he doesn't have to talk without a lawyer. I know that

much—he's been in trouble before. But this time he's as innocent as a little newborn babe."

"That innocent?"

She stood unsmiling, blocking the way to her house. The elders of the family next door, sensing the possibility of trouble, quietly came outside. They drifted in our direction like a forming audience.

Mrs. Snow gave them a long look, in which anger congealed into something very like fear. She turned to me:

"If you insist on talking, come inside."

She took me into her little front room. The tea that Mrs. Broadhurst had spilled stained the rug like the old brown evidence of a crime.

Mrs. Snow stayed on her feet, and kept me standing.

"Where's Fritz?"

"My son is in his room."

"Can't he come out?"

"No, he can't. The doctor is coming to see him. I don't want you getting him all upset, the way you did yesterday."

"He was upset before I talked to him."

"I know that. But you made it worse. Frederick is weak in his feelings. He has been since he had his nervous breakdown. And I'm not going to let you send him back to the nursing home if I can help it."

I felt a twinge of shame, simply because she was small and female and indomitable. But she was standing in my way, and the lost boy was somewhere on the other side of her.

"Do you know Al Sweetner, Mrs. Snow?"

She compressed her lips, and shook her head. "I never heard of him." But the eyes behind her spectacles were watchful.

"Didn't Al come by your house last week?"

"He may have. I'm not home all the time. What was that name again?"

"Al Sweetner. He was killed last night. The Los Angeles police told me he escaped from Folsom Prison."

Her dark eyes brightened like a nocturnal animal's caught by a flashlight. "I see."

"Did you give him money, Mrs. Snow?"

"Not much. I gave him a five-dollar bill. I didn't know that he escaped from prison."

"Why did you give him money?"

"I felt sorry for him," she said.

"Was he a friend of yours?"

"I wouldn't say that. But he needed gas to get out of town, and I could spare him five dollars."

"I heard you gave him twenty."

She looked at me without wavering. "What if I did? I had no change. And I didn't want him hanging around until Frederick got home from work."

"Was he a friend of Frederick's?"

"I wouldn't call him a friend. Al was a friend to no one, including himself."

"But you knew him."

She sat down, stiffly upright, on the edge of the platform rocker. I sat on a chair nearby. Her face was closed and intent. She looked like a woman who had taken a deep breath and submerged herself.

"I'm not denying I knew him. He lived with us here in this house for a while when he was a boy. He was already in trouble, and the county was looking for a foster home. It was either that or the Preston Reformatory. Mr. Snow was still living then, and we agreed to take Albert into our home."

"That was generous of you."

She shook her head abruptly. "I don't claim that. We

159

needed the money. We wanted to keep our home together, for Frederick, and Mr. Snow was ailing, and prices were sky-high in those days, too. Anyway, we took Albert in and did our best for him. But he was a hard case already—there wasn't much we could do to straighten him out. And he was a bad influence on Frederick. We were trying to make up our minds what to do when he solved the question for us. He stole a car and ran away with a girl."

"And Frederick was involved, wasn't he?"

She drew in a long breath like a diver coming up for air. "You've heard about it, have you?"

"Just a little."

"Then you probably heard it all wrong. A lot of people blamed Frederick for the whole thing, because he was the oldest. But Albert Sweetner was old beyond his years, and so was the girl. She was only fifteen or so but you can take my word for it, she was experienced. Frederick was easily led, like putty in their hands."

"Did you know the girl?"

"I knew her."

"What was her name?"

"Marty Nickerson. Her father was a construction man— when he worked. They lived in a motel at the end of this street. The way I got to know Marty, she used to help in the kitchen when Mr. and Mrs. Broadhurst had a party. I was keeping house for the Broadhursts at the time. Marty was a pretty little thing, but hard as nails. She was the real ringleader, if you want my opinion. And she was the one who got off scot-free, of course."

"Exactly what happened?"

"They stole a car, as I said. It must have been Marty's idea because they stole it from a man she knew—he owned the motel where she lived. Then the three of them ran off to

Los Angeles. That was her idea, too—she wanted to be a movie actress and she was crazy to go and live in Los Angeles. They lasted three days and nights down there, sleeping in the car and scrounging for food. Then the three of them got caught trying to lift some goods from a day-old bakery shop."

She was talking with a kind of unconscious gusto, as if the adventure had been hers as well as her son's. The feeling became conscious, and she repressed it, forcing iron disapproval on her face.

"The worst of it was, Marty Nickerson turned up pregnant. She was underage, and Frederick admitted he had carnal knowledge of her and the judge and probation people gave him a hard choice. He could stand trial as an adult and take his chances on going to the pen. Or he could plead guilty in Juvenile Court and get probation with six months in forestry camp. The lawyer said we shouldn't try to fight it—they bear down hard if you fight them in Juvenile Court —so Frederick went to forestry camp."

"What happened to the others?"

"Marty Nickerson got married. She married the man she stole the car from, and they never even took her into court."

"Where is she now?"

"I don't really know. The man had a business in the northern part of the county, and for all I know she's still living with him there."

"What's her married name?"

She considered the question. "I don't remember. I can find out if it's important. She sent Frederick a Christmas greeting the first year, which took some nerve on her part. I think he still has it in his keepsake drawer."

"What about Al?"

"Al is another story. It wasn't his first offense. He was

already on probation, and they sent him to Preston until he was of age. I remember when he got out. It was fifteen years ago this past summer, and the jacarandas were starting to bloom. He came here to pick up his things. I'd kept them for him in a carton—some schoolbooks and a blue suit that the county had bought for him to go to church in. But the blue suit didn't fit him any more, and he wasn't interested in the books. I gave him a good meal and a little money."

She shook her head as if I had spoken. "It wasn't generosity on my part. I wanted to get rid of him before Frederick got mixed up with him again. Frederick was working for the Forest Service at that time, and I didn't want Albert interfering with his job. But it happened anyway."

"What happened?"

"Albert lost him his job and gave him a nervous breakdown into the bargain. I don't want to go into the gory details. What's past is past, and Albert didn't set foot on my doorstep again until he showed up last week. Now you tell me he's dead."

"He was murdered in Northridge last night. We don't know who did it, or why. But it might help if you tell me what happened fifteen years ago. How did Albert give Fritz a nervous breakdown?"

"By getting him in trouble. It's always the same old story."

"What was the trouble?"

"He took Frederick's tractor and went joyriding in the hills. But of course it wasn't Frederick's, and that was the point. The tractor was U.S. Government property, and Frederick could have been sent to federal prison along with Albert. As it was, they threw him out of his job, and it was all Albert's fault."

I was getting restless. "May I talk to Frederick, Mrs. Snow?"

"I don't see any point in it. I've told you everything you asked. And I can tell you anything he can tell you."

"But there may be things that you don't know and he does."

"I'm afraid you don't understand," she said with a faintly superior look. "Frederick and I are very close." But after a moment she said: "What sort of things do you mean?"

"I'd prefer to talk to him about it. You're his mother, and you're naturally defensive."

"I have to be. Frederick doesn't stand up for himself. Ever since he had his breakdown and lost his job with the Forest Service, he blames himself for everything. You should have heard him crying in his room after you cross-questioned him yesterday."

"He didn't say anything incriminating to me."

She gave me a skeptical look. "What *did* he say?"

"I don't think I should tell you. He's a grown man."

"You're wrong. He's a boy in a man's body. He's never been the same since he had his nervous breakdown."

"Which happened fifteen years ago, is that correct?"

"That's correct. It was the summer Captain Broadhurst went away."

"Was Frederick fond of the captain?"

"He worshiped the ground he walked on. Captain Broadhurst was like a father to him. He idolized the whole Broadhurst family. And it broke his heart when the captain ran off. It was like his own father dying on him all over again. I'm not making that up. Dr. Jerome said it himself."

"Is he the doctor who's coming to see Frederick?"

She nodded. "He should be here any time now."

"Is he a psychiatrist?"

"We don't believe in psychiatrists," she said flatly. "Dr. Jerome is a good doctor. He's Mrs. Broadhurst's doctor, which means he has to be good. When Frederick had his breakdown she got him Dr. Jerome and paid the bills, including the nursing home. And when he got out of that place she gave him a job herself, in her own garden." Mrs. Snow smiled dimly, sifting what cheer she could from the memory. "But now I'm afraid he's going to lose that job, too."

"I don't see why he should, if he's done nothing wrong. As a matter of fact, I don't understand why he lost his job with the Forest Service."

"Neither do I. Albert took the key to his 'dozer without his permission. But the district ranger didn't believe my son. It all goes back to what happened in Juvenile Court three years before. Once a boy gets into trouble, he's lost his good name for all future time."

ᴠᴠᴠᴠᴠᴠᴠᴠᴠᴠᴠᴠ

XXII

ᴠᴠᴠᴠᴠᴠᴠᴠᴠᴠᴠᴠ

Mrs. Snow got up and moved toward the door, as if she was expecting to let me out. Though the atmosphere of her home depressed me, I wasn't ready to leave yet. I stayed in my chair, and after a silent struggle she came back to the platform rocker and sat down again.

"Is there something else?" she said.

"You may be able to help me. This has nothing directly to do with you or Frederick. But I gather you were working for Mr. and Mrs. Broadhurst when Mr. Broadhurst took off."

"Yes I was."

"Did you happen to know the woman?"

"Ellen Kilpatrick? I certainly did. She taught art at the high school and was married to Kilpatrick the real estate man. That was before he struck it rich with Canyon Estates. He was still living from hand to mouth like the rest of us.

"Mrs. Kilpatrick saw a chance to better herself, I guess, and she set her net for Captain Broadhurst. I saw the whole thing happen. When Mrs. Broadhurst was away, the two of them used to leave Stanley with me and go up to the Mountain House. Mrs. Kilpatrick was supposed to be teaching the captain to paint pictures. But she was teaching him other things as well. They thought they were fooling everyone, but they weren't. I used to catch the looks between them sometimes, like they were off in a secret world by themselves and nobody else existed."

"Did Mrs. Broadhurst know about the affair?"

"She must have. I could see that she was suffering. But she never said a word, at least not within my hearing. I think she wanted to avoid a break. Her family stands for something in this town—at least they used to. And then there was poor little Stanley to consider. Sometimes when I think back, I think an open break would have been better for Stanley in the long run. He used to ask me what his father and the woman were doing up there in the Mountain House. And I had to make up a story for him, but he was never entirely taken in. Children never are."

"This went on for some time, I gather."

"At least a year. It was a strange year, even for me. I was keeping house for Mrs. Broadhurst, and I was in it but not of it. After a while the two of them got careless in front of me. You'd think I was part of the furniture or something. Toward the end they didn't always bother to go to the

Mountain House. One reason for that, Frederick was working on a Forest Service trail at the head of the canyon. So the two of them stayed around the house when Mrs. Broadhurst was out. They'd lock themselves in the den and come out fiery red in the face, and I'd have to make up stories for Stanley about why the couch was squeaking." Her face blushed faintly mauve under the powder. "I don't know why I'm telling you all this. I intended to go to my grave without telling anyone."

"Do you know what made them leave?"

"I guess the strain got to be too much for them. It was almost too much for me. I was just about ready to quit my job when they finally did take off."

"Where did they go?"

"They went to San Francisco, so I've heard, and neither one of them ever did come back here. I don't know what they lived on. He had no profession, and no money of his own. Knowing both of them, my guess would be that she got a job in the Bay area, and she's probably supporting him to this day. He isn't what you call a practical man."

"What kind of a woman is she?"

"The arty type, but a lot more practical than she ever let on. She pretended to have her head in the clouds, but her feet were made of clay. Sometimes I really felt sorry for her. She used to follow him with her eyes as if she was a dog and he was her master. I've often thought about it since—how a woman with a husband of her own and a little boy could feel like that for another woman's husband."

"I gather from his picture that he was a good-looking man."

"That's true. Where did you see his picture?"

I got out Stanley's advertisement and showed it to her. She gave it a look of recognition:

"This is the clipping Albert Sweetner had the other day.

He wanted to make sure that the man was Captain Broad-hurst. I told him it was."

"Did he ask about the woman?"

"He didn't have to. Albert knew Mrs. Kilpatrick from away back. She was his home-room teacher at the high school when Albert was living in our home." She wiped her glasses and bent over the clipping again. "Who put this ad in the paper?"

"Stanley Broadhurst."

"Where would he get the cash for a thousand-dollar reward? He doesn't have one nickel to rub against another."

"From his mother. At least that was the idea."

"I see." Her eyes came up from the clipping, full of the past. "Poor little Stanley. He was still trying to find out what went on in the Mountain House."

The woman's insight continued to surprise me. Her mind had been sharpened by trouble, and exercised by years of defensive tactics on behalf of Fritz. I realized she'd been talking to me for a purpose, fending me off with stories like an aging Scheherazade, laying down a barrage of words between me and her son.

I looked at my watch. It was a quarter to one.

"Do you have to go?" Mrs. Snow said eagerly.

"If I could have a few minutes with Frederick first—"

"You can't. I won't permit it. He's always blaming himself for things he didn't do."

"I can make allowances for that."

She shook her head. "It's unfair of you to ask. I've told you a lot more than Frederick ever could." She added with a kind of angry bravado: "If there's anything more you want to know, ask me."

"There is one thing. You mentioned a Christmas card that Marty Nickerson sent Frederick."

"It wasn't a Christmas card, exactly—just a greeting on a

postcard." She got up. "I think I can find it if you want to
see it."

She went through the doorway into the kitchen. I heard a
second door open and close, and then a mumble of talk
through the thin walls. I could hear Frederick's voice rising
hysterically, his mother's voice quieting him down.

She came out with a postcard which she handed me.
The colored picture on the face of the card showed the
front of a two-story motel whose sign said: "Yucca Tree
Motor Inn." It had been postmarked in Petroleum City on
December 22, 1952. The message was handwritten in faded
green ink:

> *Dear Fritz,*
>
> *Long time no see. How are things in good old Santa Teresa?*
> *I have a little girl, born December 15, just in time to be my*
> *Christmas baby. She weighs seven lbs., six oz., and she's a*
> *dolly. We decided to call her Susan. I am very happy. Hoping*
> *you are the same. Christmas greetings to you and your mother.*
>
> *Martha (Nickerson) Crandall*

The phone rang in the kitchen. Mrs. Snow jumped as if an
alarm had sounded. But she pulled the kitchen door shut
behind her before she answered it.

A moment later she opened the door again. "It's Mr. Kelsey," she said, holding her mouth as if the name tasted bitter. "He wants to talk to you."

She stepped to one side to let me pass and stayed in the
doorway to listen.

Kelsey's voice was urgent: "The *Ariadne's* been sighted
by one of the volunteer pilots in the sheriff's aero-squadron.
She's grounded in Dunes Bay."

"What happened to the kids aboard her?"

"That isn't clear. But it doesn't sound too good. According
to my information she's breaking up in the surf."

"Exactly where?"

"Just below the state park. Do you know the place?"

"Yes. Where are you? I can pick you up."

"I'm afraid I can't leave town right now. I have a lead in the Stanley Broadhurst killing. I shouldn't leave the fire area, anyway."

"What's the lead?"

"Your man with the long black wig was seen in the area yesterday. He was driving an old white car along Rattlesnake Road. A coed from the college was taking a walk there, and she saw him shortly before the fire started."

"Is it a positive identification?"

"Not yet. I'm going to talk to her now."

Kelsey hung up. Turning away from the phone, I noticed that the door of Fritz's room was ajar. One of his moist eyes appeared at the crack like the eye of a fish in an underwater crevice. His mother, at the other door, was watching him like a shark.

"How are you, Fritz?" I said.

"I feel just terrible."

He opened the door wider. In his rumpled pajamas he looked less like a man than an ill-kept boy. His mother said:

"Go back in your room and be quiet."

He shook his frowzy head. "I don't like it in there. I keep seeing things in there."

"What do you keep seeing, Fritz?" I said.

"I keep seeing Mr. Broadhurst in his grave."

"Did you bury him?" I said.

He nodded, and began to cry, nodding and crying like a human pump. His mother moved between us. Leaning her slight weight against his amorphous body, she pushed him back into his room.

She closed the door on him and locked it and turned on

me, holding the key like a weapon. "Please get out of here now. You've got him all upset."

"If he buried Stanley Broadhurst yesterday, you can't very well hush it up. You're crazy to try."

She let out a kind of terrier noise which was meant to be a laugh. "I'm not the one that's crazy. He no more buried Mr. Broadhurst than I did. You people have got him so confused and frightened that he doesn't know what he did or what he saw. Except that I know for a fact he didn't do anything wrong. I know my son."

She spoke with such assurance that I almost believed her. "I still think he knows more than he told us."

"He knows a good deal less, you mean. He doesn't know what he knows. And I should think you'd be ashamed of yourself, badgering a widow and her only son. If the doctor finds him in this condition, he'll want to commit him to the State Hospital."

"Has he been committed before?"

"He nearly was, years ago. But Mrs. Broadhurst said she'd pay for the nursing home."

"This was in 1955?"

"Yes. Now will you please get out of my kitchen? I didn't invite you in here, but I'm inviting you out."

I thanked her, and left the house. At the curb in front of it, a middle-aged man in sports clothes was climbing out of a yellow sports car. He lifted a medical bag out of the boot and came toward me. His gray hair and light blue eyes were in contrast to his high color.

"Dr. Jerome?"

"Yes." His look was inquiring.

I told him who I was and what I was doing. "Mrs. Stanley Broadhurst hired me. How is Elizabeth Broadhurst, by the way?"

"She's suffering from exhaustion, which brought on a mild heart attack."

"Is she talkable?"

"Not today. Possibly tomorrow. But I'd stay off the subject of her son—and her grandson." The doctor took a deep breath and sighed with unexpected feeling. "I just had a look at Stanley's body in the morgue. I hate to see a young man die."

"Was it the stab wound that killed him?"

"I would say so."

"Were you his doctor?"

"I was for most of his life—as long as he lived at home. And I still saw him from time to time. He liked to check in with me when he had a problem."

"What sort of problems did he have?"

"Emotional problems. Marital problems. I really can't discuss them with a third party."

"You can't hurt Stanley. He's dead."

"I'm aware of that," the doctor said with some asperity. "The problem I'm interested in is who stabbed him to death and buried him."

"Your patient Fritz Snow says he buried him."

I watched the doctor for his reaction. His bland eyes didn't shift. His high hard color remained unchanged. He even smiled a little.

"Don't believe him. Fritz is always confessing something."

"How do you know it isn't true?"

"Because he's been my patient for over twenty years."

"Is he insane?"

"I wouldn't put it that way. He's hypersensitive, and he tends to blame himself for everything. When he gets emotionally upset, he loses all sense of reality. Poor Fritz has been a frightened boy all his life."

171

"What's he frightened of?"

"His mother, among other things."

"So am I."

"So are we all," the doctor said with a glint of amusement. "She's a powerful little woman. But she probably got that way because she had to. Her late husband was very much like Fritz. He had a hard time holding any job. I suppose their basic trouble was genetic, and there's still not much we can do about heredity."

We both glanced toward the house. Mrs. Snow was monitoring us from the front window. She let the curtain fall back into place.

"I really have to get in to see my patient," Jerome said.

"Perhaps we can have a talk about him some time when you're free. Whether or not Fritz is innocent, as you say, he has been connected with the main suspect in Stanley's death." I told him about Al Sweetner, and Kelsey's new lead. "And we know Fritz had access to the tools that were used to dig Stanley's grave. On top of that, he told me that he buried him."

The doctor shook his gray head slowly from side to side. "If the sky fell, Fritz would find a way to blame himself. As a matter of fact, there's a pretty good possibility that Stanley dug his own grave."

"The deputy coroner and I were speculating about that possibility."

"This isn't entirely speculation on my part," Jerome said. "When I examined Stanley's body just now, I noticed blisters on his hands."

"What kind of blisters?"

"Ordinary water blisters, on the insides of both hands." He touched the palm of his left hand with the wide spatulate fingers of his right. "The kind of blisters a man gets from digging he isn't used to. I admit it's hard to understand why a man would dig his own grave."

"He may have been forced to do it." I said. "Al Sweetner, the man in the wig, was a hard case when he was alive. It's possible he stood over Stanley with a gun. Or Stanley may have had some other compelling reason."

"What reason?"

"I don't know. He may have intended to bury somebody else. He had a young girl with him, as well as his son."

"What happened to them?"

"I'm on my way to find out."

XXIII

Dunes Bay was at the end of a winding county road off Highway 1. Above the wind-carved hills of sand which rose northward along the shore, clouds were streaming inland like torn pennants. It looked as if a storm was on the way.

The kiosk at the entrance to the state park was closed and empty. I drove on through to the parking lot which overlooked the ocean. About three hundred feet out, where the waves were breaking, the white sloop lay on her side. Further out a flock of pelicans circled and dived for fish.

Three people were watching *Ariadne* from the beach. They weren't the three that I was looking for. One was a man in a state park uniform. Near him but not with him, a couple of boys with long sun-faded hair leaned on their surfboards.

I got my binoculars out of the trunk of my car and focused them on the sloop. She was dismasted, and her rigging hung overside like a torn net. Her hull appeared to be sprung and heavy with water. She rose up sluggishly when the long surge lifted her, then fell back clumsily on her side. My breathing labored as if in empathy.

I went down to the beach on a wooden walkway half drifted over with sand. The state park man turned to meet me, and I asked him if the young people had been rescued.

"Yessir. They got ashore."

"All three of them?"

"Yessir. These boys here were a great help."

Following his gesture, I looked at the two surfers. They returned my look with a kind of wary pride, as if they distrusted any possible adult approval.

"They're okay," the older one said. They nodded their heads in solemn unison.

"Where are they now?"

He shrugged his limber shoulders. "Somebody came and picked them up in a station wagon."

"What kind of a station wagon?"

He pointed toward the park official. "Ask him."

I turned to the man, who looked like somebody's son-in-law. He answered me uncomfortably: "It was a blue Chevy wagon, recent model. I didn't get the license number. I had no reason to. I didn't know at the time that they were fugitives."

"The little boy isn't a fugitive. He may be a kidnaping victim."

"He didn't act like one."

"How did he act?"

"Scared. But not scared of them particularly. He went along with them without any trouble."

"Where did they take him?"

"To the station wagon."

"I know that. Who was driving it?"

"A big woman in a wide-brimmed hat."

"How did she know they were here?"

"I let the blond girl use my phone. I had no way of knowing that they—"

"Can you trace the call?"

"I don't see how, unless it was long-distance. I'll give it a try, though."

He plodded toward the walkway, shielding his face against the blowing sand. I followed him up the entrance kiosk and waited while he used the phone inside it. He came out shaking his head, with his hands spread loosely.

"They don't seem to have any record of the call."

"Have you talked to the police?"

"They came and went. The sheriff's captain came out from Petroleum City. But that was after the three of them took off in the Chevy wagon."

I went back down to the blundering edge of the sea and took another long look at *Ariadne*. She flopped in the surge like a bird made helpless by oil. When I turned away, I saw that the older of the two boy surfers had come up quietly behind me.

"I hate to see it happen to a boat. It gives me bad vibes."

"What did happen?"

"The motor conked out, he said. Before he could get the sails set, the wind blew her in and grounded her. The mast went overboard when she hit. My brother and me saw it happen. We went out on our boards and brought them in."

"Was anybody hurt?"

"*He* was. He hurt his arm when the rigging went."

"What about the little boy?"

"He's okay. He got cold, so my brother gave him his blanket. The poor little guy was shivering like he couldn't stop—I mean it." The boy was shaking with the cold himself, but maintaining a stoical expression, like a primitive youth enduring an initiation rite.

"Where did they go from here?"

He gave me another wary look. "Are you a nark, or what?"

"I'm a private detective. I'm trying to get the boy back."

"The big one with the whiskers?"

"The little one."

"When you said it was a kidnaping, were you telling it like it is?"

"Yes."

"Aren't they brother and sister? They said they were."

"What else did they say?"

"The one with the whiskers said that you—that they were after him for shooting speed. Is that right?"

"No, it isn't. I want the boy back. His father was murdered yesterday."

"By the head with the whiskers?"

"It could be. I don't know."

The boy went and talked to his brother, and started back toward me. I met him halfway:

"What's the secret?"

"I was just checking with my brother. The girl told him he could pick up his blanket in Petroleum City. She said she'd leave it for him at the office of the Yucca Tree Inn."

I went there, passing through pastures full of oil pumps and fields of derricks. Further off on the horizon stood the gantries of Vandenberg Air Force Base. Petroleum City was a country town which had grown up suddenly. It had spilled beyond its limits into miles of quick housing developments congealing in a glacier of sameness.

The Yucca Tree Inn had grown since its postcard picture was taken fifteen years ago. It was built around three sides of a short block at the southern edge of the city, with a convention center on the fourth side. The movable lettering on the marquee in front offered "Steak, Lobster and Continuous Entertainment." When I parked in front of the office, I could hear western music like the last wail of a dying frontier.

The woman behind the desk was dressed like a synthetic cowgirl in a brightly striped blouse and a western hat with an imitation rawhide band. She had a big friendly body which looked as if it didn't quite know what to do with itself, even after years of practice.

"Did somebody leave a blanket with you?" I said. "A wet blanket?"

She gave me an unsmiling look. "You aren't the one that lent Susie the blanket."

"I didn't say I was. Is Susie here?"

"No. They took off again." She paused with her lips parted, as if she'd been overtaken by sudden doubt. "I'm not supposed to be talking about it, though."

"Who said so?"

"Mr. Crandall."

"Lester Crandall?"

"Yessir. He owns this place."

"Where is he? I'd like to talk to him."

"What about?"

"His daughter. I'm a detective—a private one. I was at his house in Pacific Palisades last night, and he and I are cooperating."

"He isn't here."

"You said he gave you orders not to talk."

"On the phone. I talked to him on the phone."

"When was this?"

"A couple of hours ago. As soon as Susie called me from Dunes Bay. Mr. Crandall told me to keep her here until he arrived. That's easier said than done, though. The minute my back was turned, the three of them piled into the station wagon and took off again."

"Which way?"

"San Francisco." She moved her thumb like a hitchhiker in that direction.

I got the license number of the station wagon from her. "Did you tell the police?"

"Why should I? It's her father's car. Anyway, Mr. Crandall told me to keep the police out of it."

"When do you expect Mr. Crandall?"

"Any time now." She looked as if she wasn't looking forward to the meeting. "If you have any pull with him, do me a favor, will you? Tell him I did my best, but she got away from me."

"All right. What's your name? Mine is Lew Archer."

"Joy Rawlins." She said with the air of repeating an old joke: "I'm thinking seriously of changing it to Sorrow."

"Don't do that. Can I buy you a drink?"

"Sorry, I can't leave the desk. But thanks for the offer." She gave me a smile which gradually faded. "What goes on with Susie, anyway? She used to be a nice quiet young girl, almost too quiet."

"She isn't any more. She's on the run."

"Then why did she phone here?"

"Maybe because she needed transportation. What did she say to you when she called from the beach?"

"She said she was out for a sail, and her boat was wrecked, and she and her friends were soaking wet. She asked me not to call her father but of course I had to—he left specific orders. I brought them back here and they changed into dry clothes and had a bite—"

"Where did they get the dry clothes?"

"From the owner's suite. I opened it up for them. I thought they were staying—in fact the boy with the beard asked me about getting a doctor for his arm. He had what looked like a broken arm—hanging loose, you know? But then he changed his mind and said he'd wait until he saw his mother. I asked him where his mother was, but I didn't get an answer out of him."

"What about the little boy?"

"I have a boy of my own, and I fixed him up with some clothes."

"Did he say anything?"

"I don't think he said a word." She considered the question. "No, he didn't speak within my hearing."

"Did he cry?"

She shook her head. "No. He wasn't crying."

"Did he eat?"

"I got him to eat some soup and part of a hamburger. But most of the time he just sat like a little image." She was silent and then said as if at random: "Did you see the pelicans at Dunes Bay? They can't have any more young ones, did you know that? Their bodies are poisoned with DDT, and it makes their eggs all break."

I told her that I knew about the pelicans. "What about Susan? Did she do any talking?"

"Very little. I don't know what to make of that girl. She's changed."

"In what way?"

"Susie and I used to be pretty good friends before they moved down south. At least I thought so."

"How long ago did they move?"

"It's been a couple of years now. Les—Mr. Crandall opened a new motel in Oceano, and Los Angeles was more central for him. At least that was the reason he gave."

"Were there other reasons?"

The woman gave me a quizzical look, both friendly and suspicious. "You're pumping me, aren't you? And I'm talking too much. But I hate to see Susie kick over the traces like this. She used to be a real good girl—I mean it. Headstrong like her father, but good at heart."

She went into deep thought for a minute. Her face, forgetful of me, dreamed downward as if she had a child at her breast. I prompted her:

"What changed her?"

"She seems kind of desperate to me. I don't know why." She grimaced. "I *do* know why, really. They moved to L.A. to give her more advantages—social advantages and stuff like that. It was her mother's idea, really—she's always been hipped on L.A. It didn't work out for Susie, or for them, either. So of course they're blaming her for not being happy, and she has no one to turn to. She's a very lonely girl, and that's murder."

I winced at the word, but I found something hopeful to say. "She turned to you."

"But then she turned around and went away again."

"You care about Susan."

"Yes I do. I never had a daughter."

XXIV

I hadn't eaten for seven or eight hours. I went into the restaurant-bar from which the music emanated and hung my hat on the brass-studded tip of a mounted longhorn.

While my steak was being grilled, I shut myself up in a phone booth and put in another call to Willie Mackey.

Willie answered the phone himself. "Mackey Services."

"This is Archer. Have you put your finger on Ellen?"

"Not yet, but I've traced the dog."

"The dog?"

"The Great Dane," Willie said impatiently. "He was lost all right. I've been in touch with the owner, who lives outside Mill Valley. He advertised for his dog last week, and somebody found it in Sausalito. That's a long way from the Peninsula, Lew."

"My informant was an acid freak, I think."

"I was wondering," Willie said. "Anyway, I have a man over in Sausalito now. You know Harold."

"Can you contact him?"

"I should be able to. He has one of the radio cars."

"Tell him to watch for a blue Chevy station wagon with three young people in it." I gave him their names and descriptions, and the license number of the car.

"What is Harold supposed to do if he sees them?"

"Stay with them. Get the little boy, if he can do it without endangering him."

"I better get over to Marin County myself," Willie said. "You didn't tell me this was a snatch."

"It isn't an ordinary one."

"Then what are these people up to?"

I had no ready answer. After a moment I said:

"The little boy's father was murdered yesterday. He was probably a witness to the killing."

"The other two did it?"

"I don't know." I felt a growing ambivalence about Susan and Jerry—I wanted to end their wild flight, not only for the child's sake but for their own. "We have to go on that assumption, though."

I went back into the restaurant. My steak was ready, and I washed it down with draft beer. Behind the semi-elliptical bar four cowboys who had never been near a cow sang western songs which sounded as if they had originated in the far east.

I ordered a second beer and looked around the place. It was a noisy mixture of the real west and the imitation west. The mixture included cowboys both dude and actual, off-duty servicemen with their wives and girls, tourists, oil-workers wearing high-heeled boots like the cowboys, a few men in business suits with wide ties and narrow sun-crinkled eyes.

Some of the eyes seemed to brighten like electronic sensors when Lester Crandall came in from the lobby. Electronic money sensors. He paused in the doorway, looking around the room. I raised my hand. He came over and shook it.

"You're Archer, aren't you? How did you get here so fast?"

I told him, watching his face as I talked. His reactions

seemed dull and sluggish, as if he hadn't slept the night before. Still he seemed more at home in his motor inn than in his big house in the Palisades.

The waitresses had sprung to attention when he entered, and one of them came to the table:

"Can I get you anything, Mr. Crandall?"

"Bourbon. You know my brand. And hold Mr. Archer's check."

"That isn't necessary," I said. "But thanks."

"My pleasure." He bent forward, regarding me through puffed eyelids. "If you've told me and I've forgotten, please excuse me. I'm a little slow today. It still isn't clear to me what your interest is."

"I'm working for Mrs. Stanley Broadhurst. I'm trying to get her boy back before he's hurt—and before she goes off the deep end."

"I'm pretty close to the deep end myself." He took hold of my wrist with his work-scarred hand in a sudden gesture of intimacy. Just as suddenly, he let go. "But let me set your mind at rest about one thing. My Susan isn't the kind of girl who would hurt a little boy."

"Perhaps not intentionally. But she's exposing him to danger. It's a wonder he wasn't drowned today."

"That's what Mrs. Rawlins said. I wish she'd had the intestinal fortitude to keep them here. She said she would."

"It wasn't her fault she couldn't. Didn't you tell her not to call in the police?"

Crandall gave me a look of unguarded cold anger. "I know the police in this part of the world. I was born and brought up here. They shoot first and ask questions afterwards. I'm not turning them loose on my young daughter."

I couldn't help agreeing with him. "We won't argue. Anyway, they're well on their way to the Bay area by now."

"Where in the Bay area?"

"Probably Sausalito."

He clenched his fists and shook them as if he had dice in both hands. "Why aren't you after them?"

"I thought you might say something useful."

His eyes were still stained with anger. "Is that a crack?"

"It's the truth. Why don't you calm down? A friend of mine in San Francisco will be looking out for them."

"A friend of yours?"

"A private detective named Willie Mackey."

"What's he going to do with them if he catches them?"

"Use his good judgment. Take the boy away from them if he can."

"That sounds dangerous to me. What about my daughter?"

"It's a dangerous life she's chosen."

"Don't give me that. I want her protected, you understand?"

"Then protect her."

He gave me a dreary look. The waitress came running with his drink, smiling desperately in an effort to counteract the boss's mood. The drink was more effective than her smile. It heightened his color and made his eyes glisten with moisture. Even his sideburns seemed to take on a bristling new life of their own.

"It's not my fault," he said. "I gave her everything a girl could want. It's Jerry Kilpatrick's fault. He took an innocent girl and corrupted her."

"Somebody did."

"You mean it wasn't him?"

"I mean he wasn't the only one. One day last week—I think it was probably Thursday—she paid a visit to the Star Motel."

"The one on the coast highway? Susie wouldn't go there."

"She was seen there. She spent some time with an escaped

convict named Albert Sweetner. Does the name mean anything to you?"

"No, it doesn't, and neither does the rest of your story. I just plain don't believe it." But his face was adjusting to it like an old fighter's who had taken a lot of punishment and expected to have to take more. "Why are you telling me this?"

"You need to do some thinking, and a man can't think without the facts. Al Sweetner was murdered Saturday night."

"And you're accusing Susan?"

"No. She was probably out at sea when it happened. I'm trying to get across to you the kind of trouble she's in."

"I know she's in bad trouble." He rested his folded arms on the table and looked at me over them like a man behind a barricade. "What can I do to get her out of it? I've been running around in circles since she left home. But she keeps on moving away out of my reach."

He was silent for a minute. His gaze moved past me and grew distant as if he was watching his daughter slip away over a receding horizon. I had no children, but I had given up envying people who had.

"Have you any idea what she's running from?"

He shook his head. "We gave her everything. I thought she was okay. But something happened—I don't know what."

He moved his head obtusely from side to side, groping for his daughter in a kind of blind man's buff. It filled me with a tedious sorrow, perhaps not unlike his own.

I pushed back my chair and stood up. "Thanks for the steak."

Crandall stood up facing me, shorter, wider, older, sadder, richer.

"Where are you going, Mr. Archer?"

"Sausalito."

"Take Mother and I with you."

"Mother?"

"Mrs. Crandall." He was one of those men who seldom referred to their wives by their Christian names.

"I didn't know you had her along."

"She's freshening up in the suite. But we can be ready to leave at a moment's notice. I'll pay all expenses. In fact," he added, "let's not beat around the bush—I want to buy your services."

"I already have a client. But I'd like to talk to Mrs. Crandall."

"Of course. Why not?"

I put down a dollar tip. Crandall picked up the bill, rolled it carefully, and, rising on his toes, tucked it into my outside breast pocket.

"Your money is no good in my place."

"This is for the waitress."

I unrolled the dollar bill and put it back on the table. Crandall started to get angry, and then decided not to let himself. He wanted me to take Mother and him along.

ↄↄↄↄↄↄↄↄↄↄↄↄↄↄↄↄↄↄ

XXV

ↄↄↄↄↄↄↄↄↄↄↄↄↄↄↄↄↄↄ

I accompanied him into the lobby and waited while he went upstairs to his suite. Joy Rawlins was behind the desk, taking things out of a drawer and putting them into a leatherette case. She was heavy-eyed and sallow as if she had suffered a loss of blood.

"He fired me," she said in a flat voice. "He gave me fifteen minutes to get out. And I've been here more than fifteen years. I built this place up for him."

"I'm sure he'll reconsider."

"You don't know Les. He's been getting awfully high and mighty since he started to make real money. He's got a God complex, and it's growing on him. It was just his good luck that his daddy's ranch was between Petro City and Vandenberg AFB. But Les thinks that he did it all himself. And now he thinks he can wipe other people out like that." She made a slicing motion with her hand. Her hand was trembling. "I *need* this job. I've got a boy in school."

"What reason did he give for firing you?"

"No reason. But you know why and so do I. I was supposed to hog-tie Susie or something. He puts the blame on me because he hasn't the guts to put it where it belongs—on him and his wife. They were the ones that brought her up. I could tell you things about Susie's mother—"

Her face froze in a look of surprise, as if she had heard herself. She stopped talking. I tried to get her started again:

"What's Mrs. Crandall's background, anyway?"

"Nothing much. Her father was in the construction trades —dry-wall installation—and they batted around the state when she was a kid. She was still no more than a kid when she married Lester. He plucked her right out of high school. He was already a middle-aged man."

"I noticed the difference in ages. And I wondered why she married him."

"She had to."

"You mean she was pregnant? That's common enough."

"There was more to it than that—a good deal more. She

was running with a wild gang from Santa Teresa, and they stole Les's car. She could have gone to jail if he had wanted to prosecute. One of the others did."

"Albert Sweetner?"

Her face closed. "You've been putting me on. You already know all this."

"Not all of it. But I ran into Sweetner yesterday. How did you happen to know him?"

"I didn't, really. Only he came here last week. I've got a good memory for faces, and I remembered him from the other time. He wanted to know where to find her."

"Find Mrs. Crandall?"

"Both the Crandalls."

"And you told him?"

"No, I didn't. But their address is no secret. It's in the L.A. phone directory." She added virtuously: "I didn't even tell him that."

"You mentioned another time that he came here."

Her eyes shifted to longer focus. "It was a long time ago, when he was just a young guy hitching through. I wasn't so old myself then."

"How long ago?"

"Let's see, I was pretty new on the job. And Susan was just about three. It must have been fifteen years, at least." She grimaced. "I should have stood at home this week. Whenever that man passes through, he stirs up trouble."

"What did he stir up fifteen years ago?"

"I don't know exactly. He wanted to talk to Les—I figured he was hitting him for a loan. But after he left, all hell broke loose around here. Les and his wife had a knock-down drag-out fight."

"What was the fight about?"

"I don't know—all I heard was the shouting. You'll have

to take it up with them yourself. Only don't quote me. I've got to ask the son-of-a-gun for references."

Crandall called me from the top of the stairs. I went up, lifted by a certain excitement. I was eager for a second look at Martha Crandall, against the background I had been filling in.

The suite was furnished in cheap luxury. She was sitting in an overstuffed chair with her legs crossed in front of her and thick new makeup on her face.

I was struck again by the beauty and grace of her body. No matter how she placed herself, it seemed to organize the room around her, as a light or a fire does. But her eyes were strained and cold. They looked at me through her mask of makeup as if she had had a bad night and I had been responsible for it.

She gave me her hand and held on as she said: "You've got to get Susie back for me. She's been gone for three days now and I can't stand it."

"I'm doing my best."

"Lester says she's on her way to Sausalito. Is that right?"

"It's a fairly good possibility. Anyway, I'm acting on it. You may be able to help me."

"How?" She leaned toward me in an eager posture, but her eyes didn't change. They seemed jaded, as if she was watching her life repeat itself. "I'll do anything I can, I mean it." Her voice was rougher, taking on the accent of her surroundings.

"Do you know Ellen Kilpatrick?"

Her glance caromed off her husband, and came back to me. "It's strange you should ask me that. I was thinking of calling her."

"Why?"

"She lives in Sausalito."

"Under what name?"

"Ellen Storm. She's an artist, she uses that name."

"She calls herself an artist," Crandall said. "But she's a phony. She can't even draw."

His voice was choked, and his face reddened. I wondered if he had reason to be angry with Ellen, or if he had simply attached his general anger to her.

"Have you seen her work?" I said.

"I've seen a sample of it. She wrote us a letter in the summer offering to sell us a painting. So I sent her some money, and she sent back this painting."

"Do you have it here?"

"I chucked it out. It was just a piece of junk—an excuse to ask me for money."

"It was not," his wife said. "She said she wanted to give us first chance."

"Nobody was standing in line."

I turned to her. "Have you seen Ellen recently?"

She glanced nervously at her husband. "She was my home-room teacher. Isn't that right, Les?"

He didn't answer her. He seemed to be absorbed in his own glum thoughts.

"And she's Jerry Kilpatrick's mother," I said. "Did you know that?"

"No." She looked at her husband again and added after an embarrassed pause: "Not until I figured it out, I mean."

Crandall moved between his wife and me, standing over her like a prosecutor. "Did you invite Jerry Kilpatrick to the house?"

"What if I did? It was a nice thing to do."

"It was a lousy thing to do. You can see what's come of it. Who put you up to it? Did she?"

"It's none of your business. And don't loom over me like that."

Intent on their intramural game, they seemed to have forgotten me. Partly to break it up and partly because the question needed asking, I said to her:

"Was Albert Sweetner in your home room in high school?"

She sat very still and quiet for a time. Her husband was quiet, too, his eyes rather absent-looking as if he had been sandbagged by the past.

"It was a big class," she said. "What was that name again?"

"Albert Sweetner."

She uncrossed and recrossed her legs like soft and elegant scissors and looked up at her husband. "Don't stare at me like that. How can I think with you staring at me?"

"I'm not staring." He tried to remove his gaze from her, and couldn't.

"Why don't you go and have a drink?" she said. "I forget how to talk with you standing there staring."

He put out his hand. Without quite touching her, it traced the contour of her head. "Take it easy now, Mother. We've got to stick together—you and me against the world."

"Sure. Only give me a chance to think for a minute, will you? Go have a drink."

He left the room slowly. I waited until I heard the click of the latch behind him, and his reluctant footsteps going downstairs.

"What are you trying to do?" the woman said. "Break up my marriage?"

"It seems to be slightly bent already."

"That isn't true. I've been a good wife to Lester, and he knows it. I've done my best to make up for any harm I did him in the past."

"Such as stealing his car?"

"That was nearly twenty years ago. You've got your nerve raking it up, and throwing Albert Sweetner in my face."

"I brought him up last night. Remember? You said you didn't know him."

"All you gave me was his first name. And I haven't even seen him since high school."

"Are you sure, Mrs. Crandall? He came here to your motor inn fifteen years ago."

"A lot of people come to this place."

"And just this week he took your daughter to another motel."

She pushed the idea back with her hands. "Susan wouldn't go with a man like that."

"I'm afraid she did."

She stood up in agitation. "What was he trying to do? Get back at me for turning him in?"

"You turned him in?"

"I had to. It was that or go to Juvenile Hall. But that was before Susie was even born."

"Al wouldn't forget it, though."

"No. He wouldn't forget it. He came here fifteen years ago like you said, to try and break up my marriage. That was right after he got out of Preston."

"How did he try to break up your marriage?"

"He told my husband a lot of lies about me. I don't want to go into what he said. In fact, I don't know why I'm talking to you at all."

"Al Sweetner was murdered last night."

She looked at me in silence. Her eyes were frightened. Her body kept its feline confidence.

"I see. You think I killed him."

I neither affirmed nor denied this. Her look grew chillier: "Susan? You think it was Susan?"

"She isn't a suspect. I don't have a logical suspect."

"Then why did you throw it at me like that?"

"It's something I thought you ought to know."

"Thanks very much," she said bitterly. "What was Al doing with my daughter, anyway?"

"Mainly, I think, he was trying to use her as a source of information. Al was on the run, and he came south looking for money. He was trying to finance a trip to Mexico."

"Came south from where?"

"Sacramento. I think he stopped in Sausalito on the way."

She stood in a listening attitude, like a woman hearing footsteps in a graveyard. "Did Ellen point him in our direction?"

"I don't know what she did. But I'm reasonably certain he went to see her before he came south. He was after a reward which Stanley Broadhurst offered for her and his father."

"What kind of a reward?"

"A thousand dollars cash. Al probably hoped to get more." I produced my clipping of the ad, which was gradually wearing out. "This *is* Ellen, isn't it?"

"Yes. That's the way she used to look when she was teaching high school in Santa Teresa."

"Have you seen her since those days?"

She was slow in answering the question. "I went to see her last month after we bought that picture from her. Please don't mention this to Les—he doesn't know about it. We were in San Francisco for the weekend, and I got away from him and drove across the bridge to Sausalito." She added after a moment's hesitation: "I took Susie with me."

"Why?"

"I don't know—it seemed like a good idea. Ellen seemed to want to get in touch with me, and she did a lot for me when I was a young girl. If it wasn't for her I wouldn't even have lived all the way through my teens. And Susan was starting to show the same signs. She wasn't ever a happy girl, but she was starting to get desperate. You know?"

I didn't know, and said so. It was her first admission that something had been seriously wrong in Susan's life.

"She was scared of other people, really scared, the way I used to be when I was a kid. And they were scared of her in a way—the other kids couldn't figure what was bugging her. I knew, or I thought I knew, but I couldn't talk about it."

"Can you talk about it now?"

"I might as well. The whole thing's going to pieces anyway." She looked around the stuffy ornate room as if earthquake cracks were widening in the walls. "Les isn't Susie's father. He's done his best to be a father to her, but it just didn't get through to her. And I've felt funny about it, too—kind of embarrassed, you know? We've been sitting around like ninnies in our own house."

"Who is Susan's father?"

"It's none of your business." She regarded me levelly, without much heat. "It could be I don't even know the answer to that. My life was pretty much of a mess at one time. That was when I was younger than Susan is now."

"Was Fritz Snow her father?"

The woman's eyes grew sharper. "I'm not answering any questions on that subject, so forget it. Anyway, you're interrupting what I started out to tell you. I was worried about Susan, like I said, and I thought maybe Ellen would have some suggestions."

"Did she?"

"Not really. She did a lot of talking, and Susan did a lot of listening. But I didn't think too much of her ideas. She thought we should send Susan away and let other people look after her. Or turn her loose and let her look after herself. But you can't do that. Young people need protection in this world."

"What did Susan think about it?"

"She wanted to stay with Ellen. But it wouldn't have been a good idea at all. Ellen's changed since she was young. She lives in that creepy old house in the woods like some kind of a hermit."

"No men?"

"Not that I saw. If you mean Leo Broadhurst, he's long gone. The two of them didn't stick together. It was one of those love affairs that only lasted as long as the wife was there to keep it hot." She looked a little embarrassed by her knowledge.

"Where did he go?"

"Out of the country, she said."

"You knew Leo before he left Santa Teresa, right?"

"I worked in his house, if you call that knowing him."

"What kind of a man was he?"

"He was the kind of man that couldn't keep his hands off women."

She spoke with a certain rancor, and I said: "Did he ever make a pass at you?"

"Once. I hit him in his pretty face." She looked at me defiantly, as if I had made a pass at her myself. "He kept his hot little hands to himself after that."

Remembered anger surged up in her, and made her rosy. Perhaps it was tinged with some other passion. She was a more complex woman than had appeared at first meeting.

But I was eager to be on my way. I went downstairs and called Willie Mackey again. While I waited on the line, he looked up Ellen Storm in a Marin directory. She lived in a house on Haven Road on the outskirts of Sausalito. Willie said he would have her house watched until I got there.

I slipped out to my car without saying goodbye to either of the Crandalls. I didn't want to have to take them along, with all the years of their lives dragging behind them.

XXVI

When I got to San Francisco it was dark, and it had been raining. Out at sea beyond the Golden Gate a mass of clouds was moving in from the Farallon Islands. The offshore wind blowing across the bridge felt wet and cold on my face.

A rectangular yellow sign at the entrance to Haven Road said that it was "Not a Through Street." I turned my car around and parked it, and continued on foot along the pitted asphalt. The scattered houses were hidden from the road, but I could see their lights shining through the trees.

A voice spoke softly from the darkness. "Lew?"

Willie Mackey appeared at the side of the road. He was wearing a dark raincoat, and his mustached face looked disembodied, like something called up at a seance. I moved in under the dripping trees with him and shook his gloved hand.

"They haven't shown," he said. "How hard is your information?"

"Just medium." The hope that brought me north had turned over in my chest and was sinking heavily toward my stomach. "Is the Storm woman at home?"

"She's there, but there's nobody with her."

"Do you know that?"

"Yep. Harold can see her through the side window."

"What's she doing?"

"Nothing much. Last time I checked with Harold, he said she seemed to be waiting."

"I think I'll go in and talk to her."

Willie took hold of my arm, pinching the muscle just above the elbow. "Is that a good idea, Lew?"

"She may have heard from them. She's the older boy's mother."

"All right, don't let me stop you." Willie released my arm and stepped aside.

I made my way up the washed-out gravel drive. The twin conical towers standing up against the night sky made the house look like something out of a medieval romance.

The illusion faded as I got nearer. There was a multi-colored fanlight over the front door, with segments of glass fallen out, like missing teeth in an old smile. The veranda steps were half broken down and groaned under my weight. The door creaked open when I knocked.

Ellen appeared in the lighted hallway. Her mouth and eyes hadn't changed very much since her picture was taken all those years before, and it made the gray in her hair seem accidental. She was wearing a dress with a long-sleeved jersey top and a long full skirt on which there were paint stains in all three primary colors. Her body moved with unconscious pride.

She looked both eager and fearful as she came to the door. "Who are you?"

"My name is Lew Archer. The door blew open when I knocked."

"The latch needs fixing." She jiggled the knob. "You're the detective, aren't you?"

"You're well informed."

"Martha Crandall called me. She said you're looking for her daughter."

"Has Susan been here?"

"Not yet, but Martha spoke as if she intended to come." The woman looked out past me into the darkness. "She said my son Jerry is traveling with her."

"Right. And they have Leo Broadhurst's grandson with them."

She seemed puzzled. "How could Leo have a grandson?"

"He left a son behind him, remember. The son had a son. Ronny's six years old, and he's why I'm here."

"What are they doing with a six-year-old?"

"I don't know exactly. I was hoping to ask them."

"I see. Won't you please come in." She gestured with a kind of awkward grace, and her breast lifted. "We can wait together."

"You're very kind, Mrs. Kilpatrick."

The name displeased her, as if I'd brought it up to remind her of the past. She corrected me: "Miss Storm. I took it originally as a professional name. But I haven't used any other name for years."

"I understand you're a painter."

"Not a good one. But I work at it."

She took me into a large, high-ceilinged room. The walls were hung with canvases. Most of them were unframed, and their whorls and splotches of color looked unfinished, perhaps unfinishable.

The windows of the room were heavily draped, except for a triple window in an embrasure. Through the trees outside I could see the lights of Sausalito scattered down the hillside.

"Nice view," I said. "Do you mind if I draw the curtains?"

"Please do. Do you suppose they're out there watching me?"

I looked at her, and saw that she was serious. "Who do you mean?"

"Jerry and Susan and the little boy."

"It isn't likely."

"I know it isn't. But I've been feeling watched, tonight. Drawing the curtains doesn't really help. Whatever it is out there has X-ray eyes. Call it God, or call it the Devil. It hardly matters."

I turned from the window and looked at her face again. It had a certain nakedness, unused to the pressure of eyes.

"I've been keeping you standing, Mr. Archer. Won't you sit down?" She indicated a heavy old perpendicular chair.

"I'd rather sit in another room where we're not so visible."

"So would I, really."

She led me through the front hallway into a kind of office under the stairs, so small it was claustrophobic. The slanting ceiling at its highest part was barely high enough to accommodate my head.

Gary Snyder's broadside "Four Changes" was thumbtacked to the wall. Beside it and in contrast was an old engraving of a whaling ship beating its way through mountainous seas around a jagged black Cape Horn. There was an old iron safe in the corner with a legend on the door: "William Strome Mill and Lumber Co."

She perched on the desk beside the telephone, and I sat on a teetering swivel chair. At these close quarters I could pick up her odor. It was pleasant but rather lifeless, like wood ash or dried leaves. I wondered vaguely if she was still used up by the passion that had driven her up the mountain with Leo Broadhurst.

She caught the look in my eye and misinterpreted it, though not by much:

"I'm not as far out as you think. I have had one or two mystical experiences. I know that each and every night is the first night of eternity."

"What about the days?"

She answered shortly: "I do my best work at night."

"So I've been told."

She turned on me. She was quick on the uptake. "Has Martha been talking about me?"

"Just in the good sense. Martha said you saved her life when she was a kid."

She seemed pleased to hear this, but not to be diverted. "You know about my affair with Leo Broadhurst, or you wouldn't have brought his name up."

"I brought it up to identify his grandson."

"Am I being paranoid?"

"Maybe a little. You get that way living alone."

"How do you know that, doctor?"

"I'm not a doctor, I'm a patient. I live alone."

"By choice?"

"Not mine. My wife couldn't live with me. But now I'm used to it."

"So am I. I love my loneliness," she said rather unconvincingly. "Sometimes I paint all night. I don't need sunlight to do my kind of work. I paint things that don't reflect the light—spiritual conditions."

I thought of the paintings on the wall of the other room. They resembled serious contusions and open wounds. I said:

"Did Martha tell you about Jerry's accident? Apparently he broke his arm."

Her changeable face was pinched by compunction. "Where can he be?"

"On the road, unless he's thought of a better place to go."

"What's he running away from?"

"You'd know better than I."

She shook her head. "I haven't seen him in fifteen years."

"Why not?"

She made a gesture with her hands which seemed to say that I knew all about her. It was the gesture of a woman who spent more time in thought and fantasy than in talking and living.

"My husband—my former husband hasn't forgiven me for Leo."

"I've been wondering what happened to Leo."

"So have I. I went to Reno for my divorce, and he was supposed to join me there. But he never did. He stood me up cold." Her voice was bitter but light, like an anger that was no longer fully remembered. "I haven't seen him since I left Santa Teresa."

"Where did he go?"

"I wouldn't know. I've never heard from him."

"I heard he left the country."

"Where did you hear that?"

"Martha Crandall. She said she got it from you."

The woman seemed a little confused. "I may have said something of the sort. Leo did a lot of talking about taking me to Hawaii or Tahiti."

"He did more than talk, didn't he? I understand he booked passage for two on an English freighter going to Honolulu by way of Vancouver. The *Swansea Castle* sailed from San Francisco about July 6, 1955."

"And Leo was aboard?"

"He bought the tickets anyway. Weren't you with him?"

"No. By that time I'd been in Reno for at least a week. He must have gone with another woman."

"Or alone," I said.

"Not Leo. He couldn't stand to be alone. He had to have someone with him in order to feel really alive. Which is one reason I came back to this house after he left me. I wanted to prove that I could live alone, that I didn't need him.

"I was born in this house," she said, as if she'd been waiting fifteen years for a listener. "It was my grandfather's house, and my grandmother raised me after my mother died. It's interesting to come back to your childhood home. And creepy, too, like becoming very young and very old, both at the same time. The spirit that haunts the house."

That was how she looked, I thought, in her archaic long skirt—very young and very old, the granddaughter and the grandmother in one person, slightly schizo.

She made a nervous self-depreciating gesture. "Am I boring you?"

"Hardly. But I'm interested in Leo. I don't know much about him."

"Neither do I, really. For a couple of years I went to sleep every night thinking about him and woke up in the morning hoping to see him that day. But afterwards I realized I hardly knew him at all. He was just a surface, if you know what I mean."

"Not exactly."

"I mean, *you* know, he had no interior life. He did things well. But that's all there was to him. He was what he did."

"What did he do?"

"He took part in nine or ten landings in the Pacific, and after the war he raced his boat and competed in tennis tournaments and played polo."

"That didn't leave him much time for women."

202

"He didn't need much time," she answered wryly. "Men without insides usually don't. I know this sounds like bad-mouthing, but it really isn't. I used to love Leo, and I probably still do. I don't know how I'd feel if he walked in this minute." She looked at the door.

"Is he likely to?"

She shook her head. "I don't even know if he's alive."

"Do you have any reason to think he's dead?"

"No. But I used to tell myself he was. It made it easier to bear. He never even bothered to phone me in Reno."

"I gather you took it hard."

"I cried a lot the first winter. But I crept in here and weathered it. Whatever happens to me now happens on canvas."

"Don't you ever get lonely?"

She gave me a hard look, to see if I was trying to move in on her. She must have seen that I wasn't, because she said:

"I'm lonely all the time—at least I used to be, until I learned to live alone. You know what I mean, if you live alone. The terrible humiliation and self-pity, with no one to blame for anything but yourself."

"I know what you mean." I brought her back to the subject of her marriage, which seemed to lie hidden at the center of the case. "Why did you leave your husband?"

"It was all over between us."

"Didn't you miss him and the little boy?"

"Not Brian. He got rough with me—you can't forgive a man once he does that. He threatened to kill me if I tried to take Jerry with me, or even see him. Of course I missed my son, but I learned to live without him. I don't need anyone, literally."

"How about figuratively?"

Her smile was deep and revealing, like a glimpse of the

lights and shadows inside her head. "Figuratively is another matter. Of course I've felt like a dropout from the world. The worst loneliness I felt was for the children. Not just my own child—the children I taught in school. I keep seeing their faces and hearing their voices."

"Like Martha Crandall?"

"She was one of them once."

"And Albert Sweetner, and Fritz Snow."

She gave me a disenchanted look. "You've been doing quite a lot of research on me. Believe me, I'm not that important."

"Maybe you're not. But Albert and Fritz and Martha keep cropping up. I gather they came together in your high school class."

"Unfortunately, they did."

"Why do you say unfortunately?"

"The three of them made an explosive combination. You've probably heard about their famous trip to Los Angeles."

"I'm not quite clear about who the ringleader was. Was it Albert?"

"The authorities thought so at the time. He was the only one of the three who had a juvenile record. But I think it was originally Martha's idea." She added thoughtfully: "Martha was the one who came out of it best, too. If you can use that word about a forced marriage to an older man."

"Who was the father of her child? Albert Sweetner?"

"You'll have to ask Martha that." She changed the subject: "Is Albert really dead? Martha said on the phone that he was."

"He was stabbed to death last night. Don't ask me who was responsible, because I don't know."

She looked down sorrowfully as if the dead man was in

the room at her feet. "Poor Albert. He didn't have much of a life. Most of his adult life was spent in prison."

"How do you know that, Miss Storm?"

"I tried to keep in touch with him." She added after a little hesitation: "As a matter of fact he came here to this house last week."

"Did you know he'd escaped from the pen?"

"What if I did?"

"You didn't turn him in."

"I'm not a very good citizen," she said with some irony. "It was his third conviction, and he was due to spend most of the rest of his life in prison."

"What was he in for?"

"Armed robbery."

"Weren't you afraid of him when he came to your door?"

"I never have been. I was surprised to see him, but not afraid."

"What did he want from you? Money?"

She nodded. "I wasn't able to give him much. I haven't sold a picture for some time."

"Did you give him anything else?"

"Some bread and cheese."

I was still carrying the green-covered book. I got it out of my pocket.

"That looks like a book I used to own," Ellen said.

"It is." I showed her the book-plate in the front.

"Where did you get this, anyway? Not from Al Sweetner?"

"From your son Jerry, ultimately."

"He kept it?" She seemed starved for any dry crumb from the past she had abandoned.

"Evidently he did." I pointed out his penciled signature on the flyleaf. "But the thing I wanted to show you is inside." I opened the book and took the clipping out. "Did you give this to Al Sweetner?"

She took it in her hand and studied it. "Yes, I did."

"What for?"

"I thought it might be worth some money to him."

"That was a pretty double-edged act of charity. I can't believe your motives were entirely altruistic."

She flared up, rather weakly, as if nothing was worth getting really angry about. "What do you know about my motives?"

"Only what you tell me."

She was silent for a minute or two. "I suppose I *was* curious. I'd been holding onto this clipping all summer, wondering what I ought to do about it. I didn't know who had originated it. And of course I didn't know what had happened to Leo. I thought perhaps Albert could find out for me."

"So you turned him loose on Santa Teresa. That was kind of a crucial thing to do."

"What was so crucial about it?"

"Albert is dead, and so is Stanley Broadhurst." I spelled out the details for her.

"Then it was Stanley who placed this ad in the *Chronicle*," she said. "I'd have got in touch with him if I had known. But I thought it was probably Elizabeth."

"What made you think that?"

"I can remember when this picture was taken." She smoothed it on her knee, as if it was a feather she had found. "Elizabeth took it, before she knew that Leo and I were lovers. It brings back everything. Everything I had and everything I lost."

There were romantic tears in her eyes. My own eyes remained quite dry. I was thinking of everything that Elizabeth Broadhurst had lost.

XXVII

The gravel in the driveway crackled under the tires of a heavy car. Ellen lifted her head. I went to the front door, with her following close behind me.

Martha Crandall was already on the veranda. Her face changed when she saw me.

"They haven't come?"

"They never will if you don't keep out of sight. This place is staked out."

Ellen gave me a bright suspicious look. I asked her to go back inside and take Martha with her. Then I went down the steps to Lester Crandall's new bronze Sedan de Ville.

He hadn't moved from behind the wheel. "I told Mother it was a waste of time and energy. But she insisted on making the trip." He surveyed the front of the house with a cold eye. "So this is where the famous Ellen lives. It's practically falling down—"

I cut him short: "How about moving the car out of sight? Or slide over and let me."

"You move it. I'm slightly pooped."

He maneuvered his heavy body out from under the wheel and let me park the car behind the house. The elements of the case were coming together, and I felt crowded and excited. Perhaps I was subliminally aware of the noise of the second car.

When Lester Crandall and I went around to the front again, there was a figure at the foot of the driveway—an indeterminate bearded head surmounting a light triangle which looked like a warning sign. The figure was caught and drenched in approaching headlights. It was Jerry Kilpatrick, with one arm in a sling.

He must have recognized Crandall and me at the same time. He turned toward the moving headlights and called out: "Susie! Split!"

Her station wagon paused and went into reverse, backing up the road with a mounting roar of the engine. Jerry looked around uncertainly and ran stumbling out of the driveway into the arms of Willie Mackey and his large assistant Harold.

By the time I got to them, the station wagon was turning in the entrance to Haven Road, its headlights swiping like long paintbrushes at the tree trunks. It started off in the direction of San Francisco.

"I'll phone the bridge," Willie said.

I ran up the road to my car and followed the wagon. When I reached the near end of the bridge, traffic was beginning to line up in the right-hand lanes. The station wagon was standing empty at the head of the line.

I saw Susie out on the bridge, running hand in hand with the little boy toward the cable tower. A heavy man in patrolman's uniform was jolting along some distance behind them.

I went after them, running as hard as I could. Susie looked back once. She let go of Ronny's hand, moved to the railing, and went over. I thought for a sickening instant that she had taken the final plunge. Then I saw her light hair blowing above the railing.

The patrolman stopped before he got to her. The little boy loitered behind him, turning to me as I came up. He looked like an urchin, dirty-faced, in shorts and sweater that were too big for him.

He gave me a small embarrassed smile as if I had caught him doing something that he could be punished for, like playing hooky.

"Hello, Ronny."

"Hello. Look at what Susie's doing."

She was holding on with both hands, leaning out against the gray night. Along the wall of clouds that rose behind her, lightning flickered and prowled like somebody trying to set fire to a building.

I got a firm grip on the boy's cold hand and moved toward her. She stared at me without apparent recognition or interest, as if I belonged to a different race, the kind that lived past the age of twenty.

The patrolman turned to me: "You know her?"

"I know who she is. Her name is Susan Crandall."

"I hear you talking about me," she said. "Stop it or I'll jump."

The man in uniform backed away a few feet.

"Tell him to go further away," she said to me.

I told him, and he did. She looked at us with more interest, as part of a scene responding to her will. Her face appeared to be frozen except for her wide roving eyes. Her voice was flat:

"What are you going to do with Ronny?"

"Take him back to his mother."

"How do I know you will?"

"Ask Ronny. Ronny knows me."

The boy lifted his voice: "He let me feed peanuts to his birds."

"So you're the one," she said. "He's been talking about it all day."

She gave him a wan and patronizing smile, as if she herself had put off childish things. But with her white fingers clenching the railing, her hair blowing above it, she looked like half a child and half a bird perched over the long drop.

"What would you do to me if I came back over there?"

"Nothing."

She said as if I hadn't spoken: "Shoot me? Or send me to prison?"

"Neither of those things."

"What would you do?" she repeated.

"Take you to a safer place."

She shook her head gravely. "There is no safe place in this world."

"A safer place, I said."

"And what would you do to me there?"

"Nothing."

"You're a dirty filthy liar!"

She inclined her head to one side and looked down over her shoulder, into the depth of my lying and the terrible depth of her rage.

Toward the San Francisco end of the bridge, the tow truck that carried the roving patrol came into view. I made a pushing signal with both hands, and the patrolman repeated it. The truck slowed down and stopped.

"Come back, Susie," I said.

"Yeah," Ronny said. "Come back. I'm afraid you'll fall."

"I've already fallen," she said bitterly. "I've got no place to go."

"I'll take you to your mother."

"I don't want to see her. I don't want to live with those two ever again."

"Tell them that," I said. "You're old enough to live with

other people. You don't have to stay over there to prove it."

"I like it over here." But after a moment she said: "What other people?"

"The world is full of them."

"But I'm afraid."

"After what you've been through, you're still afraid?"

She nodded. Then she looked down once more. I was afraid I'd lost her.

But she was saying goodbye to the long drop. She climbed back over the railing and rested against it, breathing quickly and lightly. The little boy moved toward her, pulling me along by the hand, and took her hand.

We walked back to the head of the bridge, where Willie Mackey and his assistant were talking to some local officers. Willie appeared to have some clout with them. They took our names, asked a few pointed questions, and let us go.

ᓚᓂᓚᓂᓚᓂᓚᓂᓚᓂᓚᓂᓚᓂ

XXVIII

ᓚᓂᓚᓂᓚᓂᓚᓂᓚᓂᓚᓂᓚᓂ

Willie took Ronny with him in the station wagon. I hated to let the boy out of my sight. But I wanted a chance to question Susan before she saw her parents.

She sat inert while I extricated my car. The patrolman who had chased her out the walkway stopped the north-bound traffic. He looked relieved to see us go.

She said in some alarm: "Where are you taking me?"

"To Ellen Storm's house. Isn't that where you wanted to go?"

"I guess so. My mother and father are there, aren't they?"

"They arrived just before you did."

"Don't tell them I tried to jump, will you?" she said in a low voice.

"You can hardly keep it a secret. Any of it." I paused to let the fact sink in. "I still don't understand why you ran away like that."

"They stopped me at the head of the bridge. They wouldn't let me through. They started yelling at me and asking me questions. Don't you ask me any questions, either," she added breathlessly. "I don't have to answer."

"It's true, you don't. But if you won't tell me what happened, I wonder who will."

"When are we talking about? On the bridge?"

"Yesterday, on the mountain, when you went there with Stanley Broadhurst and Ronny. Why did you go up there?"

"Mr. Broadhurst asked me to. That Sweetner man told him about me—the things I said when I blew my mind."

"What things?"

"I don't want to talk about them. I don't even want to think about them. You can't make me."

There was a wild note in her voice which made me slow the car and watch her out of the corner of my eye. "Okay. Why did you go to Mr. Broadhurst's house on Friday? Did Albert Sweetner send you?"

"No. It was Jerry's idea. He said I ought to go and talk to Mr. Broadhurst, and I did. Then we went up the mountain Saturday morning."

"What for?"

"We wanted to see if something was buried there."

"Something?"

"A little red car. We went up there in a little red car."
Her voice had changed in pitch and register. It sounded as
if her mind had regressed, or shifted to a different level of
reality. I said:

"Who's 'we'?"

"Mommy and me. But I don't want to talk about what
happened then. It was a long time ago when I blew my
mind."

"We're talking about yesterday morning," I said. "Was
Stanley Broadhurst digging for a car?"

"That's right—a little red sports car. But he never got
down deep enough."

"What happened?"

"I don't know exactly. Ronny had to go to the john. I got
the key from Mr. Broadhurst and took him to the one in the
Mountain House. Then I heard Mr. Broadhurst yell. I
thought he was calling me, and I went outside. I could see
Mr. Broadhurst lying in the dirt. Another man was standing
over him—a man with a black beard and long hippie hair.
He was hitting Mr. Broadhurst with the pickax. I could see
the blood on Mr. Broadhurst's back. It made a red pattern,
and then there was a fire under the trees, and that made an
orange pattern. The man dragged Mr. Broadhurst in the
hole and shoveled dirt on him."

"What did you do, Susan?"

"I went back in and got Ronny, and we ran away. We
sneaked down the trail into the canyon. The man didn't see
us."

"Can you describe him? Was he young or old?"

"I couldn't tell, he was too far away. And he had on big
dark glasses—wraparounds—so I couldn't make out his face.
He must have been young, though, with all that hair."

"Could it have been Albert Sweetner?"

"No. He doesn't have long hair."

"What if he was wearing a wig?"

She considered the question. "I still don't think it was him. Anyway, I don't want to talk about him. He said if I talked about him he would kill me."

"When did he tell you that?"

"I said I didn't want to talk about it. You can't make me."

Her face was struck white by the headlights of a passing car. She turned away as if they had been searching out her secrets.

We were approaching the entrance to Haven Road. I pulled off the pavement and stopped under the trees. The girl crouched against the door on the far side.

"You stay away from me," she said between spasms of shivering. "Don't you do anything to me."

"What makes you think I would, Susan?"

"You're the same as that Sweetner man. He said all he wanted me to do was tell him what I remembered. But he pushed me down onto the dirty old bed."

"In the loft of the Mountain House?"

"Yes. He hurt me. He made me bleed." Her eyes looked through me as if I was made of cloud and she was peering into the night behind me. "Something went bang. I could see the blood on his head. It made a red pattern. Mommy ran out the door and didn't come back. She didn't come back all night."

"What night are you talking about?"

"The night they buried him near the sycamore tree."

"That happened in the daytime, didn't it?"

"No. It was dark night. I could see the light moving around in the trees. It was some kind of a big machine. It made a noise like a monster. I was afraid it would come and bury me. But it didn't know I was there," she said in her regressive fairy-tale voice.

214

"Where were you?"

"I hid in the loft until my mommy came back. She didn't come back all night. She told me not to tell anybody, ever."

"You've seen her, then, since it happened?"

"Of course I've seen her."

"When?"

"All my life," she said.

"I'm talking about the last thirty-six hours. Mr. Broadhurst was buried yesterday."

"You're trying to mix me up, like that Sweetner man." She hugged her hands between her legs, and shuddered. "Don't tell my mother what he did to me. I'm not supposed to let a man come near me. And I never will again."

She looked at me with deep distrust. I was overcome by angry pity—pity for her and anger against myself. It was cruel to question her under the circumstances, stirring up the memories and the fears that had driven her almost out of life.

I sat beside her without speaking and considered her answers. They had seemed at first like a flight of ideas which took off from the facts and never returned to them. But as I sorted through the ideas and images, they seemed to refer to several different events which were linked and overlapping in her consciousness.

"How many times have you been in the Mountain House, Susie?"

Her lips moved, silently counting the occasions. "Three times, that I remember. Yesterday, when I took Ronny to the john. And a couple of days ago, when that man Sweetner hurt me in the loft. And once with my mother when I was a little girl, younger than Ronny. The gun went bang and she ran away and I hid in the loft all night." The girl began to sob dryly and brokenly. "I want my mother."

XXIX

Her parents were waiting in front of the twin-towered house. Susan got out of my car and went toward them, feet dragging, head down. Her mother took her in her arms and called her pet names. Their warm coming together gave me a flicker of hope for both of them.

Lester Crandall stood off to one side, looking shut out. He moved toward me with an uncertain light in his eye, an uncertain gait, as if the world was moving away from under him and I was the one who had set it spinning.

"Your sidekick"—he gestured toward the house, and I assumed he meant Willie—"your sidekick told me you talked her in off the bridge. I'm very grateful to you."

"I'm glad I reached her in time. Why don't you say something to her, Mr. Crandall?"

He stole a sideways look at her. "I wouldn't know what to say."

"Tell her you're glad she didn't kill herself."

He shook the idea off. "I wouldn't dignify it. She had to be faking."

"She wasn't. She's attempted suicide twice in the last four days. It won't be safe to take her home unless you get her proper medical care."

He turned to look at the two women, who were moving across the veranda into the house. "Susie didn't get hurt, did she?"

"She's physically and mentally hurt. She's been drugged and raped. She's witnessed at least one murder and possibly two. You can't expect her to handle these things without psychiatric help."

"Who raped her, for God's sake?"

"Albert Sweetner."

Crandall became very still. I sensed the core of force in his aging body. "I'll kill the dirty son."

"He's already dead. Maybe you knew that."

"No."

"You haven't seen him in the past few days?"

"I only saw him once in my life. That was about eighteen years ago, when they sent him up to Preston for stealing my car. I was a witness at the trial."

"I heard he paid a visit to the Yucca Tree Inn the summer he got out of Preston. Don't you remember?"

"All right, I saw him twice. What does that prove?"

"You can tell me what happened."

"You know what happened," he said, "or you wouldn't be bringing it up. He tried to wreck my marriage. He probably spent his three years in Preston figuring out how to do it. He said he was Susie's father, and he was going to make a legal claim to her. I beat him up." He struck the palm of his left hand with his right fist, more than once. "I hit Martha, too. And she took Susie and left me. I don't blame her. She didn't come back for a long time after that."

"Did she go with Albert Sweetner?"

"I don't know. She never told me. I thought I was never going to see Susie or her again. It was like my life had gone to pieces. Now it's gone to pieces for sure."

"You have a chance to put it back together. You're the only one who can."

His eyes caught my meaning and held it. But he said: "I don't know, Archer. I'm getting old—I'll be sixty on my next birthday. I shouldn't have taken on the two of them in the first place."

"Who else would have?"

He answered me emphatically. "Plenty of men would have married Martha. She was a raving beauty. She still is."

"We won't argue about that. Have you thought about where you're going to spend the night?"

"I thought we'd drive back as far as the Yucca Tree. I'm pretty worn out myself, but Martha always seems to have something left."

"And tomorrow?"

"Back to the Palisades. One thing, it's handy to the Medical Center. I thought I'd take her in there and have her checked," he said, as if it was entirely his own idea.

"Do that, Lester. And take good care of her. She witnessed a murder yesterday, as I said, and the murderer may try to silence her." I told him about the bearded man and the false hair I had found on Al Sweetner's body.

"Does that mean Sweetner did the Broadhurst killing?"

"Whoever did it wants us to think so. But it's hardly possible. I saw Sweetner in Northridge around the time that Stanley Broadhurst was killed." I hesitated. "Where were you about that time, by the way?"

"Somewhere in Los Angeles, looking for Susie."

I didn't ask him if he could prove it. Perhaps in recognition of this, he got out his wallet and offered me several hundred-dollar bills. But I didn't want to take anything from him or owe him anything before the case was ended.

"Put your money away," I said.

"Don't you like money?"

"I may send you a bill when this thing is over."

I went inside. Willie Mackey was sitting in the front hall with Ronny on his knee. He was telling the boy about an old con he had known who had tried to swim ashore from Alcatraz.

I found Martha Crandall and her daughter in the front room. They were sitting side by side in the bay window, their pretty blonde heads close together.

An hour or so ago the big old house had been as quiet as a hermitage. Now it seemed more like a family service agency. I was hoping that the whole thing wouldn't blow up in my face.

Deciding to risk it, I caught Martha Crandall's eye and beckoned her over to my side of the room.

"What is it?" she said impatiently, with a backward look at Susan. "I hate to leave her."

"You may have to, though."

She looked at me in dismay. "You mean you're going to put her away?"

"You may decide to, temporarily. She's got a lot on her mind, and she's suicidal."

The woman's shoulders made a heavy movement which was meant to be lighter. "That was just a grandstand play, she says so herself."

"So are a lot of successful suicides. Nobody knows where the grandstanding leaves off and the thing turns dead serious. Anyone who even threatens suicide needs counseling."

"That's what I'm trying to give her. Counseling."

"I mean professional counseling, from a psychiatrist. I've discussed this with your husband, and he says he'll take her to the Medical Center tomorrow. But you're the one who will have to carry the ball and follow through. It might be a good idea if you talked to the shrinks together."

She seemed appalled. "Am I such a rotten mother?"

"I didn't say that. But I don't think you've ever leveled with her, have you?"

"What about?"

"Your own bad times."

"I couldn't," she said with vehemence.

"Why not?"

"I'd be ashamed."

"Let her know you're human, anyway."

"I am that," she said. "All right, I'll do it."

"Is that a promise?"

"Sure it is. I love her, you know. Susie's my little girl. Not so little any more, either."

She turned back toward her daughter, but I stopped her and led her into the furthest corner of the room. Ellen's canvases hung along the wall like imperfectly remembered hallucinations.

She said: "What else do you want from me?"

"A few words of truth. I want to know what happened fifteen years ago, when Albert Sweetner visited the Yucca Tree."

She looked at me as if I'd slapped her. "This is a lousy time to bring that up."

"It's the only time we have. I understand you left your husband. What happened after that?"

The woman pursed her lips and narrowed her eyes. "Has Lester been talking?"

"Some. But not enough. He knows you walked out on him and took Susan along. And he knows you came back eventually. But he doesn't know what happened in between."

"Nothing happened. I thought it through and changed my mind, that's all. Anyway, this is strictly my private business."

"Maybe it would be if you'd kept it strictly private. But other people got mixed up in it. One of them was Susan, and she was old enough to remember."

Martha Crandall looked at her daughter with guilty curiosity. The girl said:

"You're talking about me, aren't you? It isn't very nice."

Her tone was quite impersonal and remote. She sat very still in the embrasure like an actress forbidden to step out through the proscenium into the welter of reality. Her mother shook her head at her, and then at me.

"I can't take this. And I don't have to," she said.

"What do you propose to do? Let Susan work it out for herself without any help from you?"

Martha hung her head like a naughty child. "Nobody ever helped me."

"Maybe I can help you, Mrs. Crandall. Al Sweetner told your husband that he was Susan's father. But I don't think he could have been. Not even an Al Sweetner would force his own daughter."

"Who told you he did that?"

"Susan told me."

"Do we have to talk about these things?" Her look was reproachful, as if I'd made them real by naming them.

"If Susan could, we can."

"When did you talk to her?"

"Between the bridge and here."

"You had no right—"

"The hell I didn't. She's been under terrible pressure. She had to let it out some way."

"Pressure from what?"

"Too many deaths," I said. "Too many memories."

Her eyes widened like lenses, as if they were trying to pick up faint light from the past. But all I could see in their centers was my own head reflected in miniature, twice.

"What did Susan tell you?" she said.

"Not very much. She really didn't intend to tell me anything, but the memories forced their way out. Wasn't she

with you in the Mountain House one night in the summer
of 1955?"

"I don't know what night you're talking about."

"The night Leo Broadhurst was shot."

Her fringed eyelids came down over her eyes. She swayed
a little, as if the memory of the shot had wounded her. I
held her upright, and felt the warmth of her living flesh on
my hands.

"Does Susan remember? How could she? She was only
three."

"She remembers enough. Too much. Was Broadhurst
killed?"

"I don't know. I ran away and left him in the cabin. I was
drunk, and I couldn't get his car to start. But it was gone in
the morning, and so was he."

"What kind of a car was it?"

"A Porsche. A little red Porsche. It wouldn't start, so I
ran away on foot. I forgot all about Susan. I don't even
remember where I went." She moved away from my hands
as if they carried the contagion of that night. "What happened to Susie?"

"Didn't you go back for her?"

"I did in the morning. I found her asleep in the loft. How
could she remember the shooting if she was asleep in the
loft?"

"She was awake when it happened, and in the room. She
didn't make it up."

"Is Leo dead?"

"I think so."

Martha looked at her daughter, and I turned to look. The
girl was watching us intently, less like an actress now than a
spectator. Our voices were too low for her to hear, but she
seemed to know what we were talking about.

"Does she remember who shot him?" her mother said.

"No. Do you?"

"I never saw who it was. Leo and I were making love, and I was drunk—"

"Didn't you hear the shot?"

"I guess I did, but I didn't believe it. You know? I didn't know he was hurt until I tasted the blood on his face." Her tongue moved over her lips. "God, what you're dragging out of me. I thought I'd blanked out on that night. It was the worst night of my life, and I thought that it was going to be the best. We were going to go away, all three of us, and start a new life together in Hawaii. Leo bought the tickets that same day."

"Was he Susan's father?"

"I think so. I've always thought so. That's why I went back to him when Lester threw me out. He was the first man I ever let touch me."

"It wasn't Al Sweetner? Or Fritz Snow?"

She shook her head rather fiercely. "I was already pregnant when I went to L.A. with them. That was why I went."

"And you let them take the rap."

"Leo had a lot to lose. What did they have to lose?"

"Their whole lives."

She lifted her hands as though to examine them for dirt or scars. A darkness and sadness had risen in her eyes. She ducked her head and hid her face in her hands.

Susan stepped out of her niche as if a spell had broken, and came toward us. Her face was unnaturally bright, like a radiant substance with a short half-life.

"You're making my mother cry."

"It won't do her any harm. She's human like the rest of us." The girl looked at the woman in faint surprise.

〰〰〰〰〰〰〰〰〰〰〰〰

XXX

〰〰〰〰〰〰〰〰〰〰〰〰

I left them together and went out into the hallway. The little boy was lolling on Willie's knee, stunned by fatigue.

"He's just about out for the count," Willie said. "And I've got a new bride waiting for me eagerly in San Francisco."

"Give me a few more minutes. Where's Miss Storm?"

"In there with her son." He pointed his thumb at the closed door of the small room under the stairs. "He's a hardhead, which is why I'm sitting here."

"What did he do?"

"Tried to fight Harold one-handed. Harold used to play football for the Forty-Niners."

"Where's Harold now?"

"Outside watching the house, in case anybody else shows up." He made a dour face, and gave the boy a gentle poke in the ribs. "Perish the thought, eh, sleepyhead?"

I knocked on the door of the small room. Ellen told me to come in.

She was in the swivel chair. Her son was sitting on the floor beside the safe as if it was a stove that gave no heat. His face was so pale and wretched that it made his red hair and beard seem pasted on. His mouth had a nervous twitch, as if he was biting something, or being bitten.

"This is Mr. Archer," Ellen said.

With some idea of showing friendly feeling, I asked him how his arm was. He spat on the floor in my direction.

"It's broken," Ellen said. "He got it set at a clinic in the Haight-Ashbury. They asked him to check back tomorrow—"

The boy cut off her sentence with a slashing movement of his good arm. "Don't tell him anything. He was the one that made me lose *Ariadne.*"

"Sure I did. Also I broke your arm by hitting you on the gun-butt with my head."

"I should have shot you."

He was a hardhead, as Willie said. I couldn't tell how much of the hardness was his own and how much was induced by physical and mental pain.

"He's in trouble—I guess you know that," I said to Ellen.

"Do you mean you have to arrest him?"

"That isn't my job. And it isn't my job to decide what to do with him. I'm not his father."

"But you're working for him, aren't you?" Jerry said. "If you think you're going to drag me back to Slobville—"

I turned on him: "Slobville can live without you. If you think the populace is waiting on the docks for your return, think again."

That silenced him, but I felt a little cheap about talking him down, and a little dishonest. My mind threw up an image of Roger Armistead on the marina float, looking out to sea.

"He won't go back to his father," Ellen said. "I've been wondering if he couldn't stay with me, at least for the present. I can arrange to get him the care he needs."

"Do you think you can handle him?"

"I can give him shelter, anyway. I've given shelter to other troubled people." Her face was open, willing without being eager.

"I don't know what the law will have to say."

"How does he stand with the law?"

"It depends on his record, if any."

We both looked down at Jerry. He sat motionless, except for his twitch, like a sudden old man in the corner.

"Have you ever been arrested?" I said.

"No. I can hardly wait."

"It isn't funny. If the authorities wanted to throw the book at you, they could be rough. Taking the yacht could be grand larceny. Taking the boy could be child stealing or kidnaping or contributing to the delinquency of a minor."

Jerry looked up in dismay. "What do you think I did to him? I was trying to save his life."

"You almost lost it for him."

Jerry got his feet under him and rose awkwardly, grimacing with pain. "You don't have to tell me that. I know I wrecked the yacht. But I didn't steal her. Mr. Armistead left me in charge of her. Ask him."

"You better talk to him yourself. But not tonight." I said to his mother: "Why don't you put him to bed?"

He didn't argue. She walked him out with her arm around his shoulders. There was a look of acceptance on her face, almost as if she had lived too long without external trouble.

I knew it wasn't a solution. Ellen was far gone in solitude, and he was too old to need a mother, really. He had to live out his time of trouble, as she had. And there was no assurance that he would. He belonged to a generation whose elders had been poisoned, like the pelicans, with a kind of moral DDT that damaged the lives of their young.

But I had no more time to worry about Jerry. I pulled the swivel chair around to face the phone and dialed Mrs. Broadhurst's ranch in Santa Teresa. Jean answered immediately, in a voice that hung almost toneless between expectation and despair:

"This is the Broadhurst residence."

"Archer speaking. I have your boy Ronny. He's all right."

She didn't answer right away. Through the faint buzz and clamor on the line I could hear her breathing, as if she was the only life in an electronic universe.

"Where are you, Mr. Archer?"

"Sausalito. Ronny's safe and in good condition."

"Yes, I heard you." Another silence. She said in a rather grudging tone: "What about the girl?"

"I have her safe. She isn't in very good emotional shape."

"I wouldn't have thought so."

"But she didn't really intend to steal your son. She was running away from the man who killed your husband."

"All the way to Sausalito?" she said incredulously.

"Yes."

"Who was the man?"

"A bearded type with shoulder-length black hair, wearing dark wraparound glasses. Does that suggest anyone to you?"

"There are plenty of longhairs in Northridge. Here, too, for that matter. I haven't had many contacts with them in the last few years. I don't know who it would be."

"He may be one of the crazies, a random killer. I'm going to make a suggestion which I want you to act on as soon as I hang up. Call the sheriff and ask him to send a man out. Insist on having him stay there. If he won't, take a taxi downtown and check into a good hotel."

"But you told me to stay here in this house."

"That isn't necessary any more. I've got your boy. I'll bring him home tomorrow."

"Could I possibly speak to him tonight? I just want to hear his voice."

I opened the door and called the boy. He slid off Willie's knee and came running, taking the receiver in both hands.

"Is that you, Mommy? . . . The boat got sunk, but I came

in on a surfboard. . . . I'm not cold. Mrs. Rawlins gave me her little boy's clothes, and a hamburger. Susie bought me another hamburger in San Francisco. . . . Susie? She's all right, I guess. She wanted to jump off the Golden Gate Bridge. But we talked her out of it."

He listened for a moment, his face growing sober and concerned, then handed me the receiver as if it was hot. "Mommy's sad."

I said to her: "Are you all right?"

She answered in an emotion-clogged voice: "I'm fine. And I'm deeply grateful. When will I see you and Ronny?"

"About noon tomorrow, I'd say. We both need some rest before we drive south."

A short while later, after the others had left, Ellen and I put Ronny to bed in a room which she said had been hers when she was a child. An old toy phone was standing on the table beside the cot. As if to demonstrate that he never got tired, the boy picked it up and spoke into it distinctly:

"Calling Space Control. Calling Space Control. Do you hear me? Do you hear me?"

We closed the door on his fantasy and faced each other in the upstairs hall. The hanging yellow electric light, the stains of old rainstorms on the walls and ceiling, and the shadows that imitated them seemed to generate other fantasies. The rest of the world was cut off and far away. I felt shipwrecked on the dim shores of the past.

"How's Jerry?"

"He's worried about what Armistead will do to him. But he quieted down. I gave him a back rub and a sleeping pill."

"I'll talk to Armistead when I get the chance."

"I was hoping you would. Jerry's pretty tense about it. He feels terribly guilty."

"What did you do with the rest of the sleeping pills?"

"I have them."

She touched the place between her breasts. She must have seen my eyes rest there and travel down her body. Both of us moved, so that her body was resting rather sleepily against mine. I felt her hand moving on my back, giving me a kind of sample back rub.

"I don't have a bed made up for you. You can sleep with me if you like."

"Thanks, but it wouldn't be a good idea. You do all your living on canvas, remember?"

"I have a large unused canvas that I've been saving," she said rather obscurely. "What are you afraid of, Archer?"

It was hard to say. I liked the woman. I almost trusted her. But I was already working deep in her life. I didn't want to buy a piece of it or commit myself to her until I knew what the consequences would be.

Instead of answering her in words, I kissed her and disengaged myself.

She looked more rejected than deprived. "I don't sleep with many men, in case you're wondering. Leo was the only real lover I ever had."

She was quiet for a while. Then she said: "I gave you a false impression earlier. I was forgetting, lying to myself. Whatever I had with Leo was real—just about the realest thing in my life." Her eyes lit up with the memory as they hadn't lit for me. "I was in love with him. And he loved me while it lasted. I didn't believe that he would ever stop. But it ended, quite suddenly."

Her eyes closed, and opened again with a changed expression, of wary loss. She leaned on the watermarked wall. The night was running down like a transplanted heart.

"There's something I want to tell you," I said. "I don't know if I should."

"Is it something painful?"

229

"Yes. Maybe not immediately painful."

"About Leo?"

"I think he's dead."

Her eyes didn't waver. Only a kind of shadow crossed her face, as if the hanging light above her head had moved.

"How long dead?"

"The whole fifteen years."

"And that's why he never came to join me?"

"I think so." It was partly true, anyway. As for the other part of the truth, I was trying to decide whether to bring up Martha Crandall. "Unless my witnesses are hallucinating, somebody shot Leo and buried him."

"Where?"

"Near the Mountain House. Do you have any idea who might have killed him?"

"No." After a moment's hesitation, she said: "It wasn't I."

I waited for her to go on. She said finally:

"You mentioned witnesses. Who are they?"

"Martha Crandall and her daughter."

"Did he go back to Martha?"

She raised one hand to her mouth, as if she had made a damaging admission. On the heels of it, I said bluntly:

"He was in bed with Martha when he was shot. Apparently *she* was the one who came back to *him*. Her husband threw her out." I hesitated. "You knew about their earlier affair?"

"Did I not. I first got to know Leo through it. Martha came to me when she got into trouble." She was silent for a moment, then said with some irony: "I interposed my body between them."

Nearly everything had been said. But we seemed to be held together by a feeling, impersonal but almost as strong as a friendship or a passion, that there was still more to say.

The past was unwinding and rewinding like yarn which the two of us held between us.

"What about Elizabeth Broadhurst?" I said. "How did a man like Leo happen to marry a woman like Elizabeth?"

"The war brought them together. He was stationed at a military base near Santa Teresa, and she was active in the USO. She was a handsome woman when she was young. Socially prominent. Wealthy. She had all the obvious qualifications." For the first time Ellen's face was pulled to one side by malice. "But she was a failure as a wife."

"How do you know?"

"Leo told me all about their marriage, such as it was. She was a frozen woman, a daddy's girl."

"The frozen ones sometimes explode."

"I know they do."

I said carefully: "Do you think she shot Leo?"

"It's possible. She threatened to. It's one reason I left Santa Teresa and tried to take Leo with me. I was afraid of Elizabeth."

"That doesn't prove she's a murderer."

"I know that. But I'm not just being subjective. Jerry told me something as we were talking just now." Her voice wisped off, and so did her attention, as if she was listening to an internal voice.

"What did Jerry tell you?"

"He was telling me why he couldn't go back to Brian—to his father. Elizabeth Broadhurst came to their house one night this summer to talk to Brian. There was more than just talk involved. She was crying and yelling, and Jerry couldn't help overhearing everything. Brian had been extorting money from her. And not only money. He'd forced her into some kind of a real estate partnership in which she put up the land and he put up very little or nothing."

"How could he force her into it?"

"That's the question," she said.

Ellen went to bed alone. I got the sleeping bag out of the trunk of my car and slept across the door of Ronny's room.

The old house creaked like a ship sailing through the dangerous world. I dreamed I was rounding the Horn.

ᴐᴖᴖᴖᴖᴖᴖᴖᴖᴖᴖᴖᴖᴐ

XXXI

ᴐᴖᴖᴖᴖᴖᴖᴖᴖᴖᴖᴖᴖᴖᴐ

It was raining in Palo Alto, where Ronny and I had breakfast. It was raining in Gilroy and King City, and in Petroleum City it looked like rain.

I stopped at the Yucca Tree Inn to check on the Crandalls. Joy Rawlins was back on the desk. She told me Lester Crandall had rehired her that morning before he took off with his family for Los Angeles.

"Did you see Susan?" I asked her.

"Yeah. She's calmed down quite a bit. All three of them seemed to be making more sense for a change."

Before I left the Inn, I called the Santa Teresa office of the Forest Service. Kelsey wasn't there, but I left a message for him: to meet me at noon, if possible, at Mrs. Broadhurst's house. Then Ronny and I went back on the freeway for the final leg of our journey.

Using the buckle of a seat-belt as a microphone, the boy kept Space Control informed of our progress. Once he said into his imaginary mike:

"Daddy. This is Ronny. Do you hear me?"

We were just a few miles north of Santa Teresa, in what must have been familiar territory to him. He dropped the buckle and turned in the seat to speak to me directly:

"Is Daddy coming back?"

"No. He isn't."

"You mean he's dead, don't you?"

"Yes."

"Did the bogy man kill him?"

"I'm afraid he did." This was the first real evidence I'd had from another witness that the man in Susan's story of the murder was neither invention nor fantasy. "Did you get a good look at him, Ronny?"

"Pretty good."

"What did he look like?"

"A bogy man." His voice was hushed and earnest. "He had long black hair and a long black beard."

"How was he dressed?"

"All in black. He had black slacks and a black top, and he was wearing black glasses."

His voice was singsong, and it made me distrust his accuracy. "Was it anyone you knew?"

He seemed appalled by the idea. "No. I didn't know him. He was the wrong size."

"What do you mean by that?"

"He wasn't the same size as anybody I know."

"The same size as who?"

"Nobody," he said obscurely.

"Was he large or small?"

"Small, I think. I can't help it if I didn't know him."

The boy was showing signs of strain, and I dropped my questioning of him. But he had a final question to ask me:

"Is Mommy okay?"

"She's okay. You talked to her on the phone last night, remember?"

"I remember. But I thought maybe it was taped."

"It was for real."

"That's good." He fell against me and went to sleep.

He was still sleeping when we drove up the canyon to his grandmother's house. His mother was waiting on the veranda steps. She ran across the driveway and opened the car door and lifted him out.

She held him until he struggled to be free. Then she set him down and gave me both her hands:

"I'll never be able to thank you."

"Don't try. It worked out luckily for all of us. Except Stanley."

"Yes. Poor Stanley." There was a puzzled cleft, like a dry knife-cut, between her eyebrows. "What became of the blond girl?"

"Susan is with her parents. They're going to get her psychiatric care."

"And Jerry Kilpatrick? His father's been calling me."

"He's staying with his mother in Sausalito for the present."

"You mean you didn't have either of them arrested?"

"No I didn't."

"But I thought they were kidnapers."

"So did I, at one point. I was wrong. They're a pair of alienated adolescents. They seem to have thought they were rescuing Ronny from the adult world. To a certain extent it was true. The girl saw your husband murdered yesterday. Fifteen years ago, when she was younger than Ronny, she witnessed another murder. If she reacted pretty wildly to this one, you can hardly blame her."

The cleft between Jean's penciled brows deepened. "Has there been another murder?"

"It appears so. Your husband's father—Leo—didn't run off with a woman after all. Apparently he was killed in the Mountain House and buried nearby. It's what your husband and the girl were digging for yesterday."

Jean looked at me in confusion. Perhaps she understood my words, but they laid too great a load on her stretched emotions. She looked around her, saw that Ronny had disappeared, and began to call his name quite frantically.

He came out of the house. "Where's Grandma Nell?"

"She isn't here," Jean said. "She's in the hospital."

"Is she dead too?"

"Hush. Of course not. Dr. Jerome says she'll be coming home tomorrow or the next day."

"How is your mother-in-law?" I said to her.

"She's going to be all right. Her EKG was virtually normal this morning, and so was her conversation. It gave her a tremendous lift when I told her you were on your way with Ronny. If you have the time, I know she'd love to have you drop in and see her."

"Is she allowed visitors?"

"Yes."

"I may do that."

The three of us went inside. While Ronny inspected the stuffed bird collection, his mother filled me in on the past twenty-four hours. They had been mostly waiting. She had phoned the sheriff's office, as I urged her to, but they had been unable to give her any protection. Brian Kilpatrick had expressed a willingness to come over. She told him it wasn't necessary.

"Forget about Kilpatrick."

She gave me a slow look. "It wasn't exactly what you think. He intended to bring his fiancee along."

"Forget about her, too. What you need is a guard."

"I have you."

235

"But I won't be staying. I wish I could persuade you to leave town."

"I can't. Grandma Nell is depending on me."

"So is Ronny. You may have to make a choice."

"You seriously think he's still in danger?"

"I have to think so. He saw the man who murdered your husband."

"Could he describe him?"

"Not really. He had a beard and a wig that were probably false. But I got the impression that it might just possibly be someone that Ronny knows. I wouldn't press him on the subject. But if he does any spontaneous talking keep a record, will you? Every word if you can."

"I will."

She looked across the room at her son as if his round skull contained the secret meaning of her life. He said with the light of discovery on his face:

"There's been a fire around here. I can see it and I can smell it. Who started the fire?"

"That's what we're trying to find out." I turned to his mother. "I want you to think about getting out of here before dark."

"Nothing happened last night."

"Your son wasn't here last night. You'll both be safer in the Wallers' apartment in Los Angeles. Just say the word, and I'll drive you—"

She cut me short: "I'll think about it." Then she softened her answer. "I'm really very grateful for the offer. Only it's hard for me to think right now. I only know I can't go back to Northridge."

I heard the rising mutter of a car approaching the house and went outside. It was Kelsey, driving a Forest Service station wagon. He climbed out and gave me a semiofficial handshake. His suit was rumpled, and his eyes had a slight glare in them.

"I got your message, Archer. What's on your mind?"

"There's quite a lot to tell you. First, I'd like to know what you got from your witness yesterday. The coed who saw the bearded man driving the car."

"That was all she saw," Kelsey said with some disappointment. "All she could give me was a general description."

"What about the car?"

"It was an older car. She couldn't tell the make. She thought it had a California license, but she wasn't absolutely sure. I'm going to take another crack at her today. Shipstad of the LAPD asked me to."

"You got in touch with Arnie?"

"I called him this morning. He's pretty well discarded the idea that the wig and the beard belonged to Albert Sweetner. They didn't fit him at all well. Shipstad is trying to trace them through wig stores and cosmetic companies. But it's a big job and it may take a while. It would help if we could get a better description of the man my witness saw."

"He was fairly small," I said, "if I can believe *my* witness. He was wearing black slacks, some kind of black shirt or sweater, and dark glasses. And there's no doubt he murdered Stanley Broadhurst." I filled him in on what I had learned in the last twenty-four hours. "Can we get hold of a bulldozer and a man to operate it?"

"I believe we left one on the campus, in case the fire came back. I can run it myself if it's still there."

"Do you think the fire will come back?"

"Not unless the wind plays us false. We set a successful backfire above Buckhorn Meadow this morning. We should have it under control in another twenty-four hours—maybe sooner if we get the rain that's predicted." He glanced at the moving sky. "I'm hoping for just enough rain to discourage Rattlesnake but not enough to bring the mountain down on us."

Kelsey asked me to ride with him in the station wagon. In order to keep my freedom of movement I said that I would follow along in my car.

We drove out through the scorched mouth of the canyon and up into the foothills. The campus playing field, which had been swarming with men and machines the day before, was almost deserted. A couple of maintenance men were picking up bottles and scraps of paper and replacing turf.

A tractor equipped with an earth-moving blade was standing in the lot behind the bleachers. While Kelsey was getting it started, I climbed to the top of the stands and looked around.

Whitecaps stippled the surface of the ocean. Above the coastline to the southeast, smoke hung like early twilight in the sky. At the other extreme of vision, storm clouds were moving down from the northwest, trailing black rain along the coastal mountains. It looked like a day of change.

Kelsey rode the tractor down the hillside trail. I followed along in his dust, carrying a spade I had borrowed from the maintenance men.

For twenty or thirty minutes I leaned on a sycamore trunk and watched the tractor push dirt in a slow back-and-forth rhythm. When it got about as deep into the earth as a man is tall, its leading edge jarred against metal and Kelsey nearly pitched head first from his seat.

He backed out of the gradual hole he had made and let me climb down into it. In a few minutes I had spaded clear enough of the metallic obstruction to see that it was a dark red car top blotched with the lighter red of rust and shaped like a Porsche roof.

I cleared the left front window and smashed it with the spade. The odor of corruption came out, dry and thin and shocking. In the hollow of the car's body something wrapped in a rotting blanket lay on the front seat.

I stretched head down in the dirt and peered in at the dead man. The flesh was always the first to go, and then the hair, and then the bones, and finally the teeth. Leo Broadhurst was all bones and teeth.

XXXII

I left Kelsey widening and deepening the hole around the buried car and phoned the sheriff-coroner's office from the college. Then I drove down the hill and paid another visit to Fritz Snow's house.

Somewhat to my surprise, Fritz answered the door himself. He was dressed in an old brown cardigan and slacks, with worn sneakers on his feet. His shoulders were bowed and his eyes bleared as if the weekend had lasted a generation and aged him by that much.

He blocked my entrance with his soft reluctant body. "I'm not supposed to let anybody in."

"You wanted to talk to me yesterday."

"Did I?" He seemed to be trying to remember. "Mother will slay me if I do."

"I doubt that, Fritz. The secret's out anyway. We just dug up Leo Broadhurst."

His heavy gaze came up to my face. He seemed to be trying to read his future in my eyes. I could read it in his: a future of fear and confusion and trouble, resembling his past.

"May I come in for a minute?"

"I guess so."

He let me in and closed the door behind me. He was breathing audibly, as if the action had used up most of his strength.

"You told me yesterday that you buried Mr. Broadhurst. I thought you meant Stanley. But you meant his father Leo, didn't you?"

"Yessir." He looked around the sparse room as if his mother might have bugged it. "I did a terrible thing. Now I've got to suffer for it."

"Did you kill Leo Broadhurst?"

"No sir. All I did, I buried him with my 'dozer when he was already dead."

"Who put you up to it?"

"Albert Sweetner did."

He nodded in confirmation of his own statement, then looked at me to see if I believed it. I neither believed nor disbelieved it.

"Albert Sweetner made me do it," he said.

"How could Albert make you do it?"

"I was ascared of him."

"You must have had more of a reason than that."

Fritz shook his head. "I didn't want to bury him. I got so nervous I couldn't run the machine. Albert tried to take it back to the compound. He ran it in the ditch off Rattlesnake Road, and they caught him with it and sent him back to prison."

"But you got off scot-free?"

"I did that time except that I got fired and put in the nursing home. They never found out about Mr. Broadhurst."

"Does your mother know what you and Albert did?"

"I guess she does. I told her."

"When did you tell her?"

He considered the question. "Yesterday, I guess it was."

"Before I was here, or after?"

"I don't remember." Fritz was showing signs of moral strain. "You keep coming back and back. And my memory keeps jumping around on me. I keep remembering when Digger got my daddy."

"When Digger got him?"

"That's right, when they buried him out at the cemetery. I could hear the dirt plunking down on the coffin." Tears formed on his face as if it was deliquescent, drawing moisture from the air.

"Did you tell your mother before I was here, or after?"

"After, I think it was. *After* you were here. She said if I told another soul they'd send me straight off to prison." He lowered his tangled head and gave me an up-from-under look. "Will they send me to prison now?"

"I don't know, Fritz. Are you sure that you and Albert didn't kill him?"

The idea seemed to shock him. "Why would we do a thing like that?"

I could think of several reasons. Leo Broadhurst had been lucky, and they had not. He had married the richest woman around. He had tumbled the prettiest girl, and got her with child, and Albert and Fritz had taken the rap for it.

Fritz was alarmed by my silence. "I swear I didn't kill him. I swear it on the Bible." There was an actual Bible on the table, and he rested his palm on the black cloth cover. "See, I swear it on the Bible. I never killed anybody in my life. I don't even like to trap a gopher. I hate to step on a snail. They've all got feelings!"

He was weeping actively again, possibly over the deaths

of snails and the agonies of gophers. Above the watery noises he was making I heard a car in the street and looked out through the front window. An old white Rambler pulled up at the curb behind my car. Mrs. Snow got out with a heavy paper bag in her arms. She was wearing a raincoat over slacks.

I went outside, closing the door on Fritz. His mother stopped abruptly when she saw me.

"What do you think you're doing?"

"I had a talk with your son."

"Can't I leave the house without you persecuting him?"

"That's hardly the case. Fritz told me he buried Leo Broadhurst's body. I understand he told you, too, so we needn't argue about it."

"That's nonsense, he's talking nonsense."

"I don't think so," I said. "We dug Leo up this afternoon. It hasn't been established yet, but I think that he's been dead for fifteen years."

"Frederick knew all this and didn't tell me?"

"He told you yesterday, didn't he?"

She bit her lip. "He told me some kind of a story. I thought he was making it up out of whole cloth." Her face brightened alarmingly. "Maybe he *is* making it up. His head's always full of stories."

"He didn't invent the dead man, Mrs. Snow."

"Are you *sure* it's Captain Broadhurst?"

"Reasonably sure. The body was in his red Porsche."

"Where did you find it?"

"Almost directly under the place where Stanley was buried. Stanley was trying to uncover his father when he was killed. Whoever killed him probably shot his father as well."

"And you blame Frederick?"

"I wouldn't go that far. But if he buried the captain, as he says, he's an accessory."

"Does that mean he'll go to prison?"

"He could."

She was appalled. Her thin face was stretched taut across her skull. It was like a foreglimpse of her mortality, and it made me realize how deeply involved she was with her son's fate.

She stood in silence for a minute, glaring up and down the street as if to dare the neighbors to pity her. There was no one in sight except for a few brown children too young to care.

It was early afternoon, but the day had darkened. I looked up at the sky. Black clouds were moving across it like a sliding lid. Under them the town looked bright and strange. A little rain had begun to fall on the sidewalk and on my head and on the woman's.

The heavy brown grocery bag was beginning to slip out of her arms. I took it from her and followed her inside. Fritz had retreated into the back, but both of us seemed to feel his amorphous presence virtually filling the house.

His mother carried her groceries into the kitchen. When she came back into the front room she noticed that the Bible on the table was slightly out of place. She pushed it back into the exact center before she turned to me:

"Frederick is crying his heart out in his room. You can't put him in prison. He wouldn't last six months. You know what they do in prison to helpless boys—the dreadful cruelties and the wickedness."

I knew, but I didn't want to dwell on it. "He isn't a boy." I remembered that Mrs. Broadhurst had said the same thing forty-eight hours ago.

243

"He might as well be," Mrs. Snow said. "Frederick has always been my little boy. I've done my best to protect him, but he gets led astray. He does what people tell him to do, and then he has to suffer for it. He suffers terribly. He almost died when they put him in forestry camp."

Her thin body was vibrating with feeling. It was hard to believe that body, breastless and almost hipless, had mothered the large soft boy-man in the bedroom.

"What do you want me to do with him, Mrs. Snow?"

"Leave him here with me. Let me look after him, like I always have."

"That will be up to the authorities."

"Do they know what he did?"

"Not yet."

"Do you have to tell them?"

"I'm afraid so. There's a murder involved."

"You're still talking about the murder of Captain Broadhurst?"

"Yes. That's the only one your son's mixed up in. I hope."

"I'm sure you're right." She looked at me intently. "I'm going to tell you something I've never told a living soul. You say Captain Broadhurst was shot?"

"Apparently he was."

"With a .22-caliber pistol?"

"We don't know yet. What were you going to tell me?"

"I think I know who shot him. I can't swear to it, but I think I know. If I can tell you, and it turns out to be right, can you make it easier for Frederick?"

"I can try."

"They'll listen to you." She nodded her head emphatically. "Will you promise to use your influence?"

"Yes. What information do you have?"

"It's more of a general picture. Ever since Stanley was killed on Saturday, the whole thing has been coming back to me. I was at the Broadhurst house that night, looking after Stanley. It was the same night that Frederick misused his tractor and lost his job. The whole thing fits together."

"Exactly what happened?"

"Give me a chance to tell you." She sat down in the platform rocker rather abruptly, as if the effort of memory had fatigued her. "The two of them, Captain Broadhurst and Mrs. Broadhurst, had a bad quarrel at dinner. I was in and out of the dining room. They didn't say much in my presence, but I gathered they were quarreling over a woman— a woman he had stashed in the Mountain House. I thought at first it was the Kilpatrick woman, because the name of Kilpatrick came up. But it turned out it was that Nickerson girl—Marty—and she had her little girl with her. Captain Broadhurst was planning to go away with her and the little girl. He had tickets on a steamship to Hawaii which he had just bought, and Mrs. Broadhurst found out."

"How did she find out?"

"Mr. Kilpatrick told her, according to what she said. The man in the travel agency was a friend of Mr. Kilpatrick's."

I felt a change behind my eyes, as if a physical adjustment had occurred there. My witnesses were beginning to chime with each other. Mrs. Snow went on with her story:

"It was a nasty quarrel, as I said. Mrs. Broadhurst went into the long history of his womanizing. He turned around and blamed it all on her. I won't tell you the names he called her. But he claimed she hadn't been a wife to him in ten years, and he got up and stomped out.

"Poor little Stanley was sick and shaking. He was having his dinner in the kitchen with me but he couldn't help hearing the quarrel, and he was old enough to know what it meant. He ran out and tried to stop his father, but Captain Broadhurst roared away in his sports car. Then his mother got ready to leave the house. Stanley wanted to go with her, but she wouldn't take him. She asked me to put him to bed, which I did. But after that I was busy in the kitchen, and he slipped out on me. I remember the shock it gave me when I went to check his bedroom and saw his empty pillow.

"I got another shock when I was going through the rooms looking for him. Mrs. Broadhurst's pistol case—the one her father left her—was sitting on top of the desk in the study. The box of shells was lying there open, and one of the pistols was gone." She looked up, unseeing, remembering. "I didn't know what to do, so I did nothing. I waited for her and Stanley to come home."

She sat in her platform rocker, resigned but somehow expectant, as if she was still waiting for that night to end. "They were gone for well over an hour. And when they came home, mother and son, they came home together. Their feet were wet from the night grass, and they were both white and scared-looking. Mrs. Broadhurst hustled Stanley off to bed and dismissed me. When I got home my own boy was missing from his bed. It was a bad night for mothers."

"And a bad night for sons," I said. "Do you think Stanley saw his father killed?"

"I don't know. I do know he heard the shot. He told me later his mother killed an owl—that was the explanation she gave Stanley. But I think that he suspected she shot his father. I think the suspicion kept growing on him, but he couldn't face up to it. He kept trying to prove that his daddy was alive, right up until the day of his own death."

"Did he ever discuss his father's death with you?"

"Not his death. We never mentioned death. But he sometimes asked me what I thought had happened to his father. And I used to tell him stories—that his father had gone to live in another country, like Australia, and maybe he would be coming back some day." Her eyes came up to my face, clear and intense. "What else could I do? I couldn't tell him what I suspected—that his mother shot his father."

"And your son buried him."

"I didn't *know* that at the time." But her voice hurried away from the point. "Even if I had, I wouldn't have told Stanley, or anyone else. A woman's got to look out for her own flesh and blood."

XXXIII

I left her and drove through pouring rain to the hospital. It was a four-story concrete building occupying a city block and surrounded by clinics and medical office buildings. A Pink Lady in the lobby told me that Mrs. Broadhurst was able to receive visitors and gave me the number of her room on the fourth floor.

Before going up I paid a visit to the pathology department. The office and lab were on the ground floor at the end of a sickly green corridor lined with heating pipes. A sign on the door said: "Authorized Personnel Only."

A stoic-faced man in a white smock greeted me with polite

disinterest. The name board on his desk said: "W. Silcox, M.D." He told me that the body of Leo Broadhurst hadn't arrived yet, but was expected shortly.

Behind his horn-rimmed spectacles, the doctor's eyes showed a certain professional eagerness. "I understand there's quite a lot of him left."

"Quite a lot. You should look for gunshot wounds, particularly in the head. I've talked to a couple of witnesses who think he was shot there. But my witnesses aren't entirely dependable. We need concrete evidence."

"That's what I'm here for. I tend to learn more from dead people than I do from living ones."

"Do you still have Stanley Broadhurst's body?"

"It's in the mortuary. Would you like to see it?"

"I have. I wanted to check with you on cause of death."

"Multiple stab wounds, with some kind of long knife."

"Front or back?"

"Front. In the abdomen. He was also struck at the base of the skull with the pickax."

Going up in the elevator to the fourth floor, I almost envied Silcox his unliving witnesses. They were past lying, past hurting and being hurt.

I checked in with the girl at the nurses' station. She said that Mrs. Broadhurst was feeling much better, but I should limit my visit to ten minutes or so.

I tapped on the door of Mrs. Broadhurst's private room and was bidden to come in. The room was full of flowers in and out of season—roses and carnations, exotic lilacs. A vase of yellow daffodils on the dresser had Brian Kilpatrick's card standing on edge against it.

Mrs. Broadhurst was sitting up in an armchair beside the streaming window. She had on a multicolored robe which seemed to reflect the flowers in the room, and she looked quite well. But there was a basic hopelessness about her eyes which tied my tongue for a moment.

She spoke first: "You're Mr. Archer, aren't you? I'm glad to see you—to have a chance to thank you."

I was taken by surprise. "What on earth for?"

"My grandson's safe return. His mother phoned me a short time ago. With my son—my son Stanley gone—Ronny is all I have left."

"He's a good boy, and he seems to be all right."

"Where did you find him? Jean wasn't quite clear about it."

I gave her a collapsed account of my weekend and said in conclusion: "Don't blame the girl too much. She saw your son killed, and it threw her. All she could think about was saving Ronny."

I remembered as I said it that Susan had witnessed two murders, fifteen years apart. And I asked myself: if Mrs. Broadhurst killed her husband, was it possible that she had also killed her son, or had him killed? I found I couldn't ask her. Filled with her fragile gratitude, and the flowers her friends had sent her, the room wouldn't let such questions be spoken aloud.

As witnesses often do, Mrs. Broadhurst provided an opening herself. "I'm afraid I don't really understand about the girl. What did you say her name was?"

"Susan Crandall."

"What was she doing on the mountain with my son and grandson?"

"I think she was trying to understand the past."

"I don't quite follow. I'm very stupid today." Her voice and eyes divided her impatience between herself and me.

"Susan had been there before," I said, "when she was a small child. She went there with her mother one night. Perhaps you remember her mother. Her maiden name was

Martha Nickerson, and I believe she used to work for you."

The displeasure in her voice and eyes deepened. "Who have you been talking to?"

"Quite a number of people. You're just about the last one on my list. I was hoping you could help me to reconstruct what happened at the Mountain House that night about fifteen years ago."

She shook her head, and stayed with her face half-averted. Profiled against the window, her head was like a classical medallion laid over the rain-blurred image of the city.

"I'm afraid that I can't help you. I wasn't there."

"Your husband was, Mrs. Broadhurst."

The cords in her neck pulled her head around. "How can you possibly know that?"

"He never left the place. He was shot and buried there. We dug him up this afternoon."

"I see." She didn't tell me what she saw, but it seemed to make her eyes grimmer and smaller. The bones in her face became more prominent as if in imitation of the dead man's. "It's over then."

"Not entirely."

"It is for me. You're telling me that both my men are dead —my husband and my son. You're telling me that I've lost everything I held dear."

She was struggling to assume a tragic role, but there was a doubleness in her which spoiled her resonance. Her words sounded exaggerated and hollow. I was reminded of the ambivalent words that she had written about her father, staggering across the yellow foolscap toward the edge of breakdown.

"I think you've known that your husband was dead and buried for fifteen years."

"That simply isn't true." But the doubleness persisted in her voice as if she was listening to herself read lines. "I warn you, if you make this accusation publicly—"

"We're very private, Mrs. Broadhurst. You don't have to put on a front with me. I know you quarreled with your husband that night and followed him up the mountain afterwards."

"How can you know that if it isn't so?" She was playing a game that guilty people play, questioning the questioner, trying to convert the truth into a shuttlecock that could be batted back and forth and eventually lost. "Where did you get this alleged information, anyway? From Susan Crandall?"

"Part of it."

"She's scarcely a reliable witness. I gather from what you've told me that she's emotionally disturbed. And she couldn't have been more than three or four at the time. The whole thing must be fantasy on her part."

"Three-year-olds have memories, and they can see and hear. I have pretty good evidence that she was in the Mountain House, and saw or heard the shot. Her story jibes with other things I know. It also helps to explain her emotional trouble."

"You admit that she's disturbed?"

"She has a hangup. Speaking of hangups, I wonder if Stanley didn't witness the shot, too."

"No! He couldn't have." She drew in her breath audibly, as if she was trying to suck back the words.

"How do you know if you weren't there?"

"I was at home with Stanley."

"I don't think so. I think he followed you up there and heard his father shot, and for the rest of his life he tried to forget it. Or prove that it was just a bad dream he had."

She had been talking like an advocate who doubted his

client's innocence. Now she gave up on it. "What do you want from me? Money? I've been bled white." She paused, and looked at me with despairing eyes. "Don't tell Jean I have nothing left. I'd never see Ronny again."

I thought she was wrong, but I didn't argue. "Who bled you, Mrs. Broadhurst?"

"I have no wish to discuss it."

I picked up Brian Kilpatrick's card from the dresser and let her see it. "If someone has been extorting money from you, you have a chance to stop it now."

"I said I don't want to discuss it. There's no one I can trust. There never has been since my father died."

"You want it to go on?"

She gave me a closed bitter look. "I don't want anything to go on. Not my life or anything. Certainly not this conversation. This inquisition."

"I'm not enjoying it much myself."

"Then go away. I can't stand any more."

She grasped the arms of the chair so that her knuckles whitened, and stood up. The action somehow forced me out of the room.

I wasn't ready to face the dead man right away. I found the door to the fire stairs and started down to the ground floor, taking my time about it. The concrete stairs with their gray steel railings, set in a windowless concrete stairwell, were like part of a prison structure, ugly and just about indestructible. I paused on a landing halfway down and tried to imagine Mrs. Broadhurst in prison.

When I returned the boy Ronny to his mother, I had really accomplished what I set out to do. The business left unfinished was bound to be painful and nasty. I had no overriding desire to pin her husband's murder on Mrs. Broadhurst.

The hot breath of vengeance was growing cold in my nostrils as I grew older. I had more concern for a kind of economy in life that would help to preserve the things that were worth preserving. No doubt Leo Broadhurst had been worth preserving—any man, or any woman, was—but he had been killed in anger long ago. I doubted that a jury in the present would find his widow guilty of anything worse than manslaughter.

As for the other homicides, it was unlikely that Mrs. Broadhurst had had a reason to kill her son or an opportunity to kill Albert Sweetner. I told myself I didn't care who killed them. But I cared. There was a winding symmetry in the case that like the stairs themselves took me down to the sickly green corridor where Dr. Silcox consulted his dead witnesses.

I went through the office and opened the steel-sheathed mortuary door. What was left of Leo Broadhurst lay under a bright light on a stainless steel table. Silcox was probing at the skull. Its fine curve was the only remaining sign that Leo had been a handsome man in his day.

Kelsey and Purvis, the deputy coroner, were standing in the penumbra against the wall. I moved past them toward the table.

"Was he shot?"

Silcox looked up from his work. "Yes. I found this."

He picked up a lead slug and displayed it on the palm of his hand. It looked like a misshapen .22 long.

"Where did it pierce the skull?"

"I'm not sure it did. All I can find is a minor external crease which hardly could have been fatal." With the bright point of his probe, he showed me the faint groove the bullet had made in the front of Broadhurst's skull.

"What killed him then?"

253

"This."

He showed me a discolored triangle which rang on the table when he dropped it. For a moment I thought it was an Indian arrowhead. Then I picked it up and saw that it was the broken-off tip of a butcher knife.

"It was lodged in the ribs," the doctor said. "Evidently the tip of the knife snapped off when the knife was pulled out."

"Was he stabbed from the back or the front?"

"The front, I'd say."

"Could a woman have done it?"

"I don't see why not. What do you think, Purvis?"

The young deputy detached himself from the shadows and stepped forward between me and Dr. Silcox. "I think we better talk it over in private." He turned to me. "I hate to be a spoilsport, Mr. Archer, but you've got no right in here. You saw the sign on the door: 'Authorized Personnel Only.' And you're not authorized."

I thought perhaps it was just a young man's officiousness. "I am if you authorize me."

"I can't do that."

"Who says so?"

"The sheriff-coroner gives me my orders."

"Who gives him *his* orders?"

The young man flushed. His face looked porous and purplish in the raw light. "You better get out of here, mister."

I looked past him at Kelsey, who seemed embarrassed. I said to both of them:

"Hell, I located this body."

"But you're not authorized personnel."

Purvis put his hand on the butt of his gun. I didn't know him well and didn't trust him not to shoot me. I left with anger and disappointment running hot and sour in my veins.

Kelsey followed me out into the corridor. "I'm sorry about this, Archer."

"You weren't a great deal of help."

His gray eyes flinched a little and then set hard, while his mouth continued to smile. "The word came down from on high about you. And the Forest Service makes me go by the book."

"What does the book say?"

"You know as well as I do. Where local law enforcement is involved, I'm instructed to respect their jurisdiction."

"What are they planning to do? Bury this case for another fifteen years?"

"Not if I can help it. But my main responsibility is the fire."

"The killings and the fire are tied together, and you know it."

"Don't tell me what I know."

He turned and went back into the room with the dead man and the authorized personnel.

ᢒᠮᢒᠮᢒᠮᢒᠮᢒᠮᢒᠮᢒᠮᢒᠮᢒᠮᢒᠮᢒᠮᢒ

XXXIV

ᢒᠮᢒᠮᢒᠮᢒᠮᢒᠮᢒᠮᢒᠮᢒᠮᢒᠮᢒᠮᢒᠮᢒ

When I went outside the rain was coming down harder than ever. Water was running in the street, washing the detritus of summer downhill toward the sea.

The nearer I got to the mountains, the more water there was. Driving up Mrs. Broadhurst's canyon was very much like making my way upstream in a shallow watercourse. Long before I reached the ranch house I could hear the roaring of the creek behind it.

Brian Kilpatrick's black car was standing in front of the house. An artificial-looking blond whom I didn't recognize at first was sitting in the front seat. When I approached the black car I saw that she was Kilpatrick's fiancée, as he called her.

"How are you feeling today?" I said.

She lowered the electric window and peered at me through the rain. "Do I know you?"

"We met Saturday night at Kilpatrick's place."

"Really? I must have been stoned." Her lips stretched in a smile which asked for my complicity. Behind it she seemed terribly uneasy.

"You were stoned. Also you were a brunette."

"I was wearing a wig. I change them to suit my mood. People tell me I'm very mercurial."

"I can see that. What kind of a mood are you in?"

"Frankly, I'm scared," she said. "I'm scared of all this water. And the mud is coming loose above Brian's house. He's got tons of it in his patio already. That's why I'm sitting here in this car. But I don't like it here much, either."

"What's Brian doing inside?"

"Business, he said."

"With Jean Broadhurst?"

"I guess that's her name. Some woman called him and he dashed right over here." She added as I turned toward the house: "Tell him to hurry, will you?"

I went in without knocking and closed the front door carefully behind me. The noise of the creek was humming through the house, covering the small sounds my movements made.

256

There was no one in the living room. A light shone from the open door of the study. When I went nearer I could hear Jean's voice:

"I don't like this. If Mrs. Broadhurst wants these things, she could have asked me for them."

Kilpatrick answered her in a throwaway tone: "I'm sure she didn't want to bother you."

"But I am bothered. What does she want in the hospital with business papers and guns?"

"I assume she wants to get things shipshape in case anything happens to her."

"She isn't planning to kill herself?" Jean's voice was thin and breathless.

"I sincerely hope not."

"Then why does she want the guns?"

"She didn't say. I'm simply trying to keep her happy. After all, she is my business partner."

"Still I don't think I should let you—"

"But she just called me."

"I think I'll call her back."

"I wouldn't do that."

His voice had a threat in it. There was the scrape of feet and a woman's gasp. I stepped into the doorway. Jean was sprawled on the black leather couch, white-faced and breathing hard. Kilpatrick was standing over her with the telephone receiver in his hands.

"Try someone your own size," I said.

He moved as if he was going to attack me. I wanted him to, and perhaps he saw that. The color drained from his face, so that the broken veins stood out like abrasions.

He offered me a shameful little smile which didn't change his reddened apprehensive eyes. "Jean and I had a little misunderstanding. Nothing serious."

She got up, smoothing her skirt. "I think it's serious. He pushed me down. He's taking some of my mother-in-law's things."

She indicated the black briefcase standing beside the desk. I picked it up.

"I want that," Kilpatrick said. "It belongs to me."

"You may get it back eventually."

He reached for it. I swung it away from his grasp. In the same movement I leaned my shoulder into him and walked him backward. He came up hard against the opposing wall and slouched there like a man hanging on a nail. I went over him for weapons, found none, and stepped back.

For a moment his face wore the look of terrible disappointment that I had surprised on it the day before. He was losing everything, and watching it go.

"I'm going to take this up with Sheriff Tremaine," he said.

"I think you should. He'll be interested in what you've been doing to Mrs. Broadhurst."

"I'm her best friend, if you want the truth. I've been looking after her interests for many years."

"She calls it bleeding her."

He seemed surprised. "Did she say that?"

"She used the word. Don't you like it?"

He was still against the wall. His reddish-brown hair was turning dark with sweat and falling over his high freckled forehead. He pushed it back with his fingers, carefully, as if a neat appearance might make all the difference.

"I'm disappointed in Elizabeth," he said. "I thought she had more sense. And more gratitude. But that's a woman for you."

He gave me a tentative look to see if we could get together on an anti-feminist platform.

"No gratitude," I said. "No gratitude to you for blackmailing her and cheating her out of her land. Women are terrible ingrates."

He couldn't stand the unfairness of my remarks. A bright bitterness entered his eyes and changed his mouth. "Anything I did was perfectly legal. That's more than you can say for her. While she was telling you lies about me, I don't suppose she mentioned what she did."

"What did she do?"

I shouldn't have asked the direct question. It reminded him to be discreet.

"I don't believe I'll answer that."

"Then I'll tell you. Mrs. Broadhurst shot her husband. You may have put her up to it. Certainly you had a hand in it."

"That's a lie."

"Didn't you tell her about Leo's freighter bookings to Hawaii? Wasn't that what sparked their final quarrel?"

His gaze came up to mine, then moved away sideways. "I thought he was planning to take my wife with him."

"Your wife had already left you."

"I was hoping she might come back to me."

"If you could find a cat's-paw to get rid of Leo?"

"I had no such intention," he said.

"Didn't you? You incited the Broadhursts' quarrel. You watched the Mountain House that night to see what came of the quarrel. You witnessed the shot, or heard the sound of it. And when it failed to kill Leo, you finished him off with a knife."

"I absolutely did not."

"Somebody did. And you were there on the spot. You haven't denied it."

"I deny it now. I didn't shoot him and I didn't knife him."

"Tell me what you did do."

"I was an innocent bystander, that's all."

I laughed in his face, though I wasn't feeling merry. I hated to see a man, even a man like Kilpatrick, go down the tubes. "Okay, innocent bystander. What happened then?"

"I think you know what happened. But I'm not going to say it. And if you're as smart as you think you are, you'll play along with me. Right now I want my briefcase."

"You'll have to take it away from me."

He looked at me as if he was considering it. But he was running short of desire and hope. The aura of success had deserted him, and he was looking more and more like a loser.

He turned and went as far as the front door before he answered me. Just before he slammed it behind him, he called back:

"I'm going to have you run out of town."

Jean came up to me, moving quietly with one hand out as if darkness had set in and the place was unfamiliar. "Are those things true?"

"What things?"

"The things that you were saying about Elizabeth."

"I'm afraid they are."

She took hold of my arm and let me feel her weight. "I can't stand much more. How long is this going to go on?"

"I don't think there is much more. Where's Ronny?"

"He's asleep. He wanted a nap."

"Get him up and dressed. I'm going to drive you to Los Angeles."

"Now?"

"The sooner the better."

"But why?"

I had a number of reasons. I didn't want to go into the main one, which was that I didn't know what Kilpatrick might do next. I remembered the gun in his game room, and his apparent willingness to use it.

I took Jean to the big corner window and showed her what had happened to the creek. It had become a turbulent dark river, large enough to float fallen trees. Several of them had formed a natural dam which was backing up the water behind the house.

I could hear boulders rolling down the creekbed in the upper canyon. They made noises like bowling balls in an alley.

"The house may go this time," I said.

"That isn't the reason you want to take us south."

"It's one reason. You and Ronny will be safer there. And I have some things to attend to. I'm supposed to report to Captain Shipstad of the LAPD. There are certain advantages in working with him instead of the local law."

Those advantages had become clearer in the last hour, and I decided to call Arnie now. I went into the study and dialed his office number.

His voice was cool and distant: "I expected you to get in touch with me before now."

"Sorry. I had to go to Sausalito."

"I hope you had a nice weekend," he said in a flat Scandinavian tone.

"It wasn't so nice. I turned up another murder. An old one." I gave him the facts of Leo Broadhurst's death.

"Let me get this straight," he said. "You're telling me that Broadhurst was killed by his wife?"

"She shot him, but the shot may not have killed him. He had a broken knife blade in his ribs. Of course she could have put the knife in him."

"Could she have killed Albert Sweetner?"

"I don't see how. Mrs. Broadhurst was in the Santa Teresa

hospital Saturday night. It had to be someone else who did the Northridge killing."

"Who do you have in mind?"

I paused for a moment to organize my thoughts, and Arnie spoke impatiently: "You there, Lew?"

"I'm here. There are three main suspects. Number one is a local real estate man named Brian Kilpatrick. He knew that Elizabeth Broadhurst shot her husband, and I think she's been paying him off ever since. Which gives him a reason for killing Stanley Broadhurst and Albert Sweetner."

"What reason?"

"He had a large financial interest in keeping the original murder quiet."

"Blackmail?"

"Call it disguised blackmail. But it's still possible he finished off Leo Broadhurst himself. If so, he had an even stronger reason for silencing the other two. Albert Sweetner knew where Leo was buried. Stanley Broadhurst was trying to dig him up."

"But why would Kilpatrick want to knife Leo Broadhurst?"

"Broadhurst broke up his marriage. Also, there was money in it for him, as I said."

"Describe him, will you, Lew?"

"Kilpatrick's about forty-five, over six feet, around two hundred pounds. Blue eyes, wavy red hair getting thin on top. Broken veins in the nose and face." I paused. "Was he seen in Northridge Saturday?"

"Right now I'm asking the questions. Any scars?"

"None visible."

"Who are the other suspects?"

"A motel-owner named Lester Crandall is number two. He's heavy and short, about five-seven and one-eighty. Graying black hair with long sideburns. Talks like a good ole country boy, which he is, but he's shrewd and heavily loaded."

"How old?"

"He told me he'll be sixty on his next birthday. He had a motive as strong as Kilpatrick's for knocking off Leo Broadhurst."

"Sixty is too old," Arnie said.

"It would expedite matters if you laid your cards on the table. You have a description you're trying to match, right?"

"A sort of one. The trouble is, my witness may not be reliable, and I want independent confirmation. Who's your other suspect?"

"Kilpatrick's ex-wife Ellen could have done it. Leo broke up her marriage and then dropped her."

"It wasn't a woman," Arnie said. "Or if it was, my theory goes to pieces. Did any other adult male have motive and opportunity?"

I answered slowly, with some reluctance: "The gardener, Fritz Snow, who buried Leo's body with his tractor. I wouldn't have said he's capable of murder, but Leo did give him provocation. So did Albert Sweetner, for that matter."

"How old is Snow?"

"About thirty-five or -six."

"What does he look like?"

"He's five-ten, maybe one-sixty. Brown hair, moon face, green eyes which cry a lot. He seems to have emotional problems. Also genetic ones."

"What kind of genetic problems?"

"Harelip, for one thing."

"Why didn't you say so?"

Arnie's voice had risen. I held the receiver away from my ear. Jean was leaning with her hands on the door frame, watching me. Her face was pale, and her eyes were darker than I had ever seen them.

"Where is this Fritz Snow?" Arnie said.

"About a mile and a half from where I'm sitting. Do you want me to pick him up?"

"I better do it through channels."

"Let me talk to him first, Arnie. I can't believe he killed three people, or even one of them."

"I can," Arnie said. "That wig and mustache and beard that Albert Sweetner was wearing didn't belong to Sweetner. They didn't fit him. It's my hypothesis they belonged to the killer, who put them on Sweetner to confuse the issue. We've been canvassing the wig shops and supply houses. To make a long story short, your suspect bought the wig and beard at a mark-down store on Vine Street called Wigs Galore."

I didn't want to believe it. "He could have bought them for Al Sweetner."

"He could have, but he didn't. He bought them a month ago, when Sweetner was still in Folsom. And we know he bought them for his own use. He asked the salesman for a mustache that would cover the bad scar on his upper lip."

Jean spoke when I set the receiver down. "Fritz?"

"It looks that way." I told her about the wig and beard he had bought.

She bit her lip. "I should have listened to Ronny."

"Did he recognize Fritz on the mountain Saturday?"

"I don't know about Saturday. He told me several weeks ago that he saw Fritz with long black hair and a mustache. But when I questioned him further, he said that he was telling me a story."

We went into the bedroom where the boy was sleeping. He woke with a start when his mother touched him and sat up hugging his pillow, wide-eyed and shaking. It was my first naked glimpse of his hurt and fear.

He spoke with an effort: "I was afraid the bogy man would get me."

"I won't let him get you."

"He got Daddy."

"He won't get you," I said.

His mother took him in her arms, and for a little while he seemed content. Then he grew impatient of purely female comfort. He freed himself and stood up on the high bed, his eyes close to the level of mine. He bounced, and was temporarily taller than I was.

"Is Fritz the bogy man?" I said.

He looked at me in confusion. "I don't know."

"Did you ever see him wearing a long black wig?"

He nodded. "And whiskers, too," he said a little breathlessly. "And a whatchamacallit." He touched his upper lip.

"When was this, Ronny?"

"The last time that I visited Grandma Nell. I went into the barn and Fritz was there with long black hair and whiskers. He was looking at a picture of a lady."

"Did you know the lady?"

"No. She had no clothes on." He looked embarrassed, and scared. "Don't tell him I told you. He said if I told anybody that something bad would happen."

"Nothing bad will happen." Not to him. "Did you see Fritz on Saturday wearing his wig?"

"When?"

"Up on the mountain."

He looked at me in confusion. "I saw a bogy man with long black hair. He was away far off. I couldn't tell if it was Fritz or not."

"But you thought it was, didn't you?"

"I don't know."

His voice sounded strained, as if his clear childish memory had registered more than he was able to cope with. He turned to his mother and said that he was hungry.

XXXV

I dropped them off at a downtown restaurant and drove back through the ghetto to Mrs. Snow's house. Brown water was running in the road in front of it. I parked on the black-top driveway behind her old white Rambler and locked my car.

Mrs. Snow opened the front door before I could knock. She looked past me into rain as if there might be other men behind me.

"Where's Fritz?" I said.

"He's in his room. But I can do any talking that needs to be done. I always have—I guess I always will."

"He'll have to do his own talking, Mrs. Snow."

I went past her into the kitchen and opened the door of her son's room. He was crouched on the iron bed, hiding part of his face with his hands.

He was a helpless foolish man, and I hated what I had to do. A trial would make a public show of him. In prison he would be the bottom man, as his mother feared. I could feel her anxious presence close behind me.

I said to him: "Did you buy a wig a month or so ago? A wig and a beard and a mustache?"

He dropped his hands away from his face. "Maybe I did."

"I happen to know you did."

"Then what are you asking me for?"

"I want to know why you bought those things."

"To make my hair look long. And to cover this." He lifted his right forefinger to his scarred upper lip. "The girls won't let me kiss them. I only kissed a girl once in my life."

"Martha?"

"Yeah. She let me do it to her. But that was a long time ago, about sixteen or eighteen years. I read about these wigs and stuff in a movie magazine, so I went down to Hollywood and bought an outfit. I wanted to chase the chicks on Sunset Strip. And be a swinger."

"Did you catch any?"

He shook his doleful head. "I only got to go the once. She doesn't want me to have a girlfriend."

His gaze moved past me to his mother.

"I'm your girlfriend," she said brightly. "And you're my boyfriend." She smiled and winked. There were tears in her eyes.

I said: "What happened to your wig, Fritz?"

"I don't know. I hid it under my mattress. But somebody took it."

His mother said: "Albert Sweetner must have taken it. He was in the house last week."

"It was gone long before last week. It was gone about a month ago. I only got to chase the chicks the once."

"Are you sure about that?" I said.

"Yessir."

"You didn't drive down to Northridge Saturday night and put it on Albert's head?"

"No sir."

"Or wear it up the mountain Saturday morning—when you knifed Stanley Broadhurst?"

"I *liked* Stanley. Why would I knife him?"

"Because he was digging up his father's body. Didn't you kill his father, too?"

He shook his head violently, like a mop. His mother said: "Don't, Fritz. You'll do yourself an injury."

He stayed with his head hanging, as if he had broken his neck. After a time he spoke again: "I buried Mr. Broadhurst —I told you that. But I never killed him. I never killed none of them."

"Any of them," Mrs. Snow said. "You never killed *any* of them."

"I never killed any of them," he repeated. "I didn't kill Mr. Broadhurst, or Stanley, or—" He lifted his head. "Who was the other one?"

"Albert Sweetner."

"I didn't kill him, neither."

"Either," his mother said.

I turned to her. "Let him do his own talking, please."

The sharpness in my voice seemed to encourage her son: "Yeah. Let me do my own talking."

"I'm only trying to help," she said.

"Yeah. Sure." But there was a dubious questioning note in his voice. It issued in speech, though he kept his hang-dog posture on the bed: "What happened to my wig and stuff?"

"Somebody must have taken it," she said.

"Albert Sweetner?"

"It may have been Albert."

"I don't believe that. I think you took it," he said.

"That's crazy talk."

His eyes came up to her face, slowly, like snails ascending

a wall. "You swiped it from under the mattress." He struck the bed under him with his hand to emphasize the point. "And I'm not crazy."

"You're talking that way," she said. "What reason would I have to take your wig?"

"Because you didn't want me to chase the chicks. You were jealous."

She let out a high little titter, with no amusement in it. I looked at her face. It was stiff and gray, as if it had frozen.

"My son's upset. He's talking foolishly."

I said to Fritz: "What makes you think your mother took your wig?"

"Nobody else comes in here. There's just the two of us. As soon as it was gone, I knew who took it."

"Did you ask her if she took it?"

"I was afraid to."

"My son has never been afraid of his mother," she said. "And he knows I didn't take his blessed wig. Albert Sweetner must have. I remember now, he was here a month ago."

"He was in prison a month ago, Mrs. Snow. You've been blaming Albert for quite a number of things." In the ensuing silence I could hear all three of us breathing. I turned to Fritz. "You told me earlier that Albert put you up to burying Leo Broadhurst. Is that still true?"

"Albert was there," he answered haltingly. "He was sleeping in the stable near the Mountain House. He said the shot woke him up, and he hung around to see what would come of it. When I brought the tractor down from the compound, he helped me with the digging."

Mrs. Snow moved past me and stood over him. "Albert told you to do it, didn't he?"

"No," he said. "It was you. You said that Martha wanted me to do it."

"Did Martha kill Mr. Broadhurst?" I said.

269

"I dunno. I wasn't there when it happened. Mother got me up in the middle of the night and said I had to bury him deep, or Martha would go to the gas chamber." He looked around the narrow walls of the room as if he was in that chamber now, with the pellet about to drop. "She told me I should blame it all on Albert, if anybody asked me."

"You're a crazy fool," his mother said. "If you go on telling lies like this, I'll have to leave you and you'll be all alone. They'll put you in jail, or in the mental hospital."

Both of them could end up there, I was thinking. I said: "Don't let her scare you, Fritz. You won't be put in jail for anything you did because she made you."

"I won't stand for this!" she cried. "You're turning him against me."

"Maybe it's time, Mrs. Snow. You've been using your son as a scapegoat, telling yourself that you've been looking after him."

"Who else would look after him?" Her voice was rough and rueful.

"He could get better treatment from a stranger." I turned back to him: "What happened Saturday morning, when Stanley Broadhurst borrowed the pick and shovel?"

"He borrowed the pick and shovel," Fritz repeated, "and after a while I got nervous. I went up the trail to see what they were doing up there. Stanley was digging right where his father was buried."

"What did you do?"

"I went back down to the ranch and phoned *her*."

His wet green gaze rested on his mother. She made a shushing noise which narrowed into a hiss. I said over it:

"What about Saturday night, Fritz? Did you drive down to Northridge?"

"No sir. I was here in bed all night."

"Where was your mother?"

"I don't know. She gave me sleeping pills right after Albert phoned. She always gives me sleeping pills when she leaves me by myself at night."

"Albert phoned here Saturday night?"

"Yessir. I answered the phone, but it was her he wanted to talk to."

"What about?"

"They were talking about money. She said she had no money—"

"Shut up!"

Mrs. Snow raised her fist in a threat to her son. Though he was bigger and younger and probably stronger, he crawled away from her on the bed and huddled crying in the corner.

I took hold of Mrs. Snow's arm. She was taut and trembling. I drew her into the kitchen and shut the door on the dissolving man. She leaned on the counter beside the kitchen sink, shivering as though the house was chilly.

"You killed Leo Broadhurst, didn't you?"

Mrs. Snow didn't answer me. She seemed to have been overcome by a terrible embarrassment that tied her tongue.

"You didn't stay in the ranch house that night when Elizabeth Broadhurst and Stanley went up the mountain. You went up there after them and found Leo lying unconscious and stabbed him to death. Then you came back here and told your son to bury him and his car.

"Unfortunately Albert Sweetner knew where the body was buried, and eventually he came back here hoping to turn his knowledge into money. When Stanley failed to show up with the money Saturday night, Albert phoned here and tried to get some more out of you. You drove down to Northridge and killed him."

"How could I kill him—a big strong man like Albert?"

"He was probably dead drunk when you got to him. And it never occurred to him that he was in danger from you. It never occurred to Stanley, either, did it?"

She remained silent, though her mouth was working.

"I can understand why you killed Albert and Stanley," I said. "You were trying to cover up what you'd done in the past. But why did Leo Broadhurst have to die?"

Her eyes met mine and blurred like cold windows. "He was half dead already, lying there in his blood. All I did was put him out of his misery." Her clenched right hand jerked downward convulsively, reenacting the stabbing. "I'd do the same for a dying animal."

"It wasn't compassion that made you murder him."

"You can't call it murder. He deserved to die. He was a wicked man, a cheat and a fornicator. He got Marty Nickerson pregnant and let my boy take the blame. Frederick has never been the same since then."

There was no use arguing with her. She was one of those paranoid souls who kept her conscience clear by blaming everything on other people. Her violence and malice appeared to her as emanations from the external world.

I crossed the room to the phone and called the police. While the receiver was still in my hand, Mrs. Snow opened a drawer and took out a butcher knife. She came at me in a quick little dance, moving to jangled music I couldn't hear.

I caught her by the wrist. She had the kind of exploding strength that insane anger releases. But her strength soon ran out. The knife clattered on the floor. I pinned her arms and held her until the police arrived.

"You'll shame me in front of the neighbors," she said desperately.

I was the only one watching as the patrol car moved

away through the brown water with Fritz and his mother sitting behind a screen in the back seat. I followed them downtown, thinking that quite often nowadays the low-life subplots were taking over the tragedies. I gave a more prosaic explanation to a team of police detectives and a stenotypist.

My statement was interrupted by a phone call from Brian Kilpatrick's fiancee. Kilpatrick had walked into his game room and shot himself.

The briefcase I took from him, containing Elizabeth Broadhurst's guns and records, was in the trunk of my car. I let it stay there unreported for the present, though I knew all the facts of Leo Broadhurst's death would have to come out at Edna Snow's trial.

Before night fell, Jean and I and Ronny drove out of town.

"It's over," I said.

Ronny said, "That's good." His mother sighed.

I hoped it was over. I hoped that Ronny's life wouldn't turn back toward his father's death as his father's life had turned, in a narrowing circle. I wished the boy a benign failure of memory.

As though she sensed my thoughts, Jean reached behind him and touched the back of my neck with her cold fingers. We passed the steaming remnants of the fire and drove on south through the rain.

A NOTE ON THE TYPE

The text of this book is set in *Caledonia*, a Linotype face designed by W. A. Dwiggins. It belongs to the family of printing types called "modern face" by printers—a term used to mark the change in style of type letters that occurred about 1800. Caledonia borders on the general design of Scotch Modern, but is more freely drawn than that letter.

The book was composed, printed, and bound by The Haddon Craftsmen, Inc., Scranton, Pennsylvania. The typography and binding design are by Anthea Lingeman.